The Weight of Bones

Jo Reardon

LEAF BY LEAF

Published by Leaf by Leaf
an imprint of Cinnamon Press
Meirion House
Tanygrisiau
Blaenau Ffestiniog
Gwynedd, LL41 3SU
www.cinnamonpress.com

The right of Jo Reardon to be identified as author of this work has
been asserted by her in accordance with the Copyright, Designs and
Patent Act, 1988. Copyright © 2020 Jo Reardon
ISBN: 978-1-78864-910-0

British Library Cataloguing in Publication Data. A CIP record for
this book can be obtained from the British Library.

Designed and typeset in Palatino by Cinnamon Press.

Cover design by Adam Craig © Adam Craig.

Cinnamon Press is represented in the UK by Inpress Ltd and in
Wales by the Books Council of Wales.

Many thanks to the early readers of this book, George Green and Lee Horsley in particular who guided me through its beginnings through to a coherent end. Thanks also to: Jo Baker, Morgaine Merch Lleuad, Rhiannon Hooson, Elizabeth Preston, Jennie Owen and Richard Kenton Webb who read and commented on the book in its various stages.

I am grateful to have read Val McDermid's *Forensics, The Anatomy of Crime*, Helen MacDonald's *Falcon* and Stacey Horn's *The Restless Sleep* in my research and for information on Orkney and the Italian Chapel the websites: Undiscovered Scotland and About Orkney. Any inaccuracies are mine alone.

But my thanks most of all to Jan Fortune, Rowan Fortune and Adam Craig and everyone at Cinnamon Press for their unending patience, support and attention to detail. It's a joy to be part of this great publishing stable and an honour to be here.

The book is also dedicated to the memory of my schoolfriend Julie Godwin (née Stuttard) who was killed and taken from us far too young.

Jo Reardon is a writer of fiction, poetry and drama. Her short stories and poetry have been published alongside the work of contemporary artists at the Corinium Museum in Cirencester, Warrington Art Gallery and Burgh House Museum in Hampstead and her plays have been produced on BBC Radio 4. Her first novel, *The Weight of Bones,* was shortlisted for the Cinnamon Press Debut Novel Award. She is a lecturer for the Open University and lives in the North West of England on the Sefton coast.

Author website: joreardon.blog

The Weight of Bones

To my mother and in memory of my father

There's a gap between death and the moment of dying and this is where Frank is.

He doesn't know how he got here, what went wrong. But he knows it is too late to do anything about it. He's tried to move, but his body won't do what he wants it to. Only the pain tells him he's still alive. The pain cuts through his head, down deep into his neck, to where his heart is. For now, it is still beating.

He's lost track of time. It's dark, a blackness that feels like morning. The only light comes from the reflection of the mirrors around him. He's so cold he can't feel anything but the slowing beat of his blood. He doesn't want to die alone. She'll come back. She won't leave him like this.

Drifting between sleep and consciousness, every time he opens his eyes the day is still black and the cold still bitter. And he is still alone.

Monday 8 January 2007

1

Paris was empty.

Frank crossed the rue du Bercey and headed west until he reached la Bastille pulling the collar of his suit jacket high under his chin and thrusting his hands deep into his pockets. The florist on the corner of Henri IV and Saint Antoine was opening for the day and barely glanced up as he passed. The sweet dawn dampness of her flowers followed his footfall into the metro, the smell of rotting leaves and wet soil accompanying the heels of his shoes, which made the only sound, clicking their way with confidence down the steps and into the station.

The RER was three minutes late. He thought about a taxi but knew he'd have to hunt for one at this hour, so he waited one, two minutes more, undecided but knowing he was cutting it fine. Still, no need to panic. He watched the mouth of the underground tunnel breathe cold morning air onto the platform and willed the train to arrive. It did, moments later, sliding into the station smooth as a piston as though he had summoned it, and he strolled into a carriage like an early starter, keen to do his best. He took a seat by the window and watched the city evaporate behind him—across the river, past the black canals, the grey banlieues with their concrete towers and once bright port holed windows, painted in colours which had faded over time, then west towards the airport where beige apartment blocks, billboards and corporate neon took over, standing by the tracks like melancholy well-wishers—Tour Aczo, Michelin, Pepsi, the Sacré Coeur on its wedding cake hill. All watching him go.

At Charles de Gaulle the terminal was crammed.

Frank stood where he could see the queues, waiting for the girl to arrive. He bit the ends of his nails, felt their edges snag ragged on his tongue, looking like he had all the time in the world. This was the one thing he did not have. Fog was creeping in and, in an hour, maybe less, the runways would be closed and no one would be going anywhere. He'd seen this happen too many times before this winter—in France, no one would fly out in anything less than clear skies. The plane was leaving in fifty-three minutes and the girl still wasn't there. She owed him five hundred Euros, what if she didn't show? Christ he hadn't even considered it; he was sure this time he had a good one and so far his intuition had held. Dolores had vouched for her, insisted he bring her and he couldn't get a better guarantee than that.

He checked his watch, thinking he should have sent her on like the others, like he always did, but there was a reason for his going this time, which had nothing to do with the girl. He knew he was taking a risk, but it was worth it, so if this girl messed up... He counted the seconds and then, there she was, zigzagging the concourse like a ladybird, red t-shirt over black jeans. Her bony arms were dragging a suitcase on wheels. He saw a thin tattoo snaking, just visible, around her upper arm disappearing beneath the capped sleeve and into her body as though swallowing her from the inside. Her narrow heels were high and loud enough to click clack over the terminal floor. They made her seem much taller than she was. She had the canvas bag over her shoulder, the one he'd left in the locker for her with her ticket and her new passport. The Centre Pompidou logo bounced against her hip as she walked, making her look like a tourist on her way home. She didn't know what he looked like, at least he didn't think she did, but she might have been watching the locker waiting for him because as she walked by she came too close to where he was standing, glanced his way, just enough to let him know she knew, but not enough to betray any connection between them. She passed close enough for him to smell her perfume, full of earth and spice, and he was pulled back to the florist that morning, the fresh cut ends of her flowers. He marked the row of earrings circling all the way up to the top of the ear closest to him, the girl's fair hair pulled back from her skinny face, which highlighted the whiteness of her skin. The ends of her hair were fringed with red fading up to black like the face of a baby fox. She wasn't what he had expected, not the way Dolores had described her, not what he had expected at all.

She headed for the check-in desk, just like she'd been told. Frank waited as she handed the passport and ticket in at the desk, chatting with the airline girl about the weather, the fog and how spring would be a long time coming. He could hear her confident French from where he stood, a few words slipping here and there but fluid and fast with laughter thrown in for good measure. The two women looked for the world as if they had known each other for years. The girls he'd been sending over recently were older and sadder with families to keep at home somewhere in the centre of Europe. Their mothers would miss them and then forget them when the money came through so they stayed a little longer, hoped for a little more. He knew at once that this one had thicker skin. When she spoke French, her voice was hard but had a music to it, the sound of a finger running around the edge of thin glass. There was something about her—something he liked but also worried about. She was not going to be easy and that was never good.

He moved away from where he'd been watching her and went back to the locker. It was only a few corridors away, still enough time to get to the check-in line and join the queue for seats even though the screens were showing his flight as 'now boarding'. He opened the locker, rolling the security numbers, and took out the day's copy of *Le Figaro* that the girl had left behind in exchange for the ticket and passport. The paper was heavy, thick with the envelope that held his money. He flicked the pages back to check. A wad of Euro notes clung together gripped in a thick band of twine or string, he couldn't quite tell, but he had to trust that it was all there. From the thickness and the smell, it felt like the right amount. He snapped the locker door shut, swished the combination of numbers back to zero and headed for the boarding gate. The flight was busy and she was just ahead of him in the line of seats where passengers were waiting to get the call to board the plane. He shook *Le Figaro* and turned to the racing pages at the back, where they always were no matter where you were in the world. He scanned the horses, riders, times and odds, working as he always did by instinct, and fancied a horse in the 15.30 at Vincennes. He looked at his watch, would he have time to put his money down? It was a superstition he had every time he did this, one girl delivered, one bet placed. The digital display on the departures board shuffled times and gates like cards on a black jack table, changing every few seconds or so, updating or delaying. Frank tapped his mobile and placed a bet just as his gate was called—the odds were 20 to 1 on a horse called Vixen. The girl who looked like a fox was just ahead of him in the boarding queue.

On the plane, Frank settled a few seats behind her, across the aisle where he could still keep her in his sight. She must know he was watching, he could sense it from the way she moved, carefully, smiling and humming to herself, earphones in her ears tapping her blue-nail painted fingers on the arm rest. She was doing that chatting smiling thing again with the stewardess, the one she'd done with the check in girl. She ordered two miniatures of Smirnoff, ice, no tonic. The small bottles always contained doubles so that was four shots in a row, and she made it look like she was drinking water. Frank ordered a coffee. The girl read a magazine, idly twirling the dial on her MP3 player looking like she hadn't a care in the world. There was something about her, a defiance. He knew she was different but couldn't put his finger on it. He had other things on his mind, the coffee missing the sweet spot, so he ordered a whisky, leaned back in his seat and fell asleep as the plane climbed high, high into the sky. Arriving towards England, it banked low over the channel, skirting the ragged edges of Cornwall and Wales and the wild brown waves lashing against the rocky coasts. It hugged the last drop of the land before curving towards the North West, the lights on the motorways and hillsides below, had he noticed them, easing themselves flat, curling their fingers towards him and beckoning him home.

They landed in Liverpool to a dank and indifferent Monday evening. January in the North West of England never matched the rose-tinted memories of snow and red-sunsets he carried in his head, the images that had got him through these past grey winter Paris months. Sometimes he remembered snow, but he was never sure if this was something that nagged the edge of his dreams or whether it had really happened. They passed through passport control at John Lennon Airport without a hitch and then entered the arrivals terminal passing under a sign that proclaimed: *Above us only sky.* A one-line sketch of John Lennon directed visitors to imagine this, his glasses round and smiling at them. Through the plate glass windows of the arrivals lounge Frank looked at the sky, which was dark, glowering with the threat of sleet and rain. He realised now that his smart blue suit, woollen and specially tailored as it was, would not serve him well in this climate. He had already become an outsider, lacking the forethought of a native; his heavy overcoat was back in his Paris apartment. He shoved his cold hands into his pockets and thought: *Welcome home.*

2

Clemmie drove the car like she was driving a tank, slamming the gears and crunching the brakes while Tom tried to ignore the sound, staring out of the window at things that seemed submerged underwater. Distorted shoppers held their angled bodies against the sharp westerly wind and in the distance, over the sea, the sky was a thin line of pink and white, fixed on the horizon like coconut ice. He was so cold he couldn't feel his feet because the car's heater was broken and the front passenger window let icy air in through a gap that wouldn't close. It was the first time he'd been in a vehicle since the accident; the ambulance didn't count. His skull was contracting with pain, which pushed his eyes into the back of his head, and he wondered if he'd ever have the strength to help his mother lift the new TV into the car; it was the only reason he'd been persuaded to come out in the first place. His mother was too old, she said, to be shifting heavy stuff around and he was still 'young' enough to help. So here he was, doing nothing, a passenger in his mother's car while his septuagenarian mother drove; that didn't seem 'young' to him.

'I'll only be five minutes.' Clemmie was pulling over to the kerb facing the wrong way up the road, outside Curry's on the main high street. Her rally-driving father had taught her to drive and she'd never quite managed to shake off the skid and stop mentality that had characterised Tom's earliest memories of being driven around by her as a child. She stopped on a yellow line.

'You can't stop here...' he said, tried to say, but she was out of the car faster than he was able to move. 'It'll fit in the back,' she threw over her shoulder and was gone. She left the engine running.

18

She disappeared into the shop, where TVs flashed in the window showing multiple clashing channels, pictures of newsreaders and sports pundits moving their mouths silently in sync. Kids who should have been at school whizzed past him balanced on BMX bikes dodging the buskers and parked cars, weaving in and out of the Styrofoam litter from McDonalds on the corner. Tom waited, counting the minutes as the sky over the sea, which he could just glimpse beyond the grey once-stately municipal town buildings, grew steadily darker.

The street was busy, the council were always intending to pedestrianize it but no one had the conviction to push it through. Buses and lorries fought with cars and cyclists for space on what must have once been a wide boulevard in Victorian times when the town was in its heyday, but was little more than a narrow street now. Hemmed in by traffic the tall shopfronts found themselves pushed back, their gothic windows covered in mesh to keep the pigeons out, a single concession to conservation. Tom found himself scanning back and forth along the street for traffic wardens. There was no sign of Clemmie. The car was freezing, made worse by the back seats in the old Volvo being folded down to make room for the new TV, a flat screen wonder that would give Clemmie access to pictures beyond her wildest dreams. He had no idea what his mother wanted it for, the other one was perfectly good and this would only be louder, brighter, more intrusive. He wanted peace, silence, the inside world, but Clemmie wasn't concerned with what he wanted and for a while now he felt that he had overstayed his welcome. The TV might be her way of telling him to move on or, knowing his mother, her own way of making sure she was still moving into her own future.

A man came out with a large box on a trolley, followed by Clemmie giving instructions. Tom could sense the excitement in his mother's voice, which had shifted up a notch, the curve of a laugh in it, the inch of a smile, and knew this was his cue. But he couldn't move. He gripped the door handle, aware of the boot of the car behind him open to the cold air. Noise piled in from the High Street, deafening him, rooting him to the spot.

'You giving us a hand then?' Clemmie snapped.

The young man guided the TV, balancing it with one hand, manoeuvring expertly around pedestrians. He looked like he didn't need anyone's help, but with some effort Tom pushed the door wide and just caught it as a blast of wind barrelled down the street from the coastal end, meeting him off balance. He stood and staggered back down holding on to the door to save it. A cyclist in a flash and blur of bright colour clipped the door's edge as she swerved.

'Fucking watch what you're doing wanker!'

The cyclist was brought to a halt; her back wheel twisted round to the front where a mass of contorted brake wires was locking the front wheel in place. He felt his hands shake, the blood throbbing above the artery in his neck. He registered the shock on the woman's face, her eyes wide and the violent impact of the near-collision fixing her body rigid, hands gripping tight to the handlebars of the bike. She should have been more careful too and he should have moved across and got out the driver side rather than on to the road because of his mother's careless parking. There was nothing he could do now but apologise.

'I...'

'You,' the woman said, staring at him, her face beneath her helmet twisted into rage.

He looked at her; it took him a second to understand, but only a second—the yellow and black lycra, the fingerless gloves with the black nail varnish, thick eyeliner and bright, bright blue eyes. Still those blue eyes, only... Leah Barnes looked much older now. Her eyes were screwed up against the wind and the cold and showed tiny crow's feet etched into the skin, which led out to her temples. The cheek strap of her helmet was tight against the glow of sweat on her skin, half of her face thrown into shadow. It wasn't that long since he'd last seen her at his daughter's funeral, only months ago really, the months of a year, but it could have been a lifetime.

'You still alive then?' she spat.

He stared without a word in his head.

'Tom?' Clemmie's voice broke through whatever spell the sight of Leah Barnes had cast over him. She stood, hands on hips, looking between the two of them. The TV was in the car and the man with the trolley was gone.

'Tom?' she insisted as he heard the hiss of a tyre, the clang of a gear being kicked into place, upscaling as the bike took off and away from them. When he turned back from Clemmie to where Leah had been standing, there was nothing but the blur of yellow somewhere in the distance getting smaller and faster the further away it went, weaving angrily between buses and taxis. She blazed past a pedestrian who had stepped out into the street and yelled at her, she raised a finger in the air behind as a response and as quickly as she had appeared, Leah Barnes vanished.

'Get back in the car.' Clemmie said, starting the engine as he fell back on the seat and closed the door against the noise and the bitter cold outside. 'That girl was never any good,' she said, reaching for clichés because they had all, very long ago, run out of anything else to say about Leah Barnes.

The street seemed empty of colour as they drove at Clemmie's erratic pace, no yellow, no black, nothing. Tom put his fingers to his eyes and closed them. He could no longer tell what was real and wasn't. He should have stayed put inside for a while longer, he shouldn't have been blackmailed by Clemmie's emotional pull. His mother was perfectly capable of collecting the TV on her own; she was capable of doing everything she said she was unable to do.

21

He should have learned that a long time ago. He leaned his head back and felt the world move away in the slipstream of Leah Barnes's words. In his mind's eye he saw her thin, furious body melting into her racing bike and heard in his head the way she spat those words at him—*still alive*, when inside he felt he'd never come back from the dead.

3

They took a bus to Hunts Cross, which was the first time Frank spoke to the girl, pretending that they'd just met as they went through passport control then on to the bus stop where he offered directions, helpful advice. And, because they took the bus together they sat on the train together, to the seaside—she with her suitcase and stylish Pompidou bag, and he with his smart holdall of Italian leather, just like a couple on a daytrip. An odd couple to be sure, he was at least twenty years older than her for a start, but he'd worn well in his sharp suit and salt and pepper George Clooney hair, which he was especially proud of. He caught a glimpse of himself in the train window, nothing flustered, nothing getting in the way of the smart way Papa had brought him up to present himself. You could never know what might happen, who you might meet. He already knew the girl's name was Eva, but it sounded different when she said it to him.

'I am Eva,' she told him.

The name stuck to her lips like sugar on an apple and as she spoke, the sweetness of the sound came out in her strong but broken English, a singsong voice hiding the edge he'd heard when she'd spoken French at the airport. He wondered what she would sound like in her own tongue. She spoke French and English she told him because she had a good education in Rumania, but there was no money to earn in her country for clever girls like her. She had a degree in Economics, so over she comes to earn some money and plenty of kind people to help her. She lowered her eyes at this last bit and tapped her fingernails on the window ledge. She had added a leather bomber jacket to her outfit in a crazy kind of cornflour blue at the airport, against the cold and the English winter. As she leaned on the window, the startling gap of white skin in between the

23

blue of her nails and the blue of the jacket made Frank think of a puppet, the wooden joints connecting the parts of its body like bones on a string. She wouldn't stay long in England she was saying, three months at the most. That's what they all say Frank thought, but he didn't tell her this. The bright new chrome and black glass buildings being added to every corner of Liverpool's dock front, merged into blackened warehouses, remnants of its darker past. Mountains of scrap metal ripened into rust in the weak sunlight, the sweet sticky smell of barley from the brewery came in through the window and hunger hit him for the first time. Frank watched Eva's bright eyes scan the black dockland as it became sand dune, each a marker as the train pulled up the coast from the city. The train pulled north, taking Eva's dreams and Frank's plans with it.

Through the window Eva pointed at the sea when it peeped briefly between the dunes and the golf clubs, which ran in an unbroken line the length of the Sefton coast. She asked about the iron men rusting in the water on Crosby Beach; she wanted to know why couldn't she see them and he told her it was a short walk from Blundell Sands station, maybe she should try it one weekend in the summer when the sun was out.

'But I won't be here in the summer,' she said and smiled.

He couldn't work out was behind the smile; it seemed to be daring him to respond. He looked away and watched the swathes of sea grass, which lined the coastal part of the route that signalled the approach to St Marie-by-Sea; the way it draped the dunes like bunches of thick, long uncombed hair. In the distance, across the water, there was Blackpool, the tripping dippers and flashing lights of the big fairground, which made St Marie look like a child's playground. The harsh industry of Liverpool behind them, the town and the coast opened into a broad curving bay. A triangle of swans passed low over the train heading for open water and Frank felt he could hear the drumbeat of their wings through the window, beating in time to the blood in his heart. This was where he belonged, he'd been away far too long and the train couldn't get him there fast enough.

As they drew closer, Frank found that he wanted Eva to be gone, they had both kept their side of the deal and now it was over, he needed to get on with what he came for. When they pulled into the station, he felt the weight of the day behind him. The hours of travelling had made his back ache and mouth dry, he needed a drink of something to steady his nerves before he tackled his brother because he knew, before he did anything at all, he had to let him know. He put Eva in a taxi, gave the driver an address he knew by heart, wished her luck. She was on her own now.

He waited until Eva and her taxi had gone then took his phone out, tapped a few keys scrolling down to Dolores; *10pm usual place*, he texted, hesitating before he added, *business with G first*. Then pressed send.

It was still early; he had time for one drink before letting his brother see that he was still alive.

4

Clemmie was on a roll now, hooking the corner of Church Street without using her brake, never using third gear when second would do. The car screamed as she crashed the gears and people turned and looked, startled by the discordant grating of the engine that somehow managed to be louder than any other sound in the street. The Volvo ploughed its own path homewards and the box with the flat screen TV tapped a rhythm against the window as the car rode the speed bumps past the station where she swerved to take the short cut home.

Tom held the side of his head with his hands. If he took them away he felt as though the pain would seep out; pressing his temples with both thumbs numbed it for a while and held everything in place. It didn't help that Clemmie had the radio tuned to local radio where some inane debate about the planned pier development had people ringing in to argue for seafront beauty over tourist tat. She said it would take his mind off how bad the pain was. He closed his eyes and wished she were right.

When he opened them again they were stopped at the lights near the train station where his eye was drawn to a man and a woman walking together towards the taxi rank. They looked incongruous, otherwise he wouldn't have given them a second glance—the woman was small and bone-thin with kohl black eyes and hair the colour of an autumn fire startling against the porcelain of her skin. She wore pin-heeled ankle boots, a ridiculous small jacket in electric blue and pulled a suitcase behind her on wheels. The man was urging her along, guiding her, his hand cupped under the bend of her elbow even though she looked as though she didn't need help at all. She was straining against his hurrying and smiling, shrugging him off with a smile and a shake of her head. At first the man had his back to Tom, but when he turned to hail the first taxi in the rank, he raised his arm and the flourish in his movement, gallant and elegant as he opened the door for her, made Tom look more closely. And what he saw was a dead man's face. *It couldn't be...* he felt himself pulled down into the darkness he'd been trying to claw his way out of for months. *Impossible...* he tried to swallow, the saliva sticking in his throat. *It couldn't be...* the man looked like Frank Molinari, the woman he didn't recognise at all.

The lights changed and they pulled away and when Tom looked back, the taxi had gone. The man was still there however, a phone in his hand, head bent over in concentration. Tom noticed the silvered grey on the crown of his head before he straightened and melted into the crowd as the car got further away. But he had Frank's gait, Frank's height. *It couldn't be...*

'Nearly there,' Clemmie said even though they weren't.

She stayed in third gear for the final half mile, the car dragged along the asphalt like a ship on a rusty chain as Tom clenched his teeth seeing only Frank's dead face his head. He was hallucinating, he had to be, but he knew he wasn't. First Leah Barnes and now Frank, *he had to be hallucinating...* The drugs—he knew they were strong and he was trying to wean himself off them because, in truth, he didn't really need them anymore. They dulled the edge, shut the world out and now, now it had come back to find him. *Frank was dead.* Music had replaced the debate on the radio and Clemmie was humming, wittering on about how he'd have to set the TV up for her but he wasn't listening, he was going over and over what he'd just seen, feeling his hold on the present slipping further away. The girl in her blue coat, Frank in his suit, he looked like he was carrying something, maybe a holdall, but where was he going? *To his brother of course, or to Dolores...* They knew, all of them, all this time, they knew he wasn't dead and the police had been played for fools chasing round after a killer who didn't exist. *Susie,* at the back of all this was Susie, what had she thought she was doing that day, who had she thought she was rescuing, because it was clear now that it wasn't Frank. And then the question he came back to, over and over again, *why hadn't he, her father, been there to save her?*

5

The fairground at Pleasure Island was in Frank's blood. He'd lived and breathed it his whole life and even though he could see the flash in the red lights from Blackpool's big rides across the bay ripping the heart out of it, this was where he belonged. The yellow walls were like a breakwater against the ever-threatening sea just yards away. They hugged the perimeter of the fairground in an unbroken chain, meeting at the front, by the main gate, a Moroccan archway that marked the entrance into Pleasure Island. It was open, as it always was, and one glance told Frank the place was more forgotten and neglected than he'd expected. Here, at the front, the walls had faded to a mucky shade of ochre, bits of log flume and legs of iron from disconnected rides just visible over the top of the high wall. Pleasure Island looked tired, not just winter-tired waiting for a lick of paint and dust up, but dog-tired and forgotten like a battered toy truck thrown under a child's bed. The sight made his memories miss a beat and for the first time his confidence wavered, threw what he intended to do into doubt. This wasn't how he remembered it. The arch was a vast lumpen thing, built from fibreglass and plaster, peeling and chipping more each year as the wind ate it away, but once it looked like the real thing, or as close as they could get. It was intended to resemble the one Genaro had seen in *Casablanca*, a film where a man played a piano in a sun-blown bar while a beautiful woman stood by listening to the melody. The design of the fairground was supposed to bring a taste of the exotic to the faded gentility of this very English town. There was a gate of wood and rust, the fake plastic bolts that would in an ancient scenario have held off the marauding invaders, now hung off the wood like so many broken fingernails. The fairground wall, which had once seemed so impenetrable to Frank, now seemed vulnerable to any invader who cared to attack.

He stood there some minutes. He knew that as soon as he went through the arch and entered the courtyard, he would see his brother's office so when he did move he moved as slowly as he could, not wanting to be seen. He edged forward, stepping around the puddles of freezing meltwater, the tarmac giving way to potholes. The office, in an old Portakabin, was still there, cramped in the corner of the small entrance courtyard. A faded sign hanging by a thread: *Management*, lending it an air of authority. The Portakabin was only ever intended to be temporary, but this would be its tenth year or more so it was clearly going nowhere. There was one main window, the blinds were never fully closed, and through the slats Frank saw his brother hunched over his desk, angle poise lamp shedding a cone of dim orange light. The desk was piled high with a chaos of papers and Genaro looked up now and then, his fingers on the top of his head. He'd been tapping time like this since he was a young boy, listening to music in his head that no one else could hear. On his way, in the taxi, Frank had intended to go straight in, get it over with, but watching this familiar gesture he found he couldn't move. Now his return seemed like the act of madness it surely was. It hadn't occurred to him someone might see him, recognise him again and what might happen if they did. He felt so changed, so altered beyond the man he once was that he had felt he could drift through this place where he was once so well known, unnoticed and unremarked. It was only now faced with his brother, with what he had come to ask of him, that he wondered if Genaro would see it the same way.

He felt the nudge of the airplane ticket and his passport in his inside top pocket. He could turn back right now, not attempt to reopen what was closed. Even from his vantage point hidden by the archway, he could see how tired his brother looked. In the pallid glow from the lamp in the window Genaro seemed shrunk to the size of a shadow in the lamp's sad light and Frank was struck with the realisation that seeing his 'dead' brother come back to life like this could kill him. Frank hesitated and then, as he was about to turn, Genaro looked up and out of the window as though he knew Frank was waiting. His gaze was steady and strong, the light from the angle poise throwing his ragged face into relief and Frank knew he might have made a terrible miscalculation. There was something else he'd forgotten—Genaro could be unpredictable. Frank had seen it, not often, but enough to know fear of it. He stayed where he was, unable to move backwards or forwards, waiting, but Genaro did not move his gaze from where he stood.

He had made his decision the moment he stepped on that plane in Paris, there was no going back. Frank eased a foot out of the shadow and walked towards the Portakabin aware that Genaro was watching every step he took. Frank tried not to look at his brother, noticing instead everything around him trying to take in all the images he'd discarded while he'd been away. He felt as though he was committing them to memory, as though he would never see them again. The skeleton outlines of the high rides creaking in the darkness above, the snapped locks of the lower ride gates around him, the dodgem ride to his left, the canvas covers on the cars like hunched back assassins. And before him, the window of the Portakabin covered in stickers, fairground and circus posters, flyers, a crack jagged down the bottom corner of the glass, held together with brown masking tape, flapping in the wind. The sound of the angry tape was building in intensity with every step Frank took. Genaro did not move, not until Frank's hand was on the door and opening it and he could feel the harsh warmth of a fan heater blasting out stale heat as the wind caught the flimsy door and slammed it shut behind him. Genaro was still standing by the window and not until Frank was inside and facing his brother did he look up.

'Hello Franco,' Genaro said. 'I was wondering when you'd turn up.'

His voice was steady, a crack in the words like a whisper as though he'd been waiting to say them for a long time, igniting for a second the same fear Frank had felt as a kid cowering in a corner with Genaro's rage screaming itself hoarse at someone who had dared to say the wrong thing. But then he smiled and the eyes that had watched Frank make that slow journey across the courtyard, softened as he moved out from behind the desk. Frank watched Genaro bending with effort, his back uncurling bone by painful bone as he picked up the bottle of whisky from an upturned crate behind his desk without a word. He rummaged for something to drink it in, opening the drawers of a metal filing cabinet beneath the desk, slamming them closed, the metallic ring grating in irritation. The movements were clearly giving him pain, his gestures jerky, uneven, like an awkward stop-frame animation. He swung round, bottle in hand and alighted on the ancient coffee machine in the corner where a cylinder of plastic held a line of polystyrene beakers. He shook the cylinder releasing two cups to the floor and Frank darted forward to retrieve them, handing them up to his brother.

'I'm fine,' Genaro said.

'I...'

'I can see you looking; is nothing.'

'Your back again?'

Genaro pulled a blister pack from his pocket and jammed two of the pills into his mouth, swilling them down with a mouthful of water from a bottle on the desk.

'This time, I have pills,' he said. 'They tell me it helps.'

He steadied himself and poured the whisky into the two cups Frank was holding out before him.

'Highland Park,' Frank said, noticing the label.

'In honour of Papa...' Genaro said replacing the bottle, tilting his cup to his brother's. Frank took a sip, the whisky too sweet and cloying in the damp closeness of the room. 'Sit, sit,' Genaro urged him, smiling again.

Frank didn't want to sit, he didn't want the whisky, he didn't understand this 'welcome' at all. Genaro moved some papers from a battered faux leather chair with a sweep of his hand. Clearly unable to bend lower to place them with care, he threw them on the floor with a gesture for Frank to sit and Frank felt he had no choice but obey.

'What did you mean?' Frank said. 'Wondered when I'd turn up?'

Genaro manoeuvred himself back behind his desk, fell heavily into the chair and leaned so far back that the top of the chair touched the wall behind him and tilted his heavy frame. It seemed to ease him as he closed his eyes for a moment then opened them again looking straight at his brother.

'I mean,' he said, 'I knew you would be back and now here you are like nothing has happened.'

'A lot has happened...'

'Sure it has, you are dead for one!' Genaro laughed but Frank didn't. Genaro reached across and poured himself another whisky.

Behind Genaro, Frank could see that the wall was covered in a single calendar planner, long red lines across weeks and months, highlighted dates and post-it notes stickered and fading. Everything had the air of trouble about it, the piles of paper, which looked like bills, a stack of outdated flyers spilling out of shrink-wrapped plastic on the floor. Even outside, the wind hammered round the edges of the flimsy building while inside the fan heater throbbed with air, rustling the towers of papers. Frank didn't want any more to drink, he'd had enough in the pub; he wanted to leave. He could feel his hands sweat as he fiddled with the cup, destroying it in his fingers. Genaro leaned forward; Frank could smell the sweet tar of the whisky as he breathed out.

'I know why you're here,' Genaro said, his voice sinking to barely above a whisper.

'I came to see you…'

'Not for money?' There was a pause, then he added, more kindly, 'I know you Franco, I always know.'

He looked at Frank, long enough for Frank to see that his brother would do what he had come to ask of him.

'How is business?' Frank said. He had to say something, anything.

'Can you see how it is?' Genaro gestured elaborately around him. In front of him was a cashbook, the pages curled and pressed with writing. Receipts were impaled on a long spike. Frank recognised it as the same spike his father had kept for the bills, unpaid mostly until summer came and the gold coins of punters rolled in.

Genaro leaned back again, his eyes fixed on Frank's face, waiting for Frank to admit that yes he had come for money; it was always for money.

'I need your help,' Frank said. 'Your… well, your advice.'

'Advice?' Genaro smiled. He was enjoying himself. 'Up to your usual tricks I imagine?'

'No.' Frank's answer came too fast. 'No, not this time. This time it's well… it's different.'

'So you are in trouble and yet you look good,' Genaro said, 'for a dead man.'

'I like Paris,' Frank said, Genaro's tone encouraging him to try a smile.

'It suits you.'

There was a clock on the wall next to the calendar planner and Frank could see the time ebbing away. Dolores would be there by now; he had timed all this very badly. Genaro was watching his brother, the creases of his eyes stretched into a smile as he turned and looked at the clock then back at Frank.

'Go,' he said. 'Go. I know where you are going and she will be waiting.'

'How did...'

'I always know.'

Wrong footed again, Frank stood, shuffled himself in preparation nearer the door. 'I'll come back, later...'

'Sure.' Genaro shrugged. 'Sure you will. I'm counting on it.'

He leaned over, took the remains of Frank's cup of whisky, tipped it into his own and raised it to his brother.

'Welcome back,' he said and swallowed it in one. Frank's hand was already on the door and opening it into the squall of the night. He turned back as he stood in the doorway.

'It will be different this time,' he said. 'I promise.'

Genaro just nodded, he was already sinking back into his bending pain, closing his eyes, leaning back. With one final glance, Frank closed the door on the warmth behind him and faced the growing anger of the wind, pulling his jacket collar high into his face.

He could be back here in a few hours, he knew Genaro would help him; he knew that now. He was shocked at how old he looked, in the space of a year one of them had gone forwards while the other had gone back. But then, Genaro knew him better than anyone and he knew his brother was playing with him as he always did, taunting him before giving into him. Frank would explain what had happened and his brother would understand, after all, hadn't he done worse things? This was only about a bit of money, a few debts that needed clearing, the past was behind him and it was nothing, to be truthful, that he wasn't owed. But the state of the fair, the open ledger on the desk, he knew none of that boded well for what he needed, what he had expected. Still, that wasn't his problem, he was owed this and Papa always said he'd never have to worry about money, but somehow Genaro had ended up in control of the money instead of him. He was betting on blood being thicker than any past boyhood bullying, they were each all they had left and Frank knew Genaro would honour that. Frank only had one last thing to do, to see Dolores, and then he would come back here, explain everything. It was the only choice he had. It was going to be all right.

Frank had to pick his way through the darkened fairground like a dancer on a tightrope, a few intermittent low solar lights lit the odd bump in the pathway, highlighted the edges of the rides and dodgy electrical points leading up to them. He was really late now and, in the darkness, regretted agreeing to meet her here even though he knew why she had chosen it. Darkness, nighttime, a hidden room behind the mirrors where no one would see them and they could spend hours together before he spoke to Genaro again. Tomorrow he would get the first train back to the airport, back to Paris, back to where he'd started.

He had to feel his way along the pathways to the Hall of Mirrors, *their* place, the only place in the ground, which was hidden, secure. It was the place it had begun for them all those years ago, no more than children, a teenage dream that had grown and twisted into a vine that had never quite reached maturity. As he drew closer, the wooden roller coaster loomed above him, only just visible against the sky. The night glare of the town highlighted its row of wooden trucks curving upwards on the first iron rail, climbing silently in the darkness without moving. When he was a kid he used to think they moved on their own like the ghost train and was so afraid, but Genaro showed him how ordinary they were with a driver and a destination and soon he came to understand how mechanical things can seem like magic in the right light. Even so, there was the snap of ice in the air. In summer the place was full of trippers trailing sweat and hot sugar behind them, but tonight in the dead of a winter, there was no one, not even the security guards that Genaro always had around. Nothing looked as it should. Something caught Frank's eye; the glint of the new razor wire that surrounded the fairground park, the only security there now. It was there to keep intruders out, but in the blackness, in the cold, it seemed it was there only to keep him in.

As he approached the Hall of Mirrors, he could see the entrance door swinging loose and free, banging in the wind, the piece of string that held it frayed and useless. He stepped inside quickly and saw slippery images climbing up and down, his own self reflected back in different proportions, his face like a cubist painting in silver and glass. He checked the time, pulling the sleeve of his suit jacket back to reveal the hands of his wristwatch clicking round. His fingers were frozen, the skin cold and thin. He pushed his hands up to his face, breathed hot moisture into them, rubbed them together until the feeling came back then pushed them into his pockets. His feet, stamping, up then down, waiting as the time ticked away. And suddenly, there she was, just like she promised, a wraith appearing from the shadows. He wanted to hold her, he wanted to touch her, but she didn't move.

'Did he see you?' he asked.

She shook her head.

He could imagine the thin bones under her clothes, remembered the way her backbone curved towards the base of her spine like the thin tail of willow tree.

'He was shocked?' she said, inspecting him, her violet eyes in the gloom shining like a cat's.

'No,' he said. And with the words, for the first time he let the reality of this sink in.

She took this in too as her eyes skimmed over his face. She was wearing a scarf on her hair, covering it from the wind and the cold. It was made from silk, which shifted and made her look older, much older than she was, throwing her profile into shadow. She looked like a country woman ploughing the fields in the land where she came from, her lumpen man's overcoat added to the impression of heaviness and exhaustion. It looked as though at any moment the coat would pull her down into the ground. But it looked like a place he wanted to be and Frank wished he could slip inside it, feel her next to him, warming him. But there was a distance, why was she looking at him like that? This wasn't how he had imagined it at all.

'So,' she said, 'you brought Eva?

'I have, she's...'

'Thank you.'

Frank hadn't asked Dolores about Eva, he had trusted her that she was reliable and Dolores had arranged the contact, a place for Eva to go on to now that she was here. He knew that this was different in some way, but he hadn't questioned it because she had never questioned anyone he had sent over to her. So far their operation, small as it was, had run without any kind of bump in any kind of road. He didn't want to discuss it; it was just another transaction, one of many and that was not why he was here. She narrowed her eyes to look at him more closely, but he mistook it for something else, an invitation, so he moved towards her.

'No,' she said, shifting back, only a small step, but reaching her hand out to steady herself on the wall.

There was something in the way she did this that tilted him off balance. He caught her expression as the neon bulbs flashed along the top of the mirrors, catching her face. Something had caused them to light up; they must have tripped a security light by moving in front of a sensor. It felt like they were suddenly on a stage about to perform. Dolores threw her left hand up to her face, placing the flat of it against the skin and pressing it there. He put his hand out to take it away, held the bird-boned wrist in his hand so that he could see, for the first time, a scar like the claw of a tiger track gouged into the left side of her face.

'I'm sorry,' he said, but it was too little too late and they both knew that. She let him hold on to her this time without moving away.

'You have to go Franco,' she said. 'We can't stay here, I will come to you, I have enough of this now. I will come to you.'

'We can live in Paris, when Genaro...' he hesitated, going too far as he always did.

'When Genaro what?'

'Nothing,' he said. 'Nothing. It's just... nothing.' His voice came across as one he himself didn't quite recognise.

'Franco—listen to me...'

But she was cut off because something spooked her. To Frank it just sounded like the sigh of metal bending in the wind. 'Did you hear that?' She squinted out into the night. Her face was contorted now, they'd moved away from the mirrors but the flash of silver from their surfaces as they caught the light outside, brought a shift of terror to her face.

'No,' he said, calming her, stepping forward.

'There's someone there.'

'There's nothing.'

But he went to look, he had to look didn't he, for her sake, anything for her sake. He moved out into the open, into the centre of the ground where he was exposed, surrounded by the other rides, the waltzers draped in tarpaulin covering bulky bodies hiding a hundred eyes that watched him beneath in the pitch dark night as the cold air stuck in the back of his throat. Then he heard it too, there *was* someone.

'Frank!'

He tried to go back to her and dived, reached, stretched his arm out, but it was too late. He felt a crack, the sound to the side of his head, a dull jolt as his neck wrenched sideways. He felt himself falling. In the upside down mirrors, he watched his face slide down the glass like water.

He tried to move, looking for her, turning to find her, his legs gave way and he smelled the pitted earth, rotten and stale as he fell. Somewhere, he heard running, footsteps getting lighter, or maybe he didn't hear them at all, maybe he heard nothing. He thought he heard her saying his name over and over, her breath on his face, her hair falling over him, her ear listening at his mouth to see if he was all right. He did hear this didn't he? His eyes closed on the last thing he remembered before he lost consciousness, whispering her name, *Dolores*, but he knew that this time she'd gone, really gone. Out of the shadow and into the light. And in the darkness, someone watched her go—across the car park and through the archway, back the way she came.

Tuesday 9 January 2007

1

Tom Fairfax stared at the row of tablets on the bedside table. He reached out for the glass of water and counted them. Three pills—two small, one large, all white. A door banged somewhere in the house and he heard the ringing of a phone. He had no idea what time it was. He had slept solidly for hours, collapsing straight into bed when they finally got the TV set up, the cop shows loaded and the stations tuned in. Even though it was only 6pm, it had already been pitch dark outside. He looked at his watch. It was 7.36am now, another night where nothing had happened stretched back behind him, swallowed into a blanker past.

After the accident he was in a neck brace for twenty-four hours and couldn't move. He had to piss in a bottle while people checked on him every hour until he passed out. He didn't wake for three months. Here, no one came to check on him. They should, but he'd used up their sympathy and he couldn't blame them.

He flinched as he reached over for the water. Sometimes the pain was so bad it snapped his spine like the lash of wire on a mast and after Clemmie's daytrip for the TV, the things he'd seen, *thought* he'd seen, this was one of those days. He crammed the pills into his mouth all at once and gulped them down with the water. They tasted like Love Hearts: *Kiss me, Hello Sunshine, Sweetheart.*

Had he really seen those things? He saw Leah Barnes, the way she'd looked at him, spat the words at him. It was no more than he deserved. But Frank Molinari? That part he must have imagined. Frank was dead—they found him didn't they? Didn't his brother identify him? There was a funeral, he definitely remembered a funeral, but nothing was clear—was it Frank's funeral or Susie's? After you'd been to a few they pretty much blurred into each other only they didn't, no matter how much you wanted them to. He of all people should know that.

The phone had stopped ringing, but it started up again. He cursed, knowing Clemmie couldn't hear it at the best of times and with that TV blasting out it was just going to be worse, but then it stopped.

'Tom! Phone for you!' her voice shouted up from downstairs.

If he didn't answer they might go away.

'Did you hear me?'

Outside the wind was building, a wild January gale bringing the sea and the empty cry of gulls. He dragged himself off the bed, opened the curtains and watched the rain scatter-gun against the windowpane. He put his fingers to the glass to touch the drops and saw, in the garden, the broad conifer with its flat green branches being slapped around in the wind, throwing shadows across the lawn in the dawn light. The trunk of the tree was fat and solid but around its base the branches flailed, swaying down to the turf and back up again grasping for purchase, losing the fight against the building storm.

'Tom!'

'I'm coming!'

But still he didn't move. He squeezed his eyes and when he opened them again the walls were moving in focus, then out of focus, near then far. The colour of the wallpaper was the same dull brown it was forty years ago and in the desk in the corner he knew he would find broken pieces of Meccano and Airfix, a Spitfire plane he'd half-painted as a boy. He never finished anything, not even then.

'Just a minute...' He could hear Clemmie making her slow way upstairs, one difficult step at a time.

What time was it? The clock read 7.38 now, who the hell was ringing him? No one rang him these days, he ran through possibilities in the seconds before Clemmie got to him, two floors up, with the sound of the new TV

44

following her, booming up from the ground floor. He knew he should go down to her, not fair to have her climb all the way up here, but he couldn't move. He felt his head spinning then settling. When the spinning stopped he'd be able to move, but not until then so to ground himself, he watched the door, concentrated as the footsteps and the phone came closer.

'Tom!'

The door finally opened and Clemmie stood there, out of breath.

'You didn't need to come up,' he said. 'I would have come down.'

'No you wouldn't.' She handed him the phone. 'But you bloody should.'

She walked into his room without being invited and plonked herself on the bed, a hand on each thigh, puffing out steady O's with her mouth as she regained her strength. She was wearing her housecoat, the one with the deep pockets full of useful items, her Doomsday coat, the one she kept ready for any emergency. Her mobile phone that was never switched on, the number of the doctor written on a scrap of paper just in case, her wedding ring, an assortment of clinking things—an old cigarette lighter, the Swiss army knife keyring that had belonged to his father with its tiny scissors and spanners. As a boy he had longed to own that keyring, but after his father died into the big pocket it went. She was fingering it now, clipping the scissors open and closed, clicking the tweezers as she handed the phone to him.

'You should open a window in this room, wind or no wind.'

He didn't answer and seeing she wasn't going to budge, he took the phone to the window where the signal was clearer. There was turbulence in the background, shouting and a tunnel of noise bounced back at him from the handset.

'Sir, it's Ruby,' a woman's voice said. *Who else would it be?*

He was about to tell her that he was still on sick leave, but the words stuck between his teeth as he saw Frank standing beside the taxi, handing the suitcase to the girl.

'Tom?' *Tom.* That meant she was desperate. 'Sir?'

'What's happened?' he said.

'I hate to call you like this but…'

'Go on.'

'I'm at Pleasure Island…'

Frank and the girl, his arm under her elbow. Leah Barnes on her bike, pieces in a jigsaw. And now Ruby, the missing piece…

'I know it's going to be… look, I know you're not really up to it but…' she was struggling.

'What's happened?'

'We've… we've found a body.'

His voice sounded calm, even to his ears, even though he knew the answer already. 'Anyone we know?' he said.

He could almost see her shuffling her feet, side to side, not wanting to say. He could see the way her hair hung forward over one eye when she looked down, when she was avoiding a question.

'I think you should just come,' she said.

'Okay.' He knew he didn't have a choice. And in his head he saw Ruby, her red hair burning in his hand.

He put the phone down and turned back to face the room. He'd forgotten that Clemmie was still there. She was sitting on his bed, waiting, as if he'd come back from school and forgotten something. She'd taken the army knife out of her pocket and pulled the different implements from its body. They were splayed around it in a fan, which she was now carefully folding back into the body of the knife, like a deadly version of a Russian doll.

'You off then?' she said.

He didn't answer. He looked down at the phone in his hand as if staring at it would make it ring again.

'Good.' She got up. 'About time.'

She was in the doorway on her way out. The knife was safely back in her pocket, but her fingers were hovering on the edge of the fabric, lost without it.

'Was it you?' he said.

'What?'

'Did you get her to ring me?'

Clemmie didn't answer or she didn't hear him. She was already through the door; maybe he hadn't spoken loud enough for her to hear. He could have spoken louder, but he hadn't because he knew there was no answer to the question he'd just asked her.

'I'll make you a coffee and some toast,' she said over her shoulder. 'You'll need something before you go out.'

But he wasn't hungry. He pulled on the clothes he'd worn the day before, and every day before that for weeks. Cords, a shirt clean but creased, a jacket—light, too light for winter. He had no idea how cold it was outside. In his head, it was six months ago and summer.

And Susie was still alive.

2

Leah Barnes leaned on her handlebars and looked out at the cold, angry sea, well pleased because she'd won the bet. The bike, one day old, had handled well—her skin burning, face frozen from the wind, she couldn't see what she looked like but could imagine and didn't care. She breathed air into her hands and felt it move in a warm damp mist over her skin, soothing and easing the pain from the cold. It was a race but for fairness they'd split it—Mati did the first three miles on the new Rockhopper, Leah the second. Now Mati was on the all-terrain Raleigh Freeride, but he'd told Leah to go ahead. He still reckoned he'd beat her, *he wished*. There was a tenner resting on it and now Leah was the winner as she always was. *Sweet.*

As she waited for him, she counted the waves slapping against the pier, the mottled glass panes of the old Visitor Centre reflected in the mad brown foam. The doors to the end of the pier theatre clamped shut, padlocked and cobwebbed until the summer season awakened them. She loved the winter in this town—no tourists or crowds, just miles and miles of empty sand without a kid or a bucket and spade in sight. Apart from the odd dog walker, she had the coastal path to herself this morning and it was heaven even though it wasn't always like this. In the summer you couldn't move, couldn't breathe for dodging the kids and parents clogging the pavements, the sand filling every inch of the sea wall—granite, concrete and tarmac washed in heaps of sand like the Egyptian desert. In the summer she did her cycling on the country roads out towards Lancashire, owning the road, at one with her element, in the winter she had to make do with the town and it was never the same.

She'd been shaken by seeing that bastard yesterday, though. What did she think? That he was still languishing in his sweaty bed wasting away? She'd known he was out of hospital, that he'd come round. She had her sources on the wards, in one or two of the women officers down at the station, what good journalist wouldn't? He'd been out of her way for so long she hoped he'd never show up again. Always knowing that in a town of this size that, he would.

She looked out at the grey sky, the pallid light of the Irish Sea. A few seabirds hung in the droplets of air like wooden-winged puppets. She'd taken to watching the sky every day waiting for the good days, scrutinising the riffs and waves of the clouds for evidence of calm. Falcons didn't like the cold. Wind, they could deal with but cold was different and the hard edge of the Northern winter even more so. She was learning about the bird, learning everything she had only been able to observe when watching Susie. When Susie flew the falcon, Leah stood back in awe and, if she was honest, fear. That was changing. A routine report on the art of falconry had introduced her to Susie and to her falcon, Sky. It had turned a piece of casual reporting into a fascination with a creature she had never encountered and now a day without the falcon was a lost day. She had had enough of those to last her a lifetime. But seeing Fairfax the day before she was sure of only one thing now—he was not going to find out about the bird. Sky was her secret.

Something was happening. From the sea wall she could hear sirens screaming, too many for it to be nothing. The light was hazy, settling over the roofs of the red and blue beach huts like a blanket, washing them out. The white flagpole on the theatre roof carved the air needle-thin in a sliver of silver. She should go see what was happening, sirens on a dank winter morning in January meant a story. The blue lights being swallowed into the mist, beckoned her like the beacons flashing out in the bay. She couldn't ignore them.

49

As if on cue, her phone vibrated in her pocket and she had to dismount from the bike, trying to get the phone out before it stopped, sure it was Mati complaining that he'd been held up by a flock of sheep or something. He had a collection of excuses to even the bets out, determined one day to beat her. She fumbled with the zip in her tightly fitted lycra hoodie, purple and high-vis, she never took any chances these days and dragged the phone out before it stopped buzzing. But it wasn't Mati.

'Hey Mike,' she said.

'You up?'

'Well obviously…'

'Yeah well thought you might be out on some cycle path or something… Christ what's that noise?'

'Wind or sirens, take your pick.' Leah put the phone to her good ear, away from the sea wind, which roared in tune with the sirens in the background. It sounded like a very bad orchestra warming up. 'What's up?' she said

'You near Pleasure Island?'

'I am.' Resisting a quip, *how did you guess?*

'They've found a body down there…'

A beat. *Not again.*

'Don't know what is about that place. No one ever gets murdered in this town yet that place seems to rack 'em up, I don't know…'

'How do *you* know?'

'Jen called me from the station, gave us the heads up. Course they don't want anyone to know yet but…'

Leah's eye was fixed more firmly now on the fairground, its low level rides skimming the seafront skyline, the sirens definitely coming from there. She squeezed her eyes slantwise and could detect the flash of a light coming and going in the drizzle of the morning air. She looked down the coast to the larger flashier fairground in Blackpool, to the curve of the huge *Terminator* rollercoaster with its red eyes atop the rails to warn aircraft not to come too low. It looked silent as the grave over there.

'Why me?'

'Has to be you Leah,' Mike said.

Leah scuffed the heel of her thin riding shoes along the ground; her feet and calves muddy from the long ride. Mike was right. She was ready. The past was catching up—Fairfax one day scaring her shitless on the bike, a death mask walking, and now this—the one place she had never thought to set foot in again. But didn't every bike ride she went on bring her past here? She could cycle any way to avoid it, but didn't. She came past here like a pilgrim on a journey, every day of every week, every month of the year. She was ready.

'Will Tom Fairfax be there?' she asked.

'Dunno, but he's still on sick leave, isn't he…'

'I saw him yesterday.'

'Right, well then my guess is he might be.' Mike had delivered his message, given her the story even though he was probably itching to get his hands on it himself. 'Does it matter?' Leah didn't answer that.

'Do we know who's dead then?' she said, running through the possibilities in her head and landing on Genaro Molinari. She pictured the big man, the way his lip curled at the corner of his teeth like a Great White.

'Nah. Just get there soon as, yeah, don't want to lose this story.' Mike was already on to something else; he wasn't going to say more.

'Okay.' Leah let her breath out, a long stream of smoke in the foggy air. 'Okay.' But Mike had already hung up on her.

3

Tom barely glanced in the mirror before heading down to the kitchen, but knew his hair was too long, that he needed a shave. He was clean, that was all that mattered. What he looked like didn't come into it.

'You're not going looking like that are you?' Clemmie looked him up and down and passed him a cup of coffee with a plate of toast covered in red jam, which smelled like strawberry. He wasn't hungry, but found to his surprise that the sweet smell of the strawberries revived him. He was ten years old again, picking raspberries and berries for the jam, denying that he'd eaten any of them, his mouth and teeth ringed with red juice and his fingers itching with dust from the fruit. The jam would have come from the last of Clemmie's summer pots from the allotment. He'd come home from the hospital to the row of jars on the windowsill, the red syrups cooling in their glassy jackets. That was Autumn. Summer had passed him by with barely a nod, and now he was back where he started, winter-bound and aching.

He sat on, not wanting to move but Clemmie was having none of it. She gathered together things she thought he'd need: cigarettes, dented Zippo lighter (she didn't approve of his smoking even though she was addicted herself), the last remaining packets of pills—tramadol, diclofenac, codeine and aspirin. He watched her, acting as if there was still time, as if he could turn it back, then he lit two cigarettes and handed one to his mother. They sat at the table smoking in silence. The coffee was hot enough to burn the back of his throat and as he swallowed he caught a reflection of himself in the darkened kitchen window. *Who was he kidding?*

'I'll open the windows in your room while you're out,' Clemmie said. 'Let some air in.'

He nodded.

'What if I don't go? What if I'm not ready?'

'You'll never be ready,' she said. 'That's why you'll go.'

He took his time over the toast, the coffee, the cigarette. The time ticked on, the too-fast clock in the kitchen had moved on twenty minutes by the time he was ready. He could still feel the honeyed sugar of the strawberries clinging to his teeth.

He stood. 'Right then.'

Clemmie took a couple of cigarettes from his packet on the table and tucked them into her apron pocket.

'You haven't forgotten that Jack will be here tonight?' she said. 'He's going to London tomorrow for his interview?'

'No.' He had.

'So don't be late.'

He looked at the collection of items Clemmie had placed on the table. Should he put all the pills in his pockets or leave them where they were? Clemmie was pretending not to watch him as he made his decision. She was shuffling about with dishes and bottles of milk. She locked the bright summer strawberries back in the fridge; the jangle of the jars brought him back to the present. He hesitated, then took the diclofenac, just in case, leaving the rest. *One day at a time.*

'You can take the Volvo,' Clemmie said, clearing up, busy, busy, busy trying to be normal as if today was like any other. 'Go on, you don't want to keep the young woman waiting.'

He smiled, *young woman*. Making it sound as though he was off on a jaunt.

He opened the front door onto a world that had shifted several gears in less than twenty-four hours. The storm was stripping trees of their remaining leaves and shrubs in the front garden beds had wilted to brown and withered phantoms of themselves. For the first time, he realised he was noticing them. For the past few weeks, on the rare occasions he had gone out, he had looked at nothing. Now he was aware of them, he could remember the smell of the wisteria on the house when he was a boy, when these shrivelled vines were in bloom. That was better than nothing, wasn't it? It *was* better than nothing; it was something. He felt a surge in his body, the blood beating, as he slammed the front door behind him. The force of the wind took him, a sharp intake of breath, almost knocking him off his feet. He felt it in every inch of his bones.

4

It would only take a few minutes to get to the fairground, ten max, as the crow flies. The falcon would make it in about two and she imagined the flow and dip of him riding the angry skies, imagined how it must feel to do that. She could see the outline of Pleasure Island more clearly now as daylight crept around its corners. The town behind it also coming into view, the wide esplanade with its green and white shelters glinting with drizzle from the mist. Soon, even in winter, people would walk along it, dragged by reluctant dogs. The candyfloss stall had even been known to open if the sun came out, although not once had she seen it open in the middle of January.

A body could mean just some homeless guy holed up in a forgotten fairground ride. It had been known; in they go for warmth, fall asleep and before they knew it, the cold has them. But that wouldn't warrant all those sirens, a call from Mike's contact at the station to give him the heads up. She'd been waiting for something like this, hadn't she? To get to Molinari whatever it took, even if that meant crossing Fairfax again. What would Susie say if she didn't go?

Leah's hand went to her left ear, the one closest to the sea. The cold made the pain and the silence in it worse. She didn't care, she was used to it. It reminded her of everything she didn't want to forget, everything she could have had, everything she'd lost and was never, *never,* going to change now. She looked back along the coast road for Mati and saw nothing but fine rain and a line of car headlights building now that the police had closed the road to the fairground. Mati was not going to show up, he'd lost and gone home. He was always doing this and probably got side tracked along the way somewhere to make his point. She cruised slowly down the coast road and made her way up to the esplanade, looping past the cinema and the bowling alley and on to the new McDonald's, which was busy in spite of the hour. She chained the bike to the railings and went inside joining a queue of people bleary from work—the night workers, shrimpers and road workers, grubby, tired and eyeless with sleep. She needed a coffee before she hit that fairground. The body wasn't going anywhere; it would wait until she got there. No need to rush, no need to reveal her hand so soon. Staying in control was everything.

5

Detective Sergeant Ruby Miller was wearing a knee-length fuchsia coat, which didn't clash with the deep red of her hair. On anyone else, Tom thought, the effect would have been disastrous, but not on her. She was talking into her mobile phone and raised a leather-gloved hand to him, indicating that he should come over.

She looked good. She looked like she was in charge.

She was standing by the blue and white incident tape next to the Funhouse amusement arcade with its boarded-up shutters skulking behind her like guilty secrets in the dawning light. An ambulance, its engine running, idled in the cold air while the driver blew into his hands to keep them warm. Tom recognised a few faces but not most of them. Those he did know dragged their heads round to acknowledge him with an air of embarrassment. They would all have known what happened, it was probably the talk of the station for months. Now here they were greeting the man they never thought would show his face in the division again. *Wondering how he had the nerve.* The confidence he'd felt on his way over, driving the Volvo around streets that bent themselves into familiarity the more corners he turned and lights at which he stopped, had evaporated. He could have turned back, crept away as quietly as he had arrived but he saw Ruby Miller waving, waiting for him. He went forward, pulled on a thread towards her, trying to ignore the icy wind chipping away at his skull, boring through to the bone. He put his hand into his pocket to find the blister pack of pills, reassured by the bump of the tablets on the pads of his fingers. As he reached her, her phone rang and she turned away from him slightly. As she talked, she flipped her notebook over in her hand, scribbling what the caller was saying, taking charge, and

Tom found himself wrong-footed and impotent in what used to be his own familiar world.

'Hey!' she said, finishing the call and put out her hand out to touch his arm as if to say, *steady now*.

'Well,' he said, 'I'm here.'

'Good.' she smiled.

That was it? They hadn't seen each other for months. At the start, when he was in the hospital he knew she'd been many times to see him even though he would speak to no one, couldn't speak. He had heard her voice talking to someone else in the room, murmurs and whispers. Sometimes he had the feeling she was there at night when everyone had gone, sitting by his bedside. Was she reading? Sleeping in the chair? Maybe that bit had been his imagination. Later she had to interview him, for a statement about the fire, about how he knew what had happened when he wasn't even there. But she hadn't really done the talking, that had been left to the DI, Robert Nardone, who had gone easy on him. At the time he thought it was for old time's sake, they'd been together in the force for years and you didn't judge your colleagues even if sometimes you should have done, but now... now it was clear that Nardone had made a mistake. *Why had Nardone made a mistake?*

'Come on.' Ruby walked fast, her height giving her the advantage, Tom keeping up with her in long low strides.

Why did she call him? Was it something she couldn't handle? Taking in her short black boots and shoulders thrown back against the wind, he didn't think so.

Something else then...

She spoke rapidly. Tom inclined his head to hear, trying to decipher her strong Belfast accent. This morning, it sounded like part of the wild wind.

'How are you?' she said.

'I've been better.'

'You look better, a bit...'

'Do I?'

He knew she was humouring him, but it felt good to hear it.

If he was honest, it *was* good to be out in the fresh air, on the outside instead of in, away from his mother and her TV and her endless discussions about people he'd never heard of and cared about even less. It *was* better, it was. And away from the accusing gaze of his officers, people he would have to work with again, he felt the blood rush back into his reluctant heart. Above them, seagulls screamed, flung themselves into the squall, thrown back and forth on the currents of air, out of control. He thought of Hitchcock, birds sitting on wires staring at him, watching his every move, discomforting him like omens of doom if he believed that kind of thing, which he didn't. Omens were for those who had given up and couldn't find a way back and today he was somewhere in between, still hedging his bets. Because of the threatening storm, the birds were everywhere—a line of purple pigeons and black-backed gulls huddled along the edge of the old rollercoaster, which creaked and sighed in the wind, wings folded, heads down. The iron girders bent to the tune of the gale causing both Tom and Ruby to look up at the same time at the mass of metal bearing down on them. The wooden rollercoaster was over a hundred years old and had survived everything the elements had thrown at it, yet it was still at the mercy of the Irish Sea and her fury. The salt of her sorrow clung to every surface corroding and twisting the metal, which connected the wooden rails. There had been safety issues in the past, a few minor incidents, but it was solid enough. It was a hard fact that Pleasure Island and its rollercoaster was way out of step with its time and nothing, Tom thought, no amount of money or effort thrown at it by Molinari was going to bring it back to the way it had been in its heyday.

'Nothing like a bracing walk,' he said and smiled, in spite of himself.

Ruby laughed, the sound of it flying away into the brine. He watched it go, up, up and over the heads of the seagulls.

'Is that thing safe?' Ruby put her hand to her head involuntarily as though that would save her if the whole lot came down.

'It's been there long enough...' Tom said. 'But can we run fast enough...'

She smiled and they hurried their pace and then, a few feet short of the crime scene, Ruby stopped.

'You ready for this?' she said.

'For what?'

'Well, we think the body is Frank Molinari's.'

Tom looked at her, trying not to give himself away.

'You sure?'

'Pretty...'

'Fuck.'

'That's one way of putting it,' she said.

They walked on. He didn't tell her that he already knew.

The crime scene, cordoned off, was squashed between one of the fairground buildings and the exterior security fence of the ground. The glass was cracked and broken around the Hall of Mirrors, a patina of dirt and grime coating the shattered surfaces. When Tom looked down, there was no reflection in the pieces of broken glass on the floor, not mirrors at all but poor imitations of their curving undulating selves. But, as they drew closer and into the hall, he saw his body pulled out of shape, distorted and elongated one moment then shrunk and compressed the next. For the first time he felt as though he was looking at an honest impression of himself, the one that his clear bright mirror at home was always afraid to show him.

'I know this isn't easy for you—for any of us,' Ruby said, turning to him. 'But you're the link here, you knew him. And it might help you...' she hesitated, '...to find out what happened that day, with Susie and Frank. The fire...'

Why Susie died in the fire with Frank. The one Frank didn't die in after all.

He looked at her. If he'd made Clemmie stop the car, gone after Frank the day before, he'd still be alive. *Wouldn't he?*

'I saw him,' he said.

'Who?'

'Frank. In town, yesterday.'

Ruby stared at him, a shadow of disbelief passing over her face.

'You did? Did he see you?'

'No,' he said.

And it was too late to do anything about it. He was here now and Frank was dead and sooner or later Nardone would show up. *What would he do then?*

'Okay,' he said, moving forward towards the incident tent, closing down any more questions she might have. He wasn't ready to go there yet. 'Let's see him.'

6

The sirens had stopped, but morning commuter traffic was backing up now on Marine Place. Leah could see a road block ahead, a police outrider standing in the middle of the tarmac directing traffic from Pleasure Island. There must be some serious shit going on. She felt a small kick in her stomach, a shifting of the oxygen in her lungs as she breathed slowly to calm herself. She'd done the right thing not waiting any longer for that feckless bloody flatmate of hers. She'd deal with him later and make sure he coughed up her winnings, which he would, honour intact. He was never anything less than honourable, her friend Mati. The only thing was—if she pushed on further, was what would happen if she bumped into Fairfax... but if he *was* there, well then, she'd have deal with it wouldn't she? *What would Susie do?*

Susie would say life's too fucking short.

So, on she went, the back way, away from the police cordon skipping the red light down by the park, leaving a stream of car horns in her wake. She didn't care. She pushed on to hug the cycle path (which she never rode on as a matter of principle) alongside the indigo sea in its menacing cloak of daylight. Lights were coming in on container ships on their way to Liverpool from Dublin and Douglas on the Isle of Man, orange beacons in the murk, and she knew that if they had lights on at this hour it was going to be a bad storm ahead. You could always judge how bad from whether or not you could see Blackpool or Southport across the estuary and, on a good day, even the Lake District; today she could see neither. It was the same the other way—no sign of the smudge of the Welsh mountains, the inching snow-capped tip of Snowdonia, nothing but a thick wall of sea fog. Past the park the bike met the pavement and by the time she hit the corner of Albert Park, the wind felt like it was building to gale force. She double backed across the pedestrian path, which cut through the park to get to the road running directly under the pier. It was little more than a gravel track under there because the sea reached it sometimes and under normal circumstances she wouldn't let her bike tyres near it. But by now she knew that nothing about this day was normal. Cutting beneath the pier would get her to the fairground quicker. She was already starting to worry she'd lost too much time.

The car park to her left was empty apart from a couple of hardened skater kids, posing as usual even in this weather, their slicked hair limed with the wet wind. Up and down the curves and speed bumps they went, approaching them at a lick then lifting into the air as the boards hit the bumps before alighting neatly again on the other side like surefooted birds. She knew they were always there because she used to be one of them. She'd got bored of it quicker than most: bored of skimming the surface of life, pissing away most of it in the process.

There were no cars, just the one, a white VW Beetle, parked at the front of the parking slots facing the sea across the main road. The skateboarders were veering round, doing elaborate turns and spins, using it as an obstacle ignoring the woman at the wheel. Didn't matter, she didn't seem to notice them either—it was a woman, and it was the face of a woman Leah hadn't seen in a long while.

It was the car too, of course it was—Leah realised that later because who else drove a car like that? She hadn't seen her since… well, not since the day of the fire… not since then. How could she forget her? Dolores. *What's she up to?* She didn't see Leah, but why would she, she never noticed her before, why now? All wrapped in her cycling gear she would look unrecognisable, just one of the nutters along this coast who went out whatever the weather. But, all the same, in spite of what she thought about the woman, she almost stopped to ask if she was okay because she didn't look okay just staring out there into the Irish Sea. *Almost*, but didn't; Leah cycled on. She told herself Dolores wouldn't remember her anyway, *why would she*? She was not going to waste time on someone else who didn't deserve it.

She carried on under the pier bridge towards Pleasure Island and by the time she got there, Dolores in her white car had all but vanished from her mind. It was just something that she'd remember later, much later, when it was too late.

7

The crime scene had been secured, the cordon tape fastened round hurriedly, doubled over at awkward angles around posts and nails, everything surrounded by heaps of rubbish. Bottles, cans, cigarette boxes and crisp bags, logos faded by the rain and the bleaching wind were piled, looking as though a giant with a broom had brushed them there and would be back for them later. The Hall of Mirrors was a labyrinth of cramped corridors, twists and turns and Tom felt the fluid in his knee joints crack as he bent low to get inside. When he reached the centre, a wider space where there was enough room to fit several people at once, there was a thin line of blood smeared down the mirror but no body.

'He got himself out,' someone said. Dressed from head to toe in a white paper suit the person who spoke rustled and handed him a package of neatly folded protective clothing. 'You'll have to suit up, Sir.'

The final mirrored chamber led to the outside and Tom could just see the heavy outline of Frank's body propped against the exterior wall as if he was dozing in a slumber. He heard the sea thrashing against the tide barriers a few hundred yards away beyond the fairground walls and remembered when he was a kid how the tide never came in. Now it was always there, taunting the town, threatening to drag it back into the endless mud flats that lay beyond it.

Once outside, he managed to stand straighter, his head only slightly bent forward, the moisture from the top of the low chamber ceiling dripping on the back of his neck. He took his jacket off and pulled on the white suit, dragged the sleeves down over his hands as far as he could, gloves, a mask and still felt the bite of the bitter wind. He wished he'd worn something warmer, regretting his stupidity coming out dressed like this while Ruby Miller, just ahead of him getting into her own suit, looked snug as toast as she shrugged off her pink wool coat to don her protection.

Frank Molinari was well dressed, as always, in a pale blue shirt, blue serge sharp suit and shoes in polished Italian leather. The shoes were scuffed, his clothes dirty from where the living man had dragged himself out of the place he was attacked to the muddied place where he died. Ruby Miller was crouching, going through the pockets of Frank's jacket with latex-gloved hands. Tom found he couldn't move, someone pushed past him and he hardly noticed, transfixed at Frank lying on the ground, his face relaxed as though sleeping. Some track marks in the earth, from where he'd dragged himself, but not much blood; that was on the mirror and in the ground, like a joker's trick gone wrong. There was something pathetic and desperate about the way he had collapsed, crumpled into a corner, head back against the wall; he'd got himself here but no further. His mouth was dragged down and open, his death all the more banal for the finery of his impeccable clothes. Tom looked down; his own unshined shoes beneath their plastic overshoes were just visible.

'Not robbery.' Ruby straightened herself with Frank's wallet in her hands. It contained money, not much but some and a couple of credit cards: Crédit du Nord, Crédit Agricole. 'Well we can guess where he's been holed up,' she said, raising an eyebrow.

'We also found this...' One of the white suits handed her an envelope inside a newspaper; it was empty.

'Money in it, do you think?' she asked Tom, but his mind was elsewhere.

'Anyone told his brother?' Tom said, his words smaller and more hesitant than intended.

She shook her head, 'He found him.'

Unexpected but, okay, he thought. He took the envelope from her, sniffed it.

66

'Yes, money,' he said, handing it straight to the crime scene officer, a young woman he didn't recognise, steady handed, clear-eyed. They were starting younger these days. He felt the gears shift in his head, trying to recall when he started, but couldn't quite find the moment to latch on to. 'This isn't Genaro's style.'

'Usually the family...' Ruby said. 'Someone close.'

But to find his only brother in this state, that wasn't something you could come back from easily. Tom knew this. He had balanced his daughter's bones in his hands, the bag of ash in its cardboard box they carried from the crematorium was lighter than a bag of flour, there was so little left to burn. Frank was all Genaro had but there was another possibility...

'Genaro believed Frank was dead all this time so what might that do to him? Frank turning up out of the blue like that...' Tom said, more to himself.

The air was getting humid around the crime scene and he could see small shapes hovering, buzzing, in the light thrown from the arc lamps. He imagined the blowflies heading up Frank's nasal passages, into his throat, his eyes, eating him away even now from the inside. Tom sucked a breath in, felt it catch and stop, collapsing in on itself, and lunged to get away from the site. The damp air tangled with the phlegm in his tobacco sodden lungs and by the time he got outside into more open ground he was coughing too much to speak. He took a cigarette from his pocket and lit up.

'Well that's really going to help...' Ruby had followed him.

A deep drag, another gut doubling cough and he felt better. He straightened, stretching the bones in his shoulder blades together, easing the tension out. He looked around. Genaro had let security lapse—there was an attempt at security lights, the bulbs along the top of the mirrors still winking in places, a grotesque parody of a musical hall sketch with Frank slumped against his wall as the main attraction.

'Hughes interviewed Genaro,' Ruby said. 'Didn't get much from him, only he said he didn't seem that shocked.'

'Genaro never does.'

'No other witnesses, no one around...' she started to add.

'Why didn't *you* interview Genaro, why send Hughes?'

She ignored his critical tone. In spite of himself he had harked back to the rank he, strictly speaking, no longer held. He was still on sick leave and Ruby Miller had been promoted in his absence.

'Hughes can handle it,' she snapped back. 'He's a big boy now.' Making her authority clear and telling him in no uncertain terms where he stood.

She took refuge in her notebook, scribbling something, her fingers blurring across the page. He wasn't sure she was writing anything, the movements were too rapid, her pen pushing too hard and he turned to suppress a smile. He'd caught her off-guard with his challenge about Hughes, but he had made her think, touched a nerve and surprised himself in the process. He had forgotten *how* to think, how to *be*, coming here was making him remember.

There was no love lost between himself and Frank but even so, to die like that... Tom felt a stab of sadness he hadn't expected. He felt nauseous and light-headed, as though he was up on the high roller coaster looking down on Frank in his shiny shoes. His head was hammering again; he should take something to fix it. His hand went involuntarily to his pocket beneath the paper suit, located the pills. The other hand was holding the cigarette, he levelled his fingers flat, the cigarette balanced between them and watched the slight tremble he'd developed in recent months. He did that sometimes, imagining the drugs he was taking leaching out through his skin like pus. Ruby was staring at him. He'd forgotten where he was.

'You okay?' she said.

'Not really,' he said. 'But I will be.' He lowered his hand, smiled a sheepish *sorry* smile. 'That ring we found in the fire?'

'Frank's ring?'

'Genaro identified it as his brother's…'

'It was all we had, the fire took everything…'

'We had bones, we had…'

His daughter's bones, the weight of them in his hand. Ruby reached out.

'Stop.' Her tone was gentler. 'Nardone didn't think that it was worth pursuing, we had the ring, we knew Frank was there, we had witnesses, we knew…' she hesitated, 'we knew Susie was there too.'

'He didn't ask for any DNA?'

She shook her head.

'We were a man down, it was obvious it was Frank…'

'Only it wasn't was it?'

'No,' she said wearily. 'It wasn't.'

Tom realised in his gut that he had known all along the body wasn't Frank's. Frank had no reason to be there that day. He'd told no one because he thought he'd never have to come back here and identify him again. *The only question was: who else had known it too.*

The cold air settled into the back of his teeth as Tom walked and he discovered that clenching them together woke him up. He had to decide what he was going to do, what he was going to say, to *not* say. The bite of the cold was like chewing ice. He was used to that. In the hospital, confined to his bed when he couldn't move with only the flickering of his eyelids for company and the flash of a fluorescent tube over his head, ice had been his only drink. *He could do this.* The more he walked, the better he felt, so he kept walking and Ruby Miller had no choice but to follow.

More vans arrived and left. The CSIs lumbered about in their white body suits looking like they'd landed from the moon, big footed and clumsy, trying to carry bags and cases in latex-gloved fingers. There were others there now, people he didn't recognise at all this time. They were calling in the big guns, which they would for a man who was already dead, the one who had got away. He was aware that he was still looking on from the outside. *How was he to get in?* He knew there were protocols to follow, paperwork to be filled before he could have his job back to say nothing of the psychology report and whether or not anyone would allow him to. Post-traumatic stress disorder his diagnosis, one that would stick with him for the rest of his life. The last psychologist had advised he was still 'unfit for work' and maybe he was. Maybe Ruby Miller had dragged him here to give him closure; something every police officer knew didn't exist. Ruby knew that. *They all did.* Susie was dead, they'd had her birthday and a Christmas since, an Easter and then summer and now they were almost at her anniversary, each one filled with the knowledge that she was never, *never* coming back. So what kind of closure is that? There's no such thing. He had to forgive Ruby a little for trying, but it wasn't going to work.

'Good to see you back Sir,' a voice said, behind an outstretched hand. Doug Hughes was one of the people he hadn't missed. His mouth was welcoming, but his grey eyes wished him a million miles away. They'd come through the ranks together, but Tom had left him behind a long, long time ago. Doug was never going to forget that, he must have been praying he'd never come back.

'You up and about then?' Hughes said, forcing a smile.

Tom took his hand on a reflex, but he didn't smile back.

'Doug,' he said.

'Frankie boy, eh? Who'd've thought it?'

Tom could see the exit gate, the Moroccan archway emerging from the murk of the morning. He could see the

Volvo sticking out from the police cars and vans. He could feel the pressure of the keys in his pocket. All he had to do was to walk past Hughes, get in the car and go home, *give this up*. The resolve of only seconds ago evaporated at the sight of this man's resentment—was that all it was going to take to kick him off his stride?

'When you spoke to Genaro Molinari,' Tom said, 'he seem shocked about Frank?'

On the back foot, the smile on Hughes's face melted. He'd thought, as he always did, that he had a run on his old boss.

'Who wants to know?'

'I'm just interested...'

Hughes was weighing it up, not wanting to give anything away that could shift the power balance between them.

'You're sure Genaro found him?' Tom persisted.

'I'd put money on him finishing him off,' Hughes said, his lips pulled tighter and his eyes flat.

'Oh come on, that's a bit of a leap isn't it?' Ruby Miller was behind them; neither of them had seen her approach, too wrapped up in their mutual animosity.

Hughes ignored her. He moved in between her and Tom, blocking her part in the conversation.

'I reckon he just lost it when the prodigal son showed up—look around you.' He threw a careless arm wide. 'Not much left, he's on his uppers and he's not gonna share it.' Hughes folded his arms standing his ground.

'Thank you for your in-depth analysis Sergeant,' Miller said, her tone dismissed him and his face sank even further down than the jowl in his jaws had already pulled it. She handed him the empty envelope now sealed in a plastic bag. 'Can you get this checked for prints, please?'

He snatched it from her and stalked off.

'Not for me to say, but I think *you* should speak to Genaro,' Tom said quietly.

'Not for you to say, no,' she snapped shut the cover of the notebook she had been holding in her hands all morning. 'But on balance...'

'But?' he said.

'But—well, yes, okay, I think you might be right.'

'So when you speak to him—can I come with you?'

Her eyes scanned him as though she was assessing his condition, whether or not he was in any fit state, and then she put the notebook in her pocket and, back now in her cosy pink coat, pulled her leather gloves back over her hands.

'Okay,' she said. 'But don't push it, okay?'

He nodded. His first step back onto the inside.

8

If he was on leave then why was that bastard Fairfax standing by the entrance to Pleasure Island, cigarette in hand. This was serious, more serious than she'd thought and she forgot for the moment to be afraid as she ran her mind through the reasons he might be there too.

He looked really terrible she thought with some gratification, far worse than the day before. He looked washed out, smoking as usual, didn't the guy learn? What if she just walked over there and said, 'Hey guess who I've just seen sitting in her beetle car watching the sea.' Leah was starting to add the numbers up, two and two getting her closer to the identity of the dead man (because she was pretty confident now that it was a man), she just didn't know which man she was betting on.

She watched Fairfax smoke his cigarette, knowing he couldn't see her. She stood across the road in the entrance of the Winter Garden car park. The red brick and glass conservatory building was used as an art gallery in winter. In summer, the hothouse plants and foliage created a tropical world to make visitors forget the cold of winter. In the 1800's a man called Thomas Everington had grown a pineapple here; the first one to be found in the north west of England. There was a mural on one of the entrance pillars of a pineapple in a jar, like a Greek urn containing life instead of ashes. It was one of the top tourist attractions in town. When the open top bus tours went round, you could hear it proclaimed as the first pineapple to be found in England, which was a stretch. There was a coffee shop and fresh homemade cakes. Pineapple brownies were a speciality—Susie loved them. It was always a destination after a long bike ride. Leah liked to sit in the outside courtyard, which had been covered by glass and ironwork funded by some EU grant, and watch the fairground, keeping it in the corner of her eye. She brought her laptop sometimes, wrote up reports when the office was busy or just sat here watching the past. Wondering as she sat there, if Susie had lived, would things have been different and by now would they be somewhere else, living entirely altered lives.

She could see Fairfax sheltering from the drizzle beneath the ersatz archway that was supposed to represent the Casbah on account of its crenelated turrets and desert-washed sandstone effect. It was built from fibreglass and painted, repainted god knows how many times so that the bright white colour she remembered from her childhood had faded now into a dismal beige. She locked the bike up with two sets of locks, she couldn't be too careful, and made sure the back wheel was threaded through with a strong chain. Sometimes they simply removed the front wheel and left it attached to the bike park then buggered off with the rest of the bike. It had happened to her too many times and no one was having *this* new road bike.

Fairfax finished the cigarette, screwing the butt of it beneath his foot into the wet ground. There was no other way in. To get to the crime scene, to whatever it was waited for her there, she had to pass him. *Fuck.* She waited, hoping he would go away, but he didn't move. The minutes ticked away, the sirens got calmer but the backed up traffic became angrier, horns and carbon monoxide belching into the cold sea air. She watched him take another cigarette from a packet in his free hand and stand there with it, unlit, looking across, straight across to where she was standing. He'd seen her and he wasn't going anywhere. Leah had run out of choices.

9

Tom knew she'd seen him. He could see her skulking across the wide road hiding in the doorway to the Winter Garden glasshouse. In that jacket you couldn't miss her. She was waiting for him to leave, but he was going nowhere. He lit another cigarette, his—*God knows for this time of the morning* —but his chest was tight so that was too many. The match lit the flat dull walls around him pitching long black fingers of shadow under the archway. He watched the wind try to push away the clouds as the watery sun, struggling to come out, refused to give up the fight.

The ground in front of the archway was pitted with dips and holes, long past repair and last night's rainwater turned to icy sludge in its pockets. He felt a spasm in his gut. He needed to eat something. It was hours since he'd last eaten, the taste of Clemmie's strawberry jam all but a distant memory. The cigarettes were keeping hunger only temporarily at bay. He waited as the cigarette burned down in his fingers watching Leah Barnes struggling to decide whether to come over or not.

She wore her usual garb: cycling gear consisting of a bright purple jacket, black pants, red helmet. One thing was certain; you'd pick her out in a crowd. She took her time, ambling but holding his gaze. He'd give her that: she was bold faced when she wanted to be, just like his daughter.

'Alright?' she said. 'Didn't expect to see you here.'

Tom could smell her from six feet away, the cold sweat of a bike ride, unwashed trainers, muddy face and the stale trail of something more perfumed, once pleasant, just a hint of it, beneath the sweat. He put the cigarette to his lips, damp from the way he'd been gripping it, to drown the smell, to stop himself having to think about the fact that this girl was still alive and his Susie was dead. The way he was feeling had a name: *survivor's guilt* they'd called it in his counselling. But having a name for it didn't help. He wondered if Leah had been feeling it too.

'Who's dead then?' Leah said, breaking this thought.

Her face adjusted so that the light struck its angular edges emphasising the hollowed curves of her high-boned cheeks. Her fair hair was pulled back from her face, swinging free like a ragged tail. Leah Barnes looked a lot like her father, red-faced and weasel thin, but the red was from the whisky with Barnes Senior, not so with his daughter. In spite of the weather, the mud and the dreary light, Leah looked as bright and fresh as the Welsh mountains just coming into relief behind her.

'There's nothing to see,' Tom said. 'Nothing you'll be allowed to see...'

'Okay,' she said, ignoring him, moving past him to go into the fairground. *That was it? That was all she was going to say to him after...* but she stopped, turned back as though she'd forgotten something.

'Oh.' She paused, *had she read his mind?* 'Dolores.' The second hand of his watch ticked round, he could feel it on his wrist shift as the mechanism hovered above his pulse. His heart rate shifted up a notch. 'Just seen her on Marine Drive.' *Tick tock.* 'If you're interested.'

Then she made to move past him, to go straight into the ground, sure of herself as always. *Marine Drive that was only...* He put his hand out to stop her; she looked down at his fingers touching the edge of her elbow lightly as though they were the legs of a fly or a spider she wanted to shrug off. He removed it quickly.

'When... where, exactly did you see her?' he said.

He knew he'd revealed too much of himself. He saw the quick flick of her eyelids. Her rosy cheeks smiled without the balance of her lips and her blue eyes shimmered telling him she knew everything, the facts clicking around the synapses in her skin like numbers in a calculator. *She knew.* But then she smiled and took pity on him.

'About ten minutes ago, if you shift you'll probably find her.'

'Thank you.'

She shrugged. She didn't care. She turned to leave.

'So,' she said. 'Is it Genaro?'

How many of them knew the truth, how long before the chain came back to him?

'Frank.' He turned away, not wanting to see her reaction.

In the car he waited. He risked a glance in the mirror to see if she'd gone and saw that the archway behind him was empty. To his left over the sea the sky was getting brighter as the rain eased and the cold crisper air took over. Sometimes a gale could do this—blow everything away as quickly as it had arrived. There was still a line of pink hovering though, just above the sea; *red sky in the morning the sailor's warning.* It hadn't finished with them yet. He drove out of the car park and on to the main road, up to the junction with the seafront where he could have headed back for home. He went left on to Marine Drive.

There was no sign of Dolores. Nothing.

He carried on to the thin line of car park sandwiched between the sea and the road, which in summer was lined with day-trippers and their flasks of tea, Daily Mirrors on the dashboard and the rain outside for company. Today it was empty apart from a few kids on skateboards. He looked in every direction, across the bleak water of the Irish Sea that looped itself round from Southport across to St Marie-by-Sea and Lytham and then out and across to Blackpool and Morecambe hiding itself around the corner of the bay. Each seaside town was a link in an unbroken chain round this flat marshy coast. In the early days of railways and charabancs they flocked here in hordes; there were pictures in the museum showing packed railway stations, smiling girls in bathing hats posing on the board of the outdoor lido, which was St Marie's pride and joy. The lido was still there, abandoned and crumbling, waiting for a saviour, continually threatened by the sea marshlands that grew on the sandbanks abandoned by the ever-receding ocean and the treachery of the tides. One wrong step and you'd be sucked down.

Where was she?

He got out of the car, leaned against the bonnet. He knew Leah hadn't lied. Dolores had vanished again, just like she always did. *But why was she here, now, today?* He saw Frank slumped against the wall, shook away the thought.

He arched his back, extending his lower vertebrae, the pain in his lumbar spine easing as he leaned it against the cold metal and considered the sea. In a few hours there would be miles of bare quick sand. A few redshanks limbered up waiting for razor clams and shrimp to surface, their long tiptoe beaks pecking at the flat mud scribbled with sandworms and tyre tracks created by the handful of shrimpers who still came out here plying a dying trade in a dying town. A few months ago he'd wanted to come here, to walk out on the sand and will it to suck him into whatever layer of hell was down there, to take him away from what he had done. *What had stopped him?* He couldn't remember, just that he'd wanted to live, and that was enough.

He lit another cigarette, the pack was almost empty, and started to make plans in his head. A van was driving into the shopping mall at the bottom of the low hill near the cinema. The van was always here come winter come summer come spring, selling bacon butties and sausage barms and hot sweet tea. Something about it, reassuring, something that had not changed... When he'd finished the cigarette he'd go down there, eat something, drink something. He threw the still glowing butt on to the ground. Spat some threads of tobacco clinging to his tongue.

Enough.

10

Leah Barnes and DI Ruby Miller had met once before when she was still a Detective Sergeant. Quick work Leah was thinking, taking her in, making the most of a boss in meltdown, good on her. Every tall thin inch of her was draped in a bright pink coat that washed out her lovely porcelain skin. Fair play to her Leah thought, the coat sent out a statement and the place was in need of a bit of colour. Miller intercepted Leah as soon as she got inside the ground, a woman on a mission—Leah knew her mission would be to turf her out. When she spoke, the highly accented edge to her voice made every word sound like an order.

'This is a crime scene,' she said.

'Local paper. I had a tip off,' Leah clipped back.

'From?'

'One of yours, I'm afraid.' Miller looked over at the officers busy working on the crime scene. 'No one here…' Leah said.

Miller turned back, her lips set flat with determination, she opened her mouth to speak but was interrupted.

'I know I can't go in, I just want to ask a few questions,' Leah said, smiling her best smile. She could see that Miller was trying to place her, working out how she knew her.

'The fire,' Miller said, scanning the circumference of Leah's face, landing on her eyes. Leah knew it would only take her a minute or two to register her, everyone remembered Leah's eyes. She couldn't blame her for not recognising her straightaway. Everything had happened so fast that day; one thing after the other blurring even now into one of those speeded up films you see on a time delay camera. Never really believing it could happen, unable to change it, even at the inquest. It was Miller who had dragged Leah out of the mouth of the fire when she'd gone after Susie, asked her if she knew who else was in there. When she told her it was Susie Fairfax, Miller ran towards the flames just like she had. She couldn't get near though, no one could. So, of course Miller remembered her, how could she not.

'There's nothing much to see,' Miller said in a small quiet voice, almost lost in the wind.

But Leah didn't care; the words told her she was in. 'Can you tell me what's going on then?'

'Just stay back, don't get in the way,' Miller said starting to turn. She smoothed a lock of red hair from her tired, mascara-smudged eyes. If she had to put an age on Miller, Leah would say a couple of years older than her—thirty at most. She was never good at judging age though and the grey light wasn't helping.

'Robbery?' Leah persisted. 'Worse?' Miller's silence pushed her on, 'Worse is good for newspapers,' she said trying to establish a rapport. Miller glared at her, snapping her voice back to the tone of dismissal Leah was more familiar with.

'You've got ten minutes tops then you're gone…' she said and threw her head in the direction of the main track through the fairground where everything was happening. Leah could see the guys in white suits coming from there with their aluminium cases and plastic bags. Everyone jumpy. Leah could just tell from the way everyone was hovering about, and from the hush-hush silence as they moved around. From the fact there was so many of them. Frank Molinari, *fuck*, who'd have thought it, but really—all this for a man who no one had much time for in life? She was already thinking, if she could keep hold of this she could make something more of it, get away from here. If she was clever she could move from local into the BBC like she set out to do so many years ago and then, if she was lucky, maybe London. The list ticker-taped in her head, getting ahead of her as it always did. She'd missed so many chances, leaving uni she had interviews with news stations, sent tapes to every one she could think of and nothing came back to the provincial northern backwater she'd been landed in. But over time she'd learned things did happen here. People lived here and shit happened to them and they were people like anywhere else and you had to work with what you got, and she was here now. She could do something with this.

Leah followed the pathway Miller had pointed out. Her feet in their light cycling shoes, tapped a rhythm on the tarmac, the clipped metal chime of her heels ringing in the cold air.

When she reached the crime scene, she could make out what must be Frank's body on a trolley in a long black bag. This was rare, no journalist was ever allowed in this close. Miller really had taken pity. *Make the most of it.* A line of tape surrounded the area. It was right near the Hall of Mirrors where the ground was flat and muddied with blood or something else. Leah had no way of knowing what it was, but she could imagine. She was good at that. She took her tape recorder from her pocket and whispered what she could see into it. Her mouth tasted dry, ash in her throat again.

'Who's this?'

A woman came towards her in a white jumpsuit. She had a pen in one latex-gloved hand and a plastic bag in the other.

'Leah Barnes, local press, I don't think we've met,' she said as the professional in her kicked in. Leah held her hand out and the woman was so surprised she shook it, gloves and all. The action seemed to bring her back into the present. Leah wasn't going anywhere now.

'Are you allowed to be here?'

'Permission from the DI herself...'

'Is that so?' The woman said.

'…local press can be important in getting the right message out. We don't tend to go in with ten gallon boots.' *Christ listen to yourself…* she sounded Nancy fucking Drew!

'Okay,' the woman said after hesitating, clearly unsure what to make of her but smiling at the odd reference. 'Just don't let your boots, whatever size they are, get in my way please.'

'Wouldn't dream of it.'

The woman glided away in her white suit glancing in a bemused way behind her. Leah fixed a smile until she was out of sight. *Ten gallon boots…* that might be why the BBC hadn't wanted her.

The scene was being cleared up, so she made her way back, cutting around the side, off the main path towards the café, which was a shithole in the summer and didn't look much better now. In front of the café, a row of benches with rusting Fanta umbrella poles hovered over the tables on which sat tired and ragged looking, mostly young, men. They hardly noticed her, smoking, swigging out of polystyrene teacups someone was obviously supplying to them from the open door of the café.

The men were giving their names to a plain-clothes officer who was writing them down on a scrap of paper. Leah recognised Doug Hughes. She remembered him because he was the one who didn't like Fairfax, Susie told her that. Hughes was sitting, his trousers sagging, hair thinning, big coat hiding round shoulders and cold red hands. He looked like a giant mole only not so friendly.

The men didn't look local which had to mean East European if they were working, and most probably sleeping too, in here. Leah had learned from her flatmate Mati how they knew how to look invisible and she thought that if she walked towards them they might just evaporate into thin air. There was no rush, she'd get to them later and besides, Hughes had seen her now and his look said—don't even think about it so, for the moment, she didn't. She made a mental note in her head to find out what these men were doing here. She knew, of course she knew. The town was full of hopeful migrants looking for a better life. The fields around the flat ring of seaside resorts were ribbed with rows of leeks and beets, polythene tunnels of lettuce and strawberries. No one here would pick them, but plenty would come who were willing to. Rumour was Genaro had his finger in every pie, that he owned more land, more 'enterprises' than he was letting on. That's why she'd been here with Susie that day, to catch Genaro out.

If one of the men hadn't run into the ghost train, if there hadn't been a fire... Leah didn't want to think about the ghost train, didn't want to think about Susie, not now. She didn't want to think about the ghouls in the ghost train, she just hoped they were hiding and would leave her alone today.

She could come back. She made her way back to the front gate knowing Doug Hughes had seen her and would know who she was. As she walked she tilted her head back so that when she looked up beyond the height of the fairground walls she could only see white sky clearing into paler blue, clouds scudding and seagulls weaving in and out of the air currents. This place was out of step with the world, it always had been and now Genaro's past was coming back to haunt him. Last time he was one step ahead, but this time he wouldn't be so lucky. She headed back for her bike, which on a miserable day like today was in the place where she had left it, intact and half an hour later, she was knocking on her editor's door.

11

Everything was taking shape around him as sunlight pushed through the cold clouds. After he left the car park, the white VW long gone, he went back to the fairground because he had nowhere else now to go. He walked to the back of the ground this time taking the side paths, passing the dodgems which he remembered from his teenage days. He remembered the taste of Coke from warm cans, sharing them out between them, sometimes adding vodka for an extra kick. From here he could see the ghost train over the top of the log flume, the 'G' and 'T' from the title leering above the fairground in lurid lime green, just as it was on the day Susie died. He hadn't expected everything to look so much the same. It was like a film on a loop in his head— if things had been different, he'd just come when she'd called him, if he hadn't hesitated. Later, when others told him what had happened, everything became just borrowed accounts. It became what he *didn't* remember and he found himself borrowing someone else's truth because it was easier to accept than the reality. The ghost train remained there as a reproach. Rebuilt, it looked like a new pin in an old box and faker than ever.

The café was closed, but the main door propped open. A Walls Ice Cream banner flew from the doorway and behind the filthy windows, piles of paper Fanta cups waited for summer punters. A sign read 'Bucket & Spades £2' and a few men sat on benches along the far wall dressed in nylon tracksuits decades out of date, the line of them thrown in relief against the wall like a painting of dignity and endurance. They would have turned up for work and found it wanting, although God knows what work they would be doing in the dead of winter on a fairground. Genaro would no doubt have contacts, ready to bus them out to a building site or farm. They would be from Eastern Europe, the town had plenty for them and so they came in their droves. Patience was etched into the lines of their skin like cracked clay. They would have been here early so might have seen something and some—so he'd heard—slept in the empty lido buildings adjacent to the fairground so they might even have heard something the night before. Hughes was interviewing them—sitting down, writing and looking fed up. He raised his head as a flash of purple moved away out of sight round the far entrance into the café. Tom saw her too, watched as Leah Barnes disappeared again, shapeshifting like a trickster caught in the act.

'Genaro's in the Funhouse,' Ruby Miller said, suddenly at his elbow. 'Come on, he's expecting us.'

'Right,' he said. 'Right.'

The men could wait. Let Hughes talk to them first. No doubt Leah Barnes would get to them later. She'd have a different angle anyway with her crusade against the exploitation of migrant workers. She'd turn this into something else and secure the story Hughes would be unable to get out of them, the story his daughter had tried to tell before she died. *Still didn't mean he had to like her.*

He turned to Ruby and, unexpectedly, caught a breath of her perfume, which spiralled towards him on the upturned palm of the wind. She smelled of fresh air and water and sea.

The Funhouse wasn't far, but because of the CSIs milling around, the tape and the bustle blocking various exits, they had to walk the long way, round the outside. Tom was parched, another side effect of the drugs, which felt like a hangover, only worse. He wished he'd brought the other medication, the pills he needed that had been counted out for him every day. The diclofenac was not going to be enough, only realising now what a stupid idea it was to go cold turkey on a whim. It was okay at home, when he didn't

85

have to think, but in the real world he needed every ounce of strength. Easy to say now, not so easy in the middle of the night when all the bad things came into his room and stood at the end of his bed pointing—not so easy then.

Their walk took them past the outer periphery of the fairground. The air was thinning, bright and ice-clear, the wind still holding, but at bay for now. With the tide low they could see both rival grounds in Blackpool and Southport with their bigger flashier attractions—circular whirls of steel and gloss where you could cheat death not wait to see when it was coming for you in an old fashioned Fortune Teller's booth. Even Southport had resurrected itself, a grand wheel rose above the sea road, cabins dangling and swaying in the air. The wind must be throwing them around like dust, but from here they looked static and strong, like acorns on a tree. St Marie-by-Sea had never competed on these terms. In its glory days they came to take the seawater cures. Now the lido was its main attraction and in winter that was no attraction at all.

'That's what started all this.' Tom nodded towards the new place.

'The Molinaris must've been bleeding money for years,' Ruby said.

'So Hughes might have a point?'

'He might,' she conceded. 'But I'm not convinced.'

'Tell me what's going on with Hughes?' When she didn't reply he added, 'It doesn't help to make enemies, take it from me.' *He'd lost count.*

Ruby Miller had removed the leather gloves now, easing herself back into his presence and she pulled a pack of cigarettes from her pocket, offering him one. Her short nails were painted black and there was a silver filigree ring circling her thumb.

'You don't smoke...' He couldn't hide his surprise.

'Yeah well...' They stopped close to the lee of the wall to light the cigarettes. She flicked the flame close and low and Tom cupped his hands to shield it. She was inches taller than he was and the crown of her head brushed across his forehead as she bent forward.

'My father was in the RUC,' she said. 'He had plenty of enemies.'

'I didn't know that,' Tom said. He had worked beside her for three years before the accident, but there was little he knew about her. Little he had bothered to ask, afraid if he was honest, because of her accent, because of how she had suddenly appeared in his unit, on a fast track, afraid of what she might tell him, things she was running from. He felt the shame of his neglect, feeling that she must have thought the same thing of him many times in the past.

'He used to come home some nights,' she said, 'sit in front of the TV. We knew to go to bed, leave him alone. You know?'

'That why you joined us?'

'No. But it's why I joined you here.' She shrugged. 'I just didn't think I'd meet types like Hughes. Thought I'd left his kind at home.'

They walked on, quieter now, breathing in their smoke and letting it stream out into the dampness of the air, which in this more sheltered part of the ground had turned the wild wind into a little more than a breeze. It was even feeling warmer.

'You never get used to this do you?'

'You get to expect it,' Tom said, 'but that's a different thing.' He took a deep and grateful drag on his cigarette. '1991 just over there in the dunes we found a young lad, six years old. Didn't know he was dead at first,' he said. 'We knew the kid was missing; parents went on television crying and all that. You know; the usual…' Ruby nodded, of course she knew. 'Woman walking her dog found him, down there in the sand, suffocated, still wearing his Batman t-shirt.'

'I remember that,' someone said, a woman's voice behind them. Tom turned his head too fast and the pain in the crook of his neck twisted like a steel screw jammed into the nerves. *Shit!* He saw a woman he'd never met, looking at him as if she knew him.

'Father killed him didn't he?' she said.

He rubbed his neck with his free hand while the invisible screw bore down into his arm. He had to grit his teeth to block it out.

'Yes he did,' he said.

'The father killed him, but made a big fuss about paedophiles and people were out on the streets?'

All Tom could see was the box of morphine tablets beside his bed, thinking how fast he could get home to it. The pain blocked everything else. He could feel Ruby looking at the woman, waiting for the next part of the story. *What were they just talking about?* He stared at the woman, shorter than him, dark-haired and bright-eyed, about his age he guessed. He focused on a matt of hot dried hair sticking to her forehead, a peck of dirt smudged at the edge of her cheek. *The smudge of death on the living.* She rambled on about the dead boy in the Batman t shirt and what happened to him, in that endoscopic way pathologists have and, although Tom did have a point when he started the story he couldn't think what that was, because all he could hear was her voice droning on. *This was his story, wasn't it?*

Then she said, 'You're Tom Fairfax aren't you?'

'Yes.'

'I'm Linda Sweeney, the Forensic MO, you probably don't remember me.' Irritated, he was thinking, *damn fucking right I don't*, when suddenly he did.

It's six o'clock, an August morning in 1987. Nirvana is on the radio and a boy is buried in sand. She's there with him, Doctor Linda Sweeney, both of them new to the job and wondering if the rest of their career is going to be as crap as this. He's looking at this dead kid with his sunken eye sockets glued in a death sleep and mouth gaping craving for that last hopeless gasp of life, tiny grains of sand stuck to his lips and thinking of Louise at home with the twins, their open mouths screaming. Very much alive.

Then Linda says: 'I can feel him. He's still here. The boy.'

And when they bring the boy out, Tom knows what she means. He looks like he's sleeping even though his flesh is blue and there's no breath in his skinny baby body and he wants to hold him and calm him so that the warmth from his body will pour into this child and bring him back to life just as it does when he holds the twins on his shoulder to stop the shake of their cries in the middle of the night. The child has a familiarity about him, a familiarity that grows over the coming days into an instinct and then a certainty for which they require a proof. A feeling they both have that they know who killed the boy and together will find his killer.

But he only sleeps with Linda the once, that's all, just the once. It's so long ago he's almost forgotten it happened. And he stares at her wondering was this when the pattern of his life set in?

12

'Got a minute Boss?'

Leah paused while her editor Bill Higson dragged his head from the papers he was studying on his desk and tried to look interested. His door was never open these days; he lived on coffee and spent his days shouting at people down the phone. She didn't bother to hide her irritation with him, he never looked interested in anything she had to say and it was beginning to get bloody annoying.

'They've found a body in Pleasure Island.' Higson looked up, but she didn't let him get a word in. 'They're saying it's Frank Molinari.'

She had Higson's attention now even though she could see a veil of scepticism cross his face as he tried to decide whether to believe her. He was probably just furious she knew first.

'Dead Frank?'

A beat where Leah flattened her eyes like she was keeping a secret in.

'Not as simple as that,' she said, but it was enough. He was interested.

'What makes you think that?' he said.

'Well obviously they can't confirm his identity but I think I'm right.'

'And if you're not?'

Leah shrugged.

'I think I am.'

Leah knew he didn't much like her, but he was listening and that made a change. As she talked, even though she was giving him the bare bones of the story, she could see him calculating and thinking of the job cuts their new big owner had threatened them with, the negotiations still lying ahead. He thought none of them knew. They all knew, Mike had been scouring jobs for months, Arun already had something lined up, but was biding her time. This story was Leah's turn. This might give them some leverage, before it got out to bigger newspapers with more staff and revenue, and she could see him counting the time, making the minutes clear in his head.

'You've got this from Fairfax?'

The question hit where it was meant to. He knew the history, who didn't?

'Fairfax is on sick leave so it doesn't involve him,' Leah said.

'Everything involves him,' Higson snapped. 'If he's not back now then he will be when he gets wind of this. He wasn't there this morning?'

Leah shrugged indicating that, yes, he was. Higson tapped his fingers on the arm of the chair; he glanced down at the papers in front of them involuntarily moving them into a pile.

'It's not going to drag up all that fairground shit again, is it? Tell me there's no connection.'

'There might be. Need to do a bit of digging.'

'Why?'

'No one ever found what really happened over that fire, did they?' Leah said, pushing as far as she dared. 'Bit of a coincidence that we're back here again, don't you think?'

'Not forgetting your personal connection to this?'

'That has nothing to do with it,' Leah said. 'And you know what they say about criminals returning to the scene of their crime.'

'I do,' Higson shot back, 'and they don't. Only in movies.'

'Still,' Leah continued, 'this new dead guy, if it is Frank, it was Mike put the story over to me. His contact at the station said it was a murder.'

'Murder?'

'Yep.'

91

'I remember there were…' Higson searched for a word, '…*unanswered* questions back then, all cleared up pretty quickly as I recall…'

'Too quickly.'

'And I suppose if it is Molinari junior this time, if it is really him then…'

'Who died last time?' Leah finished for him.

Higson inclined his head, an attempt at a nod then sat back on his chair, his arms behind his head, feet on the filing cabinet. He was studying her. She knew she was a good reporter and so did he, but she also knew he wouldn't be sorry to see her go, not with her background—the connection to her father, the mess he'd made of *The Courier* before he drank himself out of a job. The offices needed upgrading, modernising. Higson thought he'd be the man to do it, but here they all were, three years on and nothing had changed. The paper did need a buyer, it needed the money they didn't have. All they had to work at were a pile of decrepit desks held up by piles of box files and old newspapers. The front desk was like something from the dark ages, beech wood veneer covered in sellotaped notices, price lists for photos of school proms and local show trophies. Everything needed dragging into the twenty first century. The only decent thing they had was their journalists—herself, Mike and Arun and they would all rather see the paper carry on with a new buyer than let it fold altogether. In her heart of hearts she believed Higson wanted this too.

She waited. She could tell from the way he leaned forward, folded his hands, looked, exasperated, from one side of the room to the other, weighing it up that he would give in.

'Go on then,' he said. Leah was already standing. 'And Barnes…'

'Yes?'

'Don't fuck it up.'

92

13

It was as though just one step outside had led him to the demons he'd been trying to keep at bay for months. Their hands reached towards him, devil fingers clawing their way from an infernal fire. He'd never forgotten that boy. The child continued to haunt his nightmares, the way the sand drained off his stiffened bones as they lifted him out of the hole. The blanket of dune became a cradle for his grave and it was more than his own daughter had for her last breath. There was always one that got under your skin and that boy was theirs alone, so meeting Linda Sweeney again had been the last straw. It might be the one to break his back if he allowed it, only there was one more stick of straw to come and he knew it. He'd known it as soon as he learned the body found in the fairground belonged to Frank Molinari. *Sooner or later Robert Nardone was going to show his face.*

'What did you make of our dead man then?' Linda said.

In the distance, Tom could see Frank's body, wrapped in black plastic, being loaded into an ambulance; zipped safe in its sleeping bag.

'When do you think he died?' Tom said, keeping it professional. He needed to break the tension, but from her obvious pleasure at bumping into him again, he had the feeling the tension was his alone.

'Not sure, sometime this morning by the state of the blood; I can narrow it down at the postmortem.'

The biting cold had melted into something warmer now, but Tom still shivered, a goose walking over his grave. Maybe it was the dead man's spirit leaving, on its way somewhere, brushing his shoulder as it passed. But Tom didn't believe in spirits, he believed in something else, the something he was looking for when Louise dragged him to a medium a few months after Susie died. 'I'm getting someone beginning with T, is there anyone here beginning with T?' the crooked old fraud had said and Louise was shaking his arm saying: 'That's you, that's you...' as he shrank behind her hope and her bald bloody grief on show for everyone for see.

Tom lit another, yet another, *fuck he needed to give these up*, cigarette, pressing his fingers into his eyes, creating black spots behind the lids and opened them to find Linda looking at him, concerned.

'I'm fine,' he said before she asked.

'I joined while you were on sick leave,' she said. 'Didn't know you were back at work.'

'I'm not.'

She raised an eyebrow.

'Officially,' he said smiling, rubbing his neck.

'You should take something for that. What are you on?'

He thought of the drugstore in his bathroom and laughed in spite of himself. A small gauge inside his head flickered like a speed dial on the pain register.

'Just a few painkillers.'

He wondered where Ruby Miller was and looked around, but couldn't see her.

'I'm not sure, but I don't think this man was killed by what it looks like he's been killed with,' Linda said.

'What do you mean?'

'Somebody did make sure he was dead, that explains the blows sustained after, but he was already dead when someone did this. No arterial blood near the body, which there would be if he was beaten to death. It would be everywhere.'

'How *did* he die?' Tom said.

Linda shrugged.

'I'll let you know,' she said. 'Come and see me tomorrow, I'll have something for you. And Tom...' she added. 'Good to see you again.'

'Yeah Linda, good to see you too.'
But he wasn't sure that he meant it.

'Anything we need to know?'

Ruby had her notebook out again, scribbling. Fewer people were around now, the line of CSIs had put everything they needed in the van and Frank was now on his way to a drawer in a hospital somewhere. *Probably the safest place he'd ever been in his life.* There was only one thing Tom needed to know, left unsaid.

'Nardone, is he here?'

Ruby shook her head surprised, 'No. why would he be?'

'If it's Frank Molinari, then strictly speaking it's his case isn't it?'

'*Was* his case,' she corrected him. 'He's been promoted...' she registered his confusion then, 'you didn't know?'

He *didn't* know.

'Where, how...'

'He's a Superintendent now, based in Blackpool. I thought you...'

'You thought wrong,' he said.

Nardone would still show up though promotion or not. He wouldn't let this one go, the one that got away. The one *he* allowed to get away. That word—*allowed*, it had been niggling him since this morning, since yesterday when he'd seen Frank. If Tom knew when the call came through that morning then could Nardone have known too?

'When I saw him...' Tom started to say.

'Nardone?'

'No, Frank. In town, yesterday. He was with a woman.'

'How...'

'He was at the station, just there, he was just there, I was...' he decided not to go into that. 'I was in the car.'

'Did you know her?'

'No, didn't look his type either...'

95

'It wasn't Dolores?'

'No!' Tom felt the nerve in his neck snap, synapses twitching. Ruby had overstepped her mark.

'I'm sorry,' she said.

Sooner or later Dolores was going to come up, how could she not?

'But someone should speak to her, find out who she is…'

'What did she look like?'

It was her way of saying sorry, accepting he might have been telling the truth after all because he knew that she hadn't really believed him when he'd said he'd seen Frank. *Who would take the word of a drug addict?*

'I had the impression of blue,' he said. 'A jacket, her hair was…' how was her hair? 'Different colours I think.'

An impression of blue. That could be a description of him: the blue in the veins of his hands, of the hospital ceiling as they wheeled him around immobile in his bed. He caught a glance of the sea behind Ruby, the sky opening, a small patch of blue—enough to make a sailor's underpants Clemmie would say. *A good sign.* The blue of Leah Barnes's eyes.

'Okay,' Ruby said. 'I'll see if there's any CCTV from the station, where was he?'

'The taxi rank. I think he was putting the girl into a taxi.'

'The girl?'

He'd said 'girl' without thinking, but she did look young. Something about the blue…

'She was young, I'm sure she was.'

Ruby was on the phone before he'd finished speaking, making it happen. While she waited for a reply, she turned to him.

'I suppose he might come,' she said. 'Nardone. Although in his shoes I'd not want to show my face, he got it wrong, could finish him.'

It could, which meant that sooner or later Nardone *would* show up and in Tom's experience of him it would be sooner. As for finishing him, he also knew Nardone was made of tougher stuff than that.

They found themselves in front of the Funhouse, the door ajar for them, as the sky suddenly and without warning brightened. One minute the sky was as blue as a swallow's wing, the next it flared red.

'That's not good,' Ruby said. 'Calm before the storm.'

She pushed the door open and went in.

14

The falcon was asleep, one hooked foot resting on top of the other, the claws curled down and under, her eyelids hooded over as still as though she was dead, like a proud bird on a museum plinth. Leah knew it would take only one tiny, imperceptible move to rouse her, a move the human eye wouldn't see.

'I don't think she'll be flying today,' a voice said behind her.

Rich shuffled forward, a bucket on his arm containing the bird's food. Leah turned her head. She could never get used to it, the way the birds scrapped and tore the flesh from the bones of tiny dead chicks and mice. Survival, something Susie never flinched from. The first time she'd come here, to do the article, Leah watched Susie, this self-assured young woman in her jeans and incongruous white linen shirt, pale arms as strong as a javelin thrower, dip a hand in and out of the heavy leather pouch she had slung low on her belt. Each dip would bring out a claw, a toe, a ripped beak with flesh attached. The meat would be placed on the bent forefinger of the leather glove, Susie's fingers folded into an O to allow the bird to alight. Tiny leather ties, jesses, trailing bells and music; Susie would look nonchalant, like she didn't care less what it did. Patient, ear cocked waiting for it to land. Which it did, lightly, like a firefly before taking off again, to wait for the next call, the next flight. Over and over.

Rich had taken Sky on after Susie's death, but the bird had struggled, refused at first to fly, bating every time anyone came near. It terrified Leah, the way she put her head down and splayed her wings wide like a mad Spanish fan, the feathers stretched like webs between rigid fingers. But came Leah did, she *had* to, week after week just to be with the bird, the last remnant of Susie she had. The first few weeks Sky stayed perched, hooded to calm her, the tiny jesses tangling silver in the tips of her dainty toes. Sky was as small as Susie had been tall, an incongruous pairing and, without her, the bird seemed lost and insignificant.

'You're up early today,' Rich said.

'Yeah.' Leah was looking at Sky through the bars of the aviary and knew from the slight shift in her foot that the bird knew she was there.

'She's not at her flying weight,' he continued. 'Getting there, but not quite.'

'When?'

'Tomorrow maybe, or Wednesday...'

Rich was teaching Leah to fly the bird. She watched him, feeding them all one by one, whispering and calming in turns—a barn owl with feathers so fat and broad Leah could imagine sinking a finger knuckle-deep into the down to find its bones. There was a buzzard and a Harris Hawk, balancing on their shitty branches tethered to the ground for their own safety and, in spite of the look of imprisonment, safe. Susie hated anything to be trapped, Leah had learned through her that prisons were not always as they seemed. For Sky, rescued from a house on the outskirts of St Marie where she was kept in a box of filth and earth in a front room on a council estate, these bars were her freedom.

She was getting to know the bird, bit by bit, but she wasn't sure about Leah, who hadn't earned her trust. It felt, in the early days, as though she could bring Susie back just by taming her to her will, but she knew nothing about birds of prey beyond an admiration of their beauty and the bird knew it, sensed it, so she had progressed little beyond the basics. Her greatest fear was that she would never be able to do it at all. She came to help Rich when she could, cleaning the cages, learning the ropes, but her fear was that

Susie's bird was always going to remain an elusive extension of her owner, just beyond Leah's reach.

Rich worked round her this morning, getting on quietly with what he was doing. The birds responded to him, their eyes wide, waiting for food, humming and twitting on their perches, all with the exception of Sky. The bird had kept her eyes tight shut until the moment Leah turned to go. Then she heard a slow click behind her, the slick opening of an eyelid as she moved away.

15

The Funhouse was tucked away at the back of the car park. It was housed in a purpose built corrugated building with concrete half-walls and large metal doors decorated with higgledy letters spelling out the name—*Fun* on one door, *House* on the other. It was nothing like a house nor did it look like fun. As soon as he was inside, Tom felt himself falling through a white rabbit hole in time. He was ten years old at a birthday party sitting on the high-sided wooden carousel in the middle of a vast room, which now opened out before them. The carousel was about four feet from the ground, like the base of a giant drum, old and tired with the wood on the slide sweaty from generations of children skidding down it. Arranged around it were machines made to look like gun alleys and racetracks, which pinged imaginary bullets into the stale air. Even though the place was closed, someone had forgotten to switch them off.

Genaro Molinari was nowhere to be seen.

'What is it?' Ruby Miller asked going up to the base of the carousel and peering down inside. From the edges, slats of polished wood sloped upwards to form a cone and on impulse Tom jumped in, crawled his way up to the raised platform at the top, which had a cushion big enough to accommodate several small people (children) seated back to back. He sat in the middle.

'What are you doing?' she laughed, and picked up on his instinct, a flicker of delight whisking across her face. The strangeness of the place was enough to take them out of themselves, forget for a moment why they were there.

'You sit on here,' he said, 'and someone up there spins it as fast as it will go. The last one to be thrown off is the winner.' He pointed up to a control booth, something like the projection room in a cinema, a darkened window, a row of switches.

'Okay,' Ruby said, but her voice was smaller this time, her initial enthusiasm waning as she tried to understand what was going to happen next.

'You want to try it?' A voice said from somewhere over their heads.

The window in the control booth slid open and the man himself—Genaro Molinari appeared, as though raised on a pulpit above them. He didn't wait for an answer, but started the motor. The drum turned, slowly then faster and faster as Tom clung to the edges of the platform, digging his heels into the cushion and bracing his legs the way he remembered. He remembered it was easier if someone sat behind you, then you could use their weight to anchor you, but he focused, gripped with his heels, dug in. *He was good at this*. He felt in control for the first time in a very long time.

His head was in meltdown as the room roared past, faster and faster. *Ruby, Genaro, Ruby, Genaro*—they came and went, bleeding into one another until they were the same person. He closed his eyes, threw his head back even though he could feel it slowing. He wanted it to go on and on...

'Stop it!' Ruby shouted.

He had the hang of it now, just a few more minutes... he felt like a spring winding down as he braced his feet, locked his knees, held his breath and knew that if he moved just one inch, he'd lose his grip, plummet to the bottom of the slope. This was the point of the exercise; last one sitting was the winner. He could see Ruby clinging to the sidewalls of the wheel, *now you see her, now you don't*.

'I said stop it!' she shouted and the shrillness of her voice above the noise of the wheel knocked him off balance so that he glanced up. He lost his hold, his legs went slack and he was thrown off, hurled down to the bottom. Molinari laughed, the motor slowed and Tom laughed too, a surprised shout of joy from deep in his belly. A feeling he'd forgotten he even had. Stepping off the carousel, standing upright, he felt like he was going to throw up. He leaned on one arm against the side of the drum, gaining his breath in slow steady measure.

'Too bad Mr Fairfax, so nearly...'

'I was very good at this in my day.'

'I can see that,' Molinari said laughing.

Tom registered Ruby's shocked and angry face; he winked at her. 'Never take your eye off the ball,' he said but she didn't smile back.

Molinari came down and Tom shook his hand.

'I'm sorry about Frank,' he said and the laugh faded as Molinari's eyes sunk back into themselves like pockets of air in sand. He seemed emptied out; his tall awkward frame draped in a crumpled suit jacket and mismatched trousers. His eyes were red, rimmed and rimy with sleep, the stale smell of a night unslept in. Tom had a flash of Frank, dapper in his Italian shoes, his well-cut suit. Genaro hadn't inherited the Molinari looks.

'This is Detective Sergeant Miller,' Tom said, introducing Ruby, but Molinari seemed barely aware of her. Grief clung to his throat, dragging the jowls of his cheeks down so much that it seemed genuine. It was easy to see it in another. Like being a member of an exclusive club that no one invited you to be in. Tom noticed Ruby did not shake Genaro's hand.

'Some place we can go for a chat?' she said.

Molinari gestured towards the small kiosk in the corner of the room. Unlike the café outside this was definitely open and they made their way over through the echo of the big empty amusement house, aware of the ping of the bullet machines, the high dome of its roof bearing down on them.

'Can't believe this place,' Tom said. 'Hasn't changed in what, fifty years?'

Genaro nodded.

'Used to give the people what they want,' he said. 'But tastes change.' He sounded like he couldn't care less.

'Must be expensive to run?' Ruby said, looking around at the tangle of electrics, the hanging wires and strings of old Christmas lights above their heads. Molinari shrugged.

'Can be,' he agreed.

'Must have been easier when you had Frank to help?' Tom said.

Molinari's eye twitched, only slightly, but enough for Tom and Ruby to see it. They glanced at each other, unsure how to go from here.

Taking his cue from his status as the recently bereaved, Tom said, 'I really am sorry about your brother, Genaro.' As he spoke, he realised he meant it.

'Thank you, is a shock.'

'All over again,' Ruby said, but Genaro ignored her.

'I just want to find who killed him,' was all he said.

'As do we,' she said. 'As do we.'

The kiosk had tables—fixed laminated seating laid in a square with the thick vapour of old and stale chip fat hovering over it. A microwave oven was crammed into the space between a chiller cabinet of Ginsters pasties and a vast coffee urn next to a counter with a frosted screen bulging with Mars Bars, Kit Kats and Kinder eggs. Framed black and white postcards lined the walls behind the till showing Italian scenes—a chapel, a monastery, some seascape, a family portrait. Tom went straight over to it— the woman looked familiar. *How could that be?*

'Who's this?' he asked.

Genaro flicked a glance then looked away. 'My mother.'

'It looks beautiful. Where was it taken?'

Genaro looked back at the photograph, it looked like he was trying to remember.

'Salerno,' he said looking away from it as quickly. 'Many years ago.'

The woman's eyes followed Tom when he moved away. He went back to the picture, she looked a little like Frank he supposed, the same slender shaped nose, eyes like almonds and a jaunt in her posture that suggested life was just out there waiting for her. Still, he was sure he knew her from somewhere else.

'Your mother—is she still alive?'

'No.' The answer was swift. 'She died. Long time ago.'

There was no way he could know her beyond her slight resemblance to Frank, he was seeing ghosts again, dead people at every turn. That's what happened when someone died, wasn't it? Clemmie still claimed to see his father at the end of the dinner table; she talked to him sometimes. He hadn't known this until he moved in with her after the accident. She told him about her day, what she'd done and he sat there not answering. When he'd asked her who she was talking to she'd answered without embarrassment 'Your father makes a good listener.' One day he heard her tell him about Susie and what she'd been talking to her about that day; after that he didn't listen any more.

He felt very tired. He made for one of the tables as Genaro flicked a switch, pulling the faucet on the urn releasing a cup of steaming brown liquid,

'Coffee?'

'Not for me thanks,' Ruby said.

Tom remembered—she never accepted coffee or anything else, being always strictly by the book, and Tom knew she was watching to see if *he* would accept. He did, if only to annoy her, and had his coffee served in a white glass Perspex cup, another relic from a past he'd been swimming in since he took a foot through the Fun House doors. He took a sip of the coffee and it did bring him back to his senses.

'God that tastes like piss! Thought you Italians like your coffee?'

'Can't get no decent coffee anywhere here.'

They drank for a minute or two in silence. *No rush.* He could see Ruby was getting more and more exasperated.

'I used to come here for parties,' Tom said. He brought Jack and Susie here once, *how did he remember that?* He rarely took them anywhere because he was always at work. Louise was the one who took them from place to place— swimming, scouts, school, it must have been a weekend... but Molinari cut across his thoughts and turned, arms folded, to face him.

'So I'm sure you haven't come to reminisce about the past, how can I help you Mr Fairfax?'

'Tom, please...' he said. 'But, I'm not the one in charge today...' Tom indicated Ruby Miller.

'Your brother Frank,' Ruby said. 'Obviously that's why we're here.'

Genaro shifted from one foot to the other then turned his back on them, poured another coffee, which went down as quickly as the first. Tom watched him without watching, eyes up from his coffee thinking that his throat must have been made of asbestos. His mother's voice again, speaking to his father when he downed a cup of tea in one before work. *Where did that come from?*

'You have any idea where Frank's been all this time?' she asked.

Genaro didn't have time to answer, or was saved from it as a young woman in a blue checked overall came in. Blue again, Tom thought. She looked up at them from a down-turned face, surprised to see anyone in here at all at this time of the day and particularly not with all the police around. They moved aside to let her through. Her look swept across Genaro and the two police officers without having to ask who they were. She knew who they were and they waited for an introduction, which was unforthcoming.

'Hello,' Tom said. 'Sorry we don't mean to be in the way.'

'No, is fine,' she said. Her voice small, lost in the vast cavern of the warehouse space. Her eyes were wary, expectant.

'You work in here?' Ruby said.

She looked at Genaro this time, uncomprehending.

'She does some cleaning,' Genaro said. 'In the winter there is the time. '

'I'm sure she can speak for herself,' Ruby said, then smiled at the woman who returned the smile, confused.

'What I'm wondering is,' Tom persisted. 'Was….' he reached for a name expecting it to be provided.

'Suki,' the woman said. Tom acknowledged this with a smile.

'Suki, were you here last night? You might have seen something?'

She looked confused, did she understand them or just not want to answer? Tom looked at the blue overall and remembered the girl with Frank at the station wearing the blue jacket.

'We can come back with a translator if that would help?' Ruby said kindly.

Suki looked at Genaro who shook his head.

'She was not here last night. No one was. Only me,' he said. 'Suki works for me and I have a business to run.'

Ruby smiled at Genaro.

'Course you do,' she said, then indicated to Tom that they should go. Two steps away from him, Tom turned back, as though he'd just remembered something.

'Where are you from Suki?' he said.

She looked across at Genaro then raised her head in a proud stretch.

'Rumania,' she said.

'Right, thank you,' Tom said. He turned back to Genaro. 'Was Frank still in touch with Dolores do you think? It's a bit of a coincidence, yeah? What with Dolores being Rumanian too?'

107

Not missing a beat, Molinari looked up, his face clouded with something that could have been sorrow. 'I'm not my brother's keeper,' he said. Then he hit a switch and pop music beat out of the tannoy system, echoing round the cavernous walls, bouncing off them tinny and thin. The conversation was over.

They made their way outside and in the car park, Ruby turned to Tom,

'You think he killed his brother?'

'What do you think?'

Ruby pulled the scarf up around her neck. The harsh breeze was back, Ruby had been right about the storm. The weather on this coast always did this. One minute it was over then back it came when least expected. It was easing its way in from the sea again so that when he licked his lips in the cold, Tom could taste salt on his tongue.

'It's not him,' she said.

'No.'

'But he knows who it is,' she added.

'Then why is he hiding it?'

'I don't know. Is someone threatening him maybe?'

'I can't see that, can you?'

It was doubtful Genaro Molinari had ever been afraid of anything in his life, but Tom couldn't rule it out. The memory of his father gulping that cup of tea came back— Tom hadn't thought of his father in a long time. He did not expect to think about him here of all places. That picture of Genaro's mother had brought it back.

'Why don't you get someone who can speak to Suki,' Tom said. 'It's unusual to find Rumanians here.' *Apart from*, he could have added, *Dolores*. He wasn't going to mention her again even though he knew the mention of her name had rattled Genaro. There was plenty of time for that when he knew where she was and when he was ready to face her.

Just not yet, *not yet*.

16

The news archive was down three flights of stairs below the main office in a basement no one visited. Leah pulled a few bags of recycling paper from the door and found the key hidden on a hook above the doorjamb. The papers she was looking for weren't on computer yet because Higson refused to pay someone to do it; the backlog was out of control. Most of the old issues of *The Courier* were still filed in bookcases along alcoves in the main wall of the pokey little room. Rumour was that when the paper started, this was where they worked back to back in dust and darkness. They threw stories out into the light, which filtered like whispers through a barred window at the end of the room into the world outside. Back then, the story goes, the room was thick with old cigarette smoke. That would have explained her father's hacking cough. The only sign of anything vaguely twenty first century was a HP computer blinking in the far corner attached to a dodgy-looking modem on the floor. Hard to believe, but up until a few months ago they'd relied for back research on the ancient microfiche, which stood now on a table by the window, its wheel the size of a dinner plate. Higson was a bloody dinosaur, no wonder the paper was dying; a small part of her wanted to stay and fix it, to make it great again, as it was, in her father's day in spite of his drinking, in spite of him, when journalism was about what mattered. This would have been the room from where greatness came, this cramped hole under a bland building next to a car park— great in relative terms, she had to check herself—this was only a small provincial town by the seaside—but great all the same. Great because she remembered the days she spent hanging out here as a kid, with her father, before it all went wrong.

There was a kettle and a jar of tacky Nescafe on a shelf above the sink out back, but no milk so she filled the kettle to make herself a black coffee. While it was boiling she went back out to the bookcases. She had a feeling she knew what she was looking for even though she wouldn't actually know until she found it. She pulled files on June 2004 from the big books and then several others from further back than that—2002, 2003. The kettle worked itself up into a bubbling frenzy then wound down and she went back into the kitchen, made coffee in a stained mug with a picture of St Marie's famous jaunty beach huts on the front and after some rummaging in a grubby cupboard, found dried milk powder. She stirred this into the coffee until the lumps dissolved into grease slicks on the surface. She took a sip, burnt her tongue and took the mug to where the files waited for her on the desk, waiting for it to cool down. This would take as long as it needed to.

The pages of the books and the edges of the old newspaper edged through the muffled silence in the room and after a while, when she hadn't found what she was looking for, she switched to the microfiche to go further back. She scrolled through pages so fast she could barely read what they contained looking for only one name, Molinari; it took her over an hour to find nothing. She booted up the big main frame HP computer in the corner of the room, brushing papers aside while it rattled and boned, hooking the modem to the one phone socket gaffer-taped to the wall. The dial up connection whined but then connected and within minutes, she started to search.

It was so slow going, but this time she had more luck finding company records filed in the public domain for Molinari's business interests. Nothing untoward there, and an entry for a Molinari family tree listed in Puglia, Italy, no connection because it turned out that Molinari wasn't that unusual a name and she had to scroll through lots of lists waiting when the screen froze and the internet connection came and went. At one point she went back to the kitchen to crack open the narrow window, which ran across the top of the far wall; she needed to let the outside world in. She narrowed it down to Genaro and Frank, which was when she found an interview Genaro had given years ago to the Lancashire Echo, which was much better at filing and logging their stuff than they were. The interview was from when he took over Pleasure Island from its previous owners. There was a photograph of the brothers smiling with thumbs up on the front page, the dips and dives of the fairground silhouetted behind. She could just make out the wooden rollercoaster, looking the same as it did now. What could they bring to St Marie-by-Sea that visitors couldn't get in Southport or Blackpool, they were asked. 'A sophisticated pleasure ground for a discerning public,' was what Genaro was supposed to have replied. Harking back to a long lost past.

Leah's eyes stung from staring at the screen in the airless room. She stood and forced open the back door into the small yard beyond the kitchen. It gave on the second heave, opening onto a square of concrete filled with empty drink cups, cigarette butts and garbage from where passers-by upstairs had pitched stuff over the ledge above. She looked up, aware of the footsteps going to and fro above her on the street. The beat and rhythm of so many of them, the dimming light descending into the yard, told her it must be close to evening. She'd been down here for hours. She went back into the kitchen, made another coffee and returned to the Echo interview reading as slowly as she could, making notes as she did, scribbling questions at the side and folding the corners of pages in her notebook that she wanted to come back to.

The interview was a quiet, even-toned conversation in which Molinari described how he and his brother Frank came to the town as children. Up to then they'd lived in Scotland owing to his father, Alberto, having been a prisoner of war on Orkney during World War II, captured by the British in Libya in 1943. He met a local girl as so many did, he said, and they married, moved to Glasgow where the two boys lived until their mother died. Genaro went back, attended Glasgow School of Art from 1972 to 1976. She didn't see that coming, didn't have him pegged for a man of culture, but when she googled the college there he was in the alumni listings for 1976 looking eager and hopeful. *Fuck* who'd have thought it. But then she discovered that the father, Alberto, was one of the POWs who painted the Italian Chapel on Orkney, which made him, or at least the chapel, famous apparently—so must be in the blood. Leah had no idea what the Italian Chapel was, and when she saw it, when she read about the Molinaris, she couldn't match what she knew of Genaro with what she was reading, it just didn't fit. She didn't want it to fit because the Genaro she thought she knew doled out backhanders and threats, he wasn't michel-*bloody*-angelo. The boundaries were blurring all the time and she felt herself blur with them. She read on, more fascinated now than enquiring, at his candour, his excitement in his new fairground project, which he talked about as though it was a beautiful work of art.

Genaro wanted to be an architect, but became a surveyor instead, worked on the council in Glasgow for ten years, built up a property portfolio that started with an amusement arcade on the West coast of Scotland, then another and another and finally the Pleasure Island in 1991, and that was it, nothing dodgy in any of this—nothing to pin him down, nothing to match pieces up. Genaro was turning into something legit, on the surface at least, and that was something Leah didn't want him to be.

She switched the big computer off and went into the basement room where she stacked books she'd been using back on the shelves, having copied all the information she'd gathered on to an 3GB memory stick for transferring to her laptop as soon as she got back to her desk. Her beloved notebook she kept close in her pocket. She then rinsed out the mug and left it on the draining board where it would no doubt remain until the next time she came down. She pulled the heavy back door shut, noticing as she how much darker it had become outside. This made her look over her shoulder into the room behind, an involuntary shudder that acknowledged someone might have sneaked in through a dark shadow when she wasn't looking. In her mind's eye she could see her father holding her hand, 'Time to go home sweetie,' he said. There was a long desk right at the far end of the narrow room in front of an alcove packed with filing cabinets. She hadn't taken much notice when she walked in, the place her father always sat, part of the furniture, and now dominating the room as she felt the urge to get away, flicking the fluorescent light tube off, locking the door hurriedly behind her. She hung the key back on its hook above the frame before making her way, one deep breath after another, up from the darkness and into the light.

When she got back to her desk, the offices were quiet. It was almost five fifty and the paper had been put to bed. There was only her, a couple of temps and Arun, the paper's 'commercial' correspondent. Mike had gone home hours ago. 'Think he's got himself an interview,' Arun muttered from her desk. 'Wasn't exactly keeping it quiet.'

Leah's view from her desk by the window was of Cranley Street, the clockmaker and dog's home book shop getting a lick of paint for springtime, which this year looked like it would be a long time coming. Each shop front in the tiny street was painted a different shade of pastel making it look like something from a child's painting. It was done to match the beach huts, each doorway the same pattern and colour as the Edwardian huts, which were lined neatly along the promenade like rows of sweets. There were pockets in this town that were as quaint and comforting as a book of seaside postcards where history and nostalgia seeped into every corner. It wasn't really Leah's style, nostalgia, but sometimes, looking up instead of down at the uneven cobbled pavements, she saw beauty soaring into the sky, the flat shop fronts transformed into works of art. She loved how the apex of the Halifax Bank building on Queen Street was scattered in sapphire and white mosaic against red brick looking as exotic as lapis lazuli on the robe of a Madonna. No wonder Genaro had liked it here, thought he could build a future. But no one looked up any more, that was the problem; no one cared enough to patch a window when it was broken, paint a wrought iron portico when the white paint fell and settled on passers-by like dandruff. No one cared enough to turn the town back on itself. These days it was easier just to give up and let St Marie-by-Sea crumble into its uncertain future.

She turned from the window where the evening was bedding in now, the double-glazing covered in a fine mist as the cold outside tried to force its way in. She tapped her thumb on the touch pad of her laptop, scrolling through the information she'd copied on to the memory stick. She looked at photo after grainy photo for details and didn't have enough of them, none that added up. She scrolled and tapped, read of Susie: *loved by everyone, all her life ahead of her, blah-blah, cliché after fucking cliché*. Why did every death leave behind someone who was loved by everyone? Leah knew this wasn't true, so why did everyone say it? Susie was hard to love and Leah thought that only she and Susie's twin brother Jack had truly loved her. Tolerate was a better word for how most people thought of Susie, even her father, and even though she might have mellowed with age, which Leah doubted (and hoped she wouldn't) this was enough to make her smile. She flicked to the next page, occasionally moving stuff from the portable to the hard drive into a new folder, backing everything up.

She found more about the accident, the fire in the fairground, but it was stuff she already knew. Genaro asking for privacy, respect for the family's grief, etcetera, etcetera, and then Susie again—daughter of a senior officer in the local police force, 'a known activist who cared passionately about local causes.' Hmm... that sat better, that was true. As for Frank, well everyone knew Frank was a low level crook. The report didn't dwell on him in any significant way apart from a hint between the lines that suggested: who would be sad he was dead, apart from his brother? Maybe that was why they decided to let it be him? No one cared enough to take it further.

Leah read through the article looking for any mention of herself and found only one brief line—'A friend of the victim, educated at Oxford University...' it read, like that was the only thing that mattered. It made no mention of her injury, her burned out ear, but then how would they know? She remembered saying she was okay then fainting or some other embarrassing thing and the guy in the ambulance car, the backup, insisting she came with him to A&E for a check-up. Heat damage, they said but how can the inside of your ear be damaged by fire if it never touches it? They discharged her within hours, said there was nothing wrong, but there was. Sometimes she could only hear voices like a low rumble, which sounded like seawater swishing about in the canal of her ear. She'd done nothing about it, just learned to sit on the right side of people so she could hear them, pretend nothing was wrong. It was easier that way and would always remind her of what she'd lost.

Leah hit the down arrow looking for something else but not sure what, only that she'd feel certain she'd know it when she saw it, but it meant that she had to keep seeing Susie's face. It was the same photo every time—the one

Louise had given the paper, where she was looking away down at something laughing. Her hair fell on one side and something, a light or maybe the sun, lit up the side of her face. It caught the row of earrings, which circled her ear, the bleached black/blonde hair caught behind it, the butterfly tattoo peeping out. Susie was the story, in some senses Frank was very much sidelined, so she was in every issue until the story died down. In the end she became one small 'news in brief' paragraph on the inside pages. Then nothing at all. Leah stopped when she reached the end of the reports. There was nothing beyond this even though she knew there should be. There was a small mention of the coroner's report where the fairground tragedy was pronounced as 'death by misadventure' only it wasn't, was it? It was manslaughter, at the very least.

She closed her eyes, pushing her fists into her eye sockets until she saw stars and dots, pushing the exhaustion away and when she looked up, Arun was hovering over her with a sheaf of papers in her hand. She had her long slick black hair curled in a ponytail on top of her head and held in place with a pencil. She was chewing gum and the look on her face said she knew it all.

'Bloody hell you doing haunting in your spare time?' Leah said, 'Sneaking up on me there!'

Arun ignored her and slapped the papers on the desk beside Leah proceeding to leaf through them until she found a glossy brochure. It was some kind of promotional thing a new Casino and apartment block being built on the site of the old Victorian seawater baths on Marine Parade, right next to the fairground. Arun scrolled through until she found a page, which listed two developers, one of whom was Molinari. The other wasn't named, just a company, Orpheus Holdings. Now Arun had Leah's attention. The digital design for the casino was interesting, given what Leah now knew about Genaro's background, hinting at the Victorian elegance St Marie's had always been known for, the combination of a forgotten and just tangible past, and the neon twang of a Vegas strip. Leah had seen pictures of what St Marie-by-Sea used to look like —the old casino, a beautiful domed and round-edged building in white and pink brick, which had once stood at the head of the pier. Visitors were fooled into thinking they were in Monte Carlo or Monaco when they stepped inside. It had been there until the 60s, she even remembered her father describing what it was like inside—green stained glass and plush carpets, gold brass railings and maître d's in smart uniforms, the first time he had ever gambled he once told her. So what? Time moved on, the new casino looked flashier than the old one even if it had none of its charm. She didn't give the brochure much credence.

'What about it?' Leah said. 'He's probably expanding his portfolio.'

Arun snorted and stabbed a finger on a name at the bottom of the page.

'This Orpheus Holdings,' she said. 'Can't find out a thing about them.'

'Not his style.' Leah wanted to get back to her search. 'Too flash, grubby fairgrounds and cash in envelopes that's more his style.'

'That's what I thought,' Arun said. 'Yet, here he is.'

Arun sat on the desk, dangling her feet over the edge. Whatever desk or chair she sat on, her feet never reached the floor and Arun loved to sit on desks. She was pretty in a pixie-ish way, but always looked like she was wired with something. Her hair pulled back from her temples gave the impression of a woman always on the alert, but she was teetotal and drug free and Leah had never seen her drink a coffee in her life so God knows what she took to keep her going. She once confided to Leah that she hated local newspapers but knew she had to go through the motions, work her way up and this one with its past reputation and very little internal competition was perfect. Besides, she wasn't from round here, she was from Manchester, more urban and plugged in and she was ambitious so she was the perfect reporter for stories with that extra bit of edge like this one. She just wasn't that bothered about getting all her facts right; in Arun's view the gist was good enough. The story was always what she created from her carefully crafted prose and anyway, it was mostly right here and there, nothing to get sued over. Her stories attracted a good readership and Bill Higson loved her. Anything inside you needed to know, Arun was your woman and there was nothing she couldn't find out from her web of contacts, most of whom worked in the town's market or on the council. The rest she simply made up to make it more interesting than it was. She knew something else, Leah could tell.

'Knowing your love of the fairground king I thought it might interest you.'

Leah turned the pages of the brochure where flashy pictures invited investment—cash up front and a promise of return on investment later, that kind of thing, all enquiries to Orpheus Holdings, not to Molinari. *That was odd, wasn't it?*

'Genaro has to be Orpheus Holdings, don't you think?' Arun said. 'The rest is just a front.'

'No. He just hasn't got this kind of money. That's someone else...'

'Okay,' Arun said, 'I took the liberty while you were out of looking up said Orpheus Holdings in Company's House and turns out, they don't exist. Course no one ever checks in this town so you can call yourself any bloody thing.'

'So?'

'Guess what else?' she said, jumping down from the desk, Leah just wished she would go, she was tired, she wanted to go home.

'What?' she said reluctantly.

'Pleasure Island is up for sale.'

118

'How do you…'

'So the money could be earmarked for this casino thing…' Arun cut across her.

Leah thought hard.

'What has this to do with Frank Molinari though?'

It was Arun's turn to be confused.

'Well it doesn't, does it? He's dead…'

'Turns out he wasn't…' Leah said. It was going to leak out soon anyway, she might as well tell her; she'd said it without thinking and had to go on '…but he is now. That's who they found this morning.'

'You're fucking kidding me!'

'Straight up, but quiet for now okay?'

Arun was chewing her pencil.

'Wonder if he got wind of this, wanted in and…'

'Could be…' Leah said, 'Or…' but Arun was running on.

'It'll be the same old shit, of course,' she reflected. 'People invest—cash, promises are made, places never get built and the whole thing is just a front anyway. My guess, when he's got all the cash he's going to do a runner because boy does he need the cash—you've seen the place. So if Frank shows up after cash…'

'Yeah but…' Leah leafed through the brochure back and forth, reading the promises and ideas, the beautiful buildings and carpets shiny bright and promising.

'What?'

'What if it isn't him, what if it's someone else using this as a front?'

'Like who?' Arun scoffed.

'I was hoping for something else.' Leah knew she should be grateful to Arun for bringing this to her, but she wasn't. 'This is nothing, well nothing new. We see this all the time…'

Arun looked at her, head on one side.

'Something like what?'

'Well... I dunno, something to do with the workforce he uses,' Leah said.

'Such as?'

'Trafficking, something like, something but not this. Maybe that was what Frank was doing here? Running something for Genaro?'

Arun studied her.

'Don't think that's the story,' she said. 'Trust me, it will be much more mundane; someone wanting to rob a load of greedy gits of their pensions investments. This is St Marie's remember? Not Morecambe, no gang masters here. But,' she conceded, 'if you wanna check it out wouldn't your mate Mati know something?'

'He might.'

Leah had already thought of this, but she didn't want to drag Mati into it. Mati was a mate, but the mention of his name made her realise she still hadn't heard from him since the morning. She hoped the bike was safe. It might be the older one, but she was very attached to it. He had a habit of forgetting to lock it up or leaving it in plain sight wherever he happened to end up for the day. She could do with a friendly face after the day she'd had, she hadn't realised until now how tired and hungry she was.

'Call him,' Arun said, thinking about it. 'Could be something like that I s'pose. Doubt it though. Frank Molinari was definitely capable of that... but.' Arun jumped off the desk. 'I bet you'll find it's more like money laundering, planning committee backhanders that kind of thing, which isn't sexy but is newsworthy, ruins small lives, much more satisfying for us to crack.'

'And be careful yeah?' Arun added. 'Makes some people a lot of money but it don't always harm anyone that kind of stuff even if it is annoying.' *Annoying?* Leah watched her busy little back, bending to pick her papers with the brochure, scrolling through her phone. Was that all it was, exploiting people desperate for work? Like a wasp on your collar you couldn't shake?

'You want me to do some more digging for you on this Molinari thing?' Arun said.

'Sure, why not.'

Arun spun round, away, and before she even reached her desk she was on her mobile, on another story, rattling facts out faster than the caller could take in.

Leah wanted, oh she so wanted this to be connected to Susie's crusade, her search for justice. Those workers at the Pleasure Island were not operating rides, it wasn't the season, the place only had a few rides open and how did any of this connect to Frank Molinari's death? And a casino, well where was the harm? And in a way Arun was right, if folks were gullible enough to hand over their hard earned money thinking they were going to make more cash in some hare-brained casino thing they were greedy bastards who deserved to lose every penny they owned. What was going to be in it for her though? Was she doing this for Susie, or herself?

Arun was right, she had to have something to back her theories up. It was still early and she had time while the office was quiet to look round a bit. She googled migrant workers in Lancashire and Merseyside and first up—of course, the Morecambe cockle pickers. No news there, everyone knew that story, what she was looking for were smaller things, individuals, one-offs, anything she could connect to Molinari, but there was nothing local. The only local story she could find was about a Rumanian man called Vasil living in a tent in Victoria Gardens down near the big Sainsbury's who paid €500 for a flight to a man in Bucharest, had a job for a bit he said, in a bar, but it didn't pay enough so he was looking for something else. The bar was called 'Columbo's', down by the pier where the old casino used to be; Mati used to work there not that long ago. Mati might remember.

She dialled his mobile: nothing. She sent a text: *call me!* then narrowed her search. The local town.com's website was useless—'We like to welcome our EU neighbours' it proclaimed. But there was nothing about the migrants themselves, nothing about how they made a living in this town, how they got here or why and of course nothing about local opportunities and casinos and people living in tents in the park. But still something didn't add up and she was basing it all on something intangible, something she couldn't explain to anyone. Somewhere in all of this was her father and his relationship, if she could call it that, with Genaro Molinari. All roads in Leah's life led back to Genaro Molinari, they always had, but she was no closer to knowing what to do about that than she ever had been. She copied as much as she could to her memory stick and closed the computer. She would talk to Mati and visit Genaro Molinari in the morning using her father, the great newspaper man, as the 'in'. Ultimately that was what this was all about, wasn't it? Before Genaro came into her father's life everything had been so simple and she was never going to get a chance like this again.

She switched the light off as she left the office, Arun had gone, but Bill Higson was still at his desk. He raised his head and nodded looking knackered, like someone had sneaked in roughed him up then ran out again before he'd even realised what was happening. Leah wasn't going to waste time feeling sorry for him. You made your own luck and it wasn't her fault that Higson's was long gone.

She unlocked the bike from the front of the building and hooked her iPod in her ears, flicking it to find something that would reflect how she felt. She alighted on Verdi. She hit the Requiem and took off to the wrath of the *Dies Irae,* the day of reckoning, reverberating in her one good ear.

17

Tom parked the Volvo in the visitor's space at the station. He'd been away so long it seemed the obvious place for him to go. He parked next to a silver Jaguar XJS, a classic, in good condition, polished to within an inch of its life and realised before he was aware he was registering it, that he knew who it belonged to. Robert Nardone.

Fuck it. Always one step ahead of him, come back to finish what he had got wrong all those months ago, make sure someone else took the blame instead of losing his own head, which he would make sure was not going to roll anywhere. Tom came through the back way because he didn't want Nardone to see him first, to know he was even there. He needed the edge, no more surprises and from now on, he knew he had to keep one step ahead of them all without treading on any toes. Without treading on his own.

His office felt lived in despite his months of absence. There was a trace of perfume trapped in limbo; the scent of fresh air and seawater told him who it belonged to. There were neat piles of files and papers, cases and photographs, a small pot filled with colourful pens, a notebook spiral-bound and doodled on with curlicues of leaves and trees. A green scarf was tossed over the back of the chair and as he picked it up he disturbed a scatter of fibres from its surface. They lifted in the air on touch, the feel of the fabric as soft as a handful of warm feathers.

'Oh.' Ruby was in the doorway and did not look happy.

Tom put his finger to his lips, replaced the scarf on the chair.

'What's he doing here?' she hissed, but not before he'd seen the brown jacket behind the door—classy, well cut and the brogues, shiny.

'Why are *you* here?' Ruby said, unsmiling. He tried a smile, hoping for pity of some kind but she didn't flinch. 'Can I have my scarf back?'

He picked it off the back of his chair and handed it over. Even though it was too warm in the airless room, she wrapped it round her neck, tucking the ends in, then folded her arms and stood waiting for him to explain himself.

'So?' she said. 'You saw whose name was on the back of the door?'

'No, I...' he stopped dead. Of course, what a bloody fool. Nothing in here was as it was, nothing was left from a year ago. This was the new DIs office, Ruby Miller's.

'Oh never mind,' she snapped. 'Sit down for goodness sake.'

Nardone's low bass voice reverberated through the wall and someone was laughing, probably Hughes. He'd want to get on Nardone's right side, be the right hand man, there when he needed him. Nardone was telling a joke; Tom could hear the pauses, the exaggerated laugh (it *was* Hughes), and the tailing off at the end. Nardone liked to tell jokes; it was part of his carefully constructed Glaswegian persona even though he'd never been near the city in, like, thirty years, getting one up on the Scousers he used to say. Glaswegians *knew* how to tell a joke. Tom imagined him swaggering out there like he owned the place, thinking there was no chance the disgraced DI was ever dragging his sorry arse back in here to reclaim his life, his job. If nothing else would get him back in here, the thought of that would. Just the timbre of Nardone's voice, the way it hooked up at the end before swooping downwards too low to hear, made Tom want to march out and punch him in the face.

'He says Region sent him,' Ruby said. 'You were right.' She nodded. 'He couldn't keep away. Says he's here to keep an eye on things while Superintendent Coulter is away on conference.'

'Coulter doesn't need to be here, and neither does he, we have *you*,' Tom said and Ruby softened, she could see he was trying to make up for his mistake with the office. 'And me, I'm here now too.'

'Well,' Ruby started with a slow voice as though she was talking to a child. 'You can't just walk back in Tom, you know that…'

'You called me to come in.'

'I called you because…'

'Then *he* can go.'

'It's not for me to tell him.' Ruby's face, for the first time since the confident pink coat of the morning, faltered. She looked disappointed and that gave him hope. 'And,' she hesitated, swooping her eyes past his, avoiding them. 'You have to be signed back to work, you can't just show up as if nothing's happened.' Tom drew in a deep breath, looked her in the eye. 'Don't you?' she added, there was no way round that one.

'In theory,' he acknowledged. 'I suppose I do.'

The joke was over; they could hear the people in the room outside settling. Phones were ringing and being answered, a door slammed and the low hum of office work resumed like the easy rumble of traffic, the joke no more than a pit stop.

'Look,' she relented, 'do you want a coffee?'

He nodded, allowed a small apologetic smile to cross his face. 'But don't let *him* see you, I need some quiet before it all kicks off.'

'God's sake Tom, what do you mean *kicks off*?' Her voice caught that edge of irritation again, the one he'd managed to puncture and now re-inflate. If he was going to stay here he had to be careful, *very*.

'I don't know yet, but it will.'

'He's here because *he* didn't get it right, you know that,' Ruby said. 'And you know how he hates to get things wrong. We all do. In the end it reflects badly on us too.'

'*He* didn't get it right,' Tom emphasised. 'He's covering his own backside. *That'll* be why he's here.'

Tom didn't add: *and he wouldn't care who else got savaged along the way.* And then there was Dolores, of course—the elephant in the room, when was she going to turn up? Had she really been at the seafront, had Leah Barnes told the truth? Why wouldn't she? Whatever else that girl did, she didn't lie, unless... Ruby folded her arms, fingers clasping her elbows in a tidy knot, gloss-varnished and only slightly chipped at the edges. How did women always find time to paint their nails, he wondered, hooking his fingers over to hide his own. She had that face—he'd forgotten that face, the one that was going to tell him as it was, give him the lecture he needed to push him to a point of decision. He watched her building up to what she was going to say, reaching in her mind for the words.

'He needs to sort it, Tom, he did let it slip and the wrong man was identified, which almost certainly, given the location, might be connected to Frank's death...'

'And what about Susie?' Tom stabbed. He sounded petulant, he hadn't meant to. It came out of his mouth the way he felt it, ripped in half. Who else was going to speak up for her if not him?

When she spoke, Ruby's voice was so quiet he had to strain to hear. He watched her lips move as the words came out in a calm whisper. 'This isn't about Susie.'

Or maybe it was his imagination, maybe she didn't say anything, maybe neither of them had spoken at all. His hand went to his pocket, where his thumb pushed a pill through the foil bubble in one of the packets. It weighed as much as a Smartie and he felt it in his fingers, imagined the colours coming off on his skin like they did when he was a kid—red, yellow, green, purple, the sugar still clinging to the sweet dyed colours. Only these pills, when they reached his mouth, were always disappointingly soft and bitter. He was just aware that Ruby was speaking, her voice coming through the pressure of the pill on his fingertips as he tried not to drag the tablet out of his pocket and swallow it. He struggled to leave it where it was.

'I was six years old when they shot my father,' she said. 'Someone called in the night and I thought it was my Nan. She lived two doors down and always came round at all hours for a cup of tea. You know, sat for ages wanting to discuss everything under the sun and nothing, kind of thing. But it wasn't her. I heard the shots, two of them, and him falling. He was a great man, over six feet so the sound of him was like a... well what I thought was... it was like a horse falling. You ever heard a horse when it falls?'

Tom shook his head.

'My uncle had a farm out near Larne, up the coast. I used to spend summers there as a kid and my cousin had this horse, a small one mind, but big you know? It got some sickness, some horse cancer or other and it had to be shot. We were sent to feed the others, us little kids, keep them busy because animals can sense. Anyway, we heard it. The thud of the gun, and then nothing and then the horse... it's like the worst sound you can imagine.'

'I've forgotten what he looked like; I don't remember him at all now. The smell of and feel of him, you know? I was only a wee girl, but I remember the sound. The men who shot him are dead now, not the kind of justice I would have wanted. Or my mother. The men who shot them were let out in the Good Friday Agreement. A Protestant shoots a Catholic shoots a Protestant. So who's the winner? Where's the justice? I joined the Police Force, because I kept hearing that sound, every day. The only way I could silence it was to listen to it until I couldn't hear it any more.'

The noise from the office outside seemed to have disappeared, absorbed into the air. In the beat between her words Tom realised that the stillness seemed to come from Ruby. It came through her hands and eyes and settled on him like an out breath.

'Do you hear it now?' he asked.

'Sometimes,' she said. 'But less and less. Thing is, it doesn't go away just because you turn your back on it.'

And again the sounds from the people on the other side of the wall, the telephones and voices, the stuttering calls of the police radios, filtered back again as though someone had released a pause button. Low murmurs tethered the fraying edges of his memory in place.

'I'll get you some coffee then go home Tom. Come back in the morning, I'll make some phone calls, clear it. And…' she was almost out the door. '…get some sleep, you look awful.' Then she was gone.

Tom listened to her footsteps disappearing down the corridor. He leaned back, closed his eyes until he couldn't hear them anymore.

18

'Tom!'

They shook hands, Robert Nardone, looking older than Tom remembered, was dressed as immaculately as always. The coffee Ruby had brought in steamed on the desk and her eyes swept Tom's as she closed the door behind her, leaving them to it. Tom picked up the coffee and elaborated a charade of pouring sachets of sugar he didn't take, into his drink.

'That your Jag outside, is it?'

'God, no! I did come in it, but it's not mine.' Nardone didn't expand, which was typical. 'What are *you* driving now?' he asked.

Tom pictured his classic red Mercedes 190 mashed to a pulp in some scrap yard and then he pictured Clemmie's heap parked next to the gleaming Jag.

'I don't drive much now,' he said, 'I'm a bit of a liability.'

Nardone ignored the bait and settled in the room's only chair. 'So, what do we know about this murder? Pretty brutal,' Nardone said, stating the obvious as always.

Tom played back what Nardone had just said—brutal, murder. He broke the words up in his head so that backwards it spelled: r-e-d-r-u-m. He put a bet on Red Rum in 1977 and won five quid, the only time he ever won anything in his life. Nardone was still talking, but Tom had missed most of what he said.

'Robert,' Tom said, stopping him in mid-flow. 'What are you doing here?'

Nardone squeezed his blue eyes together and smiled. 'I don't want to make this any more awkward than it is.'

'No.'

'I'm not here through choice, Tom. Superintendent Coulter has to attend Conference in Milton Keynes, no one knew you were coming back and there was no senior rank here.'

'DI Miller is here,' Tom said.

'DI Miller has only been in post for seven weeks.' Nardone spoke as though he was addressing a child. And then, quite suddenly, he changed tack. 'We are aware that there might be overlaps in this case...'

'Such as?'

'It could be linked to another case on my patch in Blackpool.'

'How?'

'Similar MO, similar location.'

'Is it really,' Tom said, hearing his own voice, strong and steady, which surprised him because he'd forgotten what that sounded like.

Robert Nardone stood, raised his hand in the air as if he were about to hit something, rubbed the back of his neck, then lowered it again.

'Look, let's start again,' he said. 'You've all had a long day. I didn't expect you to be here, but now you are, well that obviously changes things. Why don't we grab something to eat before we start. You hungry?'

Start what?

Tom took a cigarette from his jacket pocket, tapped it on his knee, looked out at the January sun and blustering sky and realised he was starving, which had to be a good sign and he was fairly certain Nardone would pay. He thought about where they could go.

'Shrimper's Rest' does a good pint,' he said pulling a long coat from the back of the door. He had no idea who it belonged to but beneath it he found his fur hat, the one with flaps which he always left in the office, which Susie had bought for him a couple of Christmases ago to keep his almost bald head warm. The coat fitted, he looked down at it—it seemed familiar. He pulled it around him, after this morning's cold he was taking no chances; he

130

dragged the fur hat on to his head. He could tell Nardone wanted to laugh, but he didn't. Too much had changed.

'What?'

'Nothing,' Nardone said. 'Nice hat.'

The wind battered the shop fronts outside the police station and the sleet was turning to snow. In the summer the streets stank of chip fat and petrol, the pavements sparkled only if the sun shone, which it didn't, not often. In the winter on a day like today, everything was the colour of stagnant water, the clouds black as pockets. All the shops were closed for the season and piles of faded sugar rock with the name of the town hammered drunkenly all the way through, wilted in the windows. When his son Jack was little they used to sneak here on Sundays, the two of them, buy a stick of rock each, which Jack liked to suck down to a pointed stump until he couldn't read what was written on it. Louise would never have approved so they never told her. Susie never came; Susie didn't like sweets. Tom wondered where Jack was now, what he was doing and then he remembered with a bump of sickness that Clemmie had reminded him he would be there later. He barely saw his son these days and half wondered if he might not turn up at all. Part of Tom didn't want him to, but the rest of him, the main part, hoped he would. They existed in a bubble where the past knocked in from the outside, neither mentioning it; Susie a shimmer in the surface of the bubble.

They made their way along the promenade where the skeletons of new hotels were being thrown up in a seismic vomit of tarmac and grey metal. The sea churned its frustration beneath the pier and the painted horse carousel cowered like a child from the bitter North wind. They passed joke emporiums, amusement arcades with penny grabbers luring punters with cheap soft toys in the window, which by the summer would be long past their best.

'Does the sun shine here?' Nardone asked.

Across the bay, Blackpool and Southport glinted, two beacons in the mad sea where a faint haze of sunshine hovered over them like a halo. It could be sunny there and raining here at the same time—the mud flats in between sucking the sunshine down as it tried to cross.

'At least we have a bit of class here,' Tom said.

The hat let him down on that last point, but he didn't care; his cheeks were stinging from the cold, but his head was warm. He knew what to expect from the wind and it pleased him that Nardone was shivering without a coat or hat, but when he caught sight of himself in a shop window as they neared the pub, furry ear flaps tucked tightly on his ears, he did wonder if he'd made a wise decision. He looked like a bloody yeti.

'I think the hat's rather fetching,' Tom said.

Nardone looked at him.

'Do you care?'

'Not a bit.'

They went in taking the smell of the sea with them. Inside the pub was warm, the benches along the back absorbing the heat from the open fires. As soon as Tom walked in he thought of Louise and the Sundays they came here for Guinness after long cold walks on the beach, before the children were born, a bloody lifetime ago. He looked at Robert Nardone standing at the bar ordering the drinks, shrimp and chips, all those years ago, what did Louise ever see in him? Robert and Louise had had a thing first; Tom met them at one of those awful police dances they had to go to. Tom went alone; Robert brought Louise. Tom went home with Louise. He couldn't picture them together now, but he knew Robert had never forgotten it.

'Fresh this morning these are,' Tom said when Nardone brought them over. He heard his stomach rumble, but Nardone said nothing, placing the pots of tiny brown sea shrimp before them, shimmering in their yellow butter and flanked by thick slices of brown bread.

'Crack of dawn they're out then they come back with these. Magic.' Tom said stuffing a forkful into his mouth; he couldn't think how else to stop himself talking.

Nardone was watching him, not eating.

'You still having grief from the cockle pickers?' Tom asked.

'Some,' Nardone said, but he looked bored.

'I would have thought they'd lie low for a bit.'

'Not where there's money to be made.'

Tom carried on eating, waiting for Nardone to make whatever point he wanted to make.

'I thought it was a good idea for us to talk first,' Nardone said. 'Clear the air. This is...' he searched for the words '...going to be a difficult business.'

Nardone creased his eyes in the gloom. Crow's feet gathered at the edges, his skin had a grey pallor, a North of the Border tint that made him look older than he was.

'You don't need to be here now though, do you,' Tom said, watching him. 'Two DIs plus a Superintendent?' He waited for an answer, but none was forthcoming so he went on, 'Bit of a waste of resources, isn't it? Aren't there any criminal masterminds to look out for in Blackpool?'

Nardone ignored the sarcasm. 'You think you're well enough to be back Tom?' he said, 'Just like that?'

Tom took a large swig of beer, gas filled his mouth and he wanted to burp, which made him want to laugh, but he knew it wasn't funny, any of this.

'I wouldn't be here if I wasn't well enough,' Tom said.

'Have you been given the all clear?'

'You make it sound like I have cancer.'

Nardone smiled. Tom watched his eyes swivel away, scanning the room. In the dim light of the pub he looked like a matinee idol—slicked back black hair with silver edges and dark eyes; the low lighting suited him. Nardone raised a few shrimp on his fork then put them down again.

'You know that in a few days we'll know whether Blackpool will get the licence to have the first Super Casino in the country?' Nardone said.

'And?'

'Do you know of plans to build one here?'

'I don't.'

Nardone tapped his fingers on Tom's box of cigarettes. He flipped the lid of the packet open and closed, curling the edges of his nails under as he did so. He had a large silver ring on his little finger, not unlike the one Ruby Miller was wearing, decorated with small braids of plaited silver.

'There's been the usual movement of personnel in advance of the announcement. Russian gangster by the name of Boris Oledsky was found three days ago, as I said. Similar MO to your man here. '

Tom nodded.

'I've heard that Genaro Molinari has plans for a Casino here,' Nardone said.

'I wouldn't know.'

'I don't think it has anything to do with him.' Nardone measured his words. 'This is bigger. Frank's murder could be connected with Oledsky.'

'Frank Molinari and Russian gangsters, you've got to be joking!' But it occurred to Tom that he could be wrong, even as he said it. Frank was always full of surprises.

'Why did he come back? Someone knew he was here. Maybe he was planning to double cross his brother?'

'Who thought he was dead...'

'Who thought he was dead, yes,' said Nardone.

'As did we.' Tom waited for that one to land, then added, 'So, who killed him the first time? Maybe Genaro *knew* he wasn't dead?'

'The fire was an accident,' Nardone snapped. 'He obviously just took advantage of that to get away. Why?'

'You had a body though—presumably you ID'd it? That would have been the first thing I would have done.'

Nardone looked at him, eyes narrowed. 'You weren't there though, were you?' His fingers fiddled with his gold watch strap, undoing it, redoing it over his tanned wrist, the silver ring appearing and disappearing. 'Dolores and Genaro identified him from his ring and there were his gold teeth.'

'You didn't do a full dental check?'

'Not much left to do it with.'

'Looks like you should have,' Tom said.

Nardone removed the watch and Tom saw that his skin was whiter beneath the strap. He must have been on holiday; maybe he rushed back to get here when he heard. This was no time to be talking about mistakes and both of them knew it, but Tom did not want to let it go.

'There's a lot we should have done but didn't,' Nardone said. 'But that was then, this is now.'

Nardone was keeping something back. Tom knew him too well.

'Anyway, how do I know *you* didn't kill him,' Nardone added. 'You have the motive.'

Tom glared at him. 'I don't like being watched.'

'You're not being watched.'

'I don't think this has anything to do with a casino at all,' Tom said, 'Or with Frank being in the wrong place.'

When he spoke again, Nardone's voice had a slow measure to it. 'It's possible,' he said. '*We* think it's possible there's a connection that's all. But, with it all happening where it did and you being so connected...' he stopped. 'Tom, maybe you're too close to it all. Maybe it's too early to come back. Leave it to me.'

'What? And let you fuck it up all over again? It was my daughter died in that fire too, remember?'

'This is just one avenue I'm pursuing,' Nardone said calmly. 'If it turns out to have no connection then I'll go. No harm done.'

Tom placed his fork on his plate. 'Not an avenue *I'm* pursuing. It's a murder of a local man. It's not linked to anything else. Knowing Frank, he probably got himself involved in some fight. He will have owed debts, he always did. He probably came home to borrow cash he was that desperate. The obvious suspect is his brother and you know it!'

'I don't think it was Genaro,' Nardone said again.

Something shifted. Tom wanted this to end; it was going nowhere.

'You Italians sticking together?' Tom's voice sounded nastier than he'd intended, but he couldn't take it back.

'Meaning?'

'All I meant is, why did he pretend to be dead in a fire and then saunter back just when his brother decides he's moving into the casino business—*if* as you say he *is* moving into the casino business, and there's money to be made?'

'It's not Genaro Molinari.' Nardone shifted in his seat and his voice had an edge to it now, Tom wasn't imagining it. 'This isn't about settling old scores, Tom. I made a mistake, I missed something, but in my place you would have done the same, we did all we could because you were unable to.'

There it was again, the unspoken truth. Tom could run and run all his life, but he was never going to get away from this; still, he was not going to let Nardone blame him for mistakes he had made.

'I'm going to question Genaro Molinari again,' Tom said quietly. 'Would be remiss if I didn't. After letting Frank get away last time, I'm sure you at Regional HQ will be looking for a thorough job this time, won't you?' He'd been away too long, but he wasn't losing his touch and he felt the balance of power shifting. 'Frankly, I'm surprised they can spare you.'

Nardone coughed and Tom tapped his cigarette packet, which was empty. He leaned across and took a cigarette from Nardone's lying on the table. He hated Silk Cut, but needs must. He didn't light up, but tapped it upended on the table one way then the other.

'You know why they call this pub the Shrimper's Rest?'

Nardone shook his head.

'1886, shipwreck just off the coast here, lifeboat went out to save a fishing boat. Don't know what happened, maybe the tides, no one knows. No survivors. Locals brought them in here, laid them out side by side on the floor under canvas. Right here. Right where we're sitting.'

Nardone's face narrowed; Tom could see his jaw tighten, that square Cary Grant jaw with its perfect profile. He knew Nardone wanted to slug him, but he didn't care.

'And the point of this story is…' Nardone said.

'Never let the truth get in the way of a good story is my point.' Tom smiled.

'Tom,' he said, 'If this is about Susie. If you're looking for closure…'

Tom laughed, almost choked on his drink. 'You thought I might find closure? Finding out who killed Frank Molinari?'

'Something like that.'

Tom put the cigarette down carefully along the length of the packet. His phone vibrated in his coat pocket and without taking his eyes off Nardone he looked at the screen: Ruby. The phone to his ear he heard her voice: 'It's me,' she said, 'Postmortem, first thing tomorrow.'

'Okay…'

'I'll meet you at the hospital at 8.30? I've cleared it with Region, for now.'

He didn't answer.

'Is everything okay?' she said, her voice concerned. 'Please don't tell me you're with Nardone?' Still he didn't answer. 'Tom! Where are you?'

'Everything's fine, I'll see you then.' He clicked the phone shut.

'I'm sorry, I have to go' he stood. His head was aching again and he felt the room sway. For a moment he thought Nardone was going to hit him. It would have been long overdue, but Nardone only stood too, he'd put his hand out, to shake it. Tom wavered for a second then took it.

'Closure,' he said. 'No such bloody thing. It's like chasing shadows.'

Then he left the pub, letting the swing doors slam shut behind him. His back was to Nardone who stayed standing where he was.

19

The newsreader looked out from the screen fixing Leah with a sympathetic and tearless eye.

'Police are appealing for information following the death of a man in one of the North West's major visitor attractions. The man, who hasn't been named, was found in the early hours of Tuesday morning in the Pleasure Island fairground in St Marie-by-Sea. A year ago, fire destroyed a ghost train in the same amusement park killing two people, including the brother of the owner, Genaro Molinari. Molinari, who took over the site from his father in 1991, said he was devastated at this latest incident. Pleasure Island has been closed pending further investigation. Police are treating the man's death as suspicious.'

'Bet they bloody are.'

She stomped into the kitchen in disgust, a half-eaten bacon sandwich clenched between her teeth. The coffee in her mug was bitter and strong and she'd added an extra spoon to the filter in the jug without cleaning out the old one, ignoring the musty smell clinging to the filter paper. She'd hardly eaten a thing all day, the sides of her cheeks stuck to her teeth and her mouth was stale and sour. There were dishes everywhere. Ginny and Mati's post-clubbing feast from last night was still scattered over the kitchen— congealed Pot Noodle cartons and manky slices of toast buried under empty cans of Red Bull and Stella. It was late in the evening, Mati would have gone straight to the fields picking from the bike ride, but he was back by three latest and had all afternoon to clear this shit up.

Leah moved things into the bin, shoved all the dirty dishes in the sink to clear surfaces. The kitchen was small and narrow and as soon as she did this it seemed to ease out, expanding its breath as though she was clearing space into its lungs. The tall wall cupboards looked down on her as she rinsed mugs, replaced them on shelves and when she snapped the doors shut, they clicked neatly in approval. The sink faced the big window at the far end of the kitchen. Outside, the wind was battering the panes, rattling the mechanisms of the old sash frames with their strong arms holding the outside world in check, just. In the summer, the sun streamed through the glass, picked out the bubbles of defect in the old panes, twisted the garden beyond into a distortion of crazy foliage. In the summer evenings, light just failing, the view created a perspective like a watercolour, the colours sliding and blending in the pale easy light. Now, as she looked through it, washing and stacking dishes, it looked in the darkness like a painting of one of those medieval pastoral landscapes that, when you looked closer, were filled with fire and anger. It was easy to imagine helpless creatures slaughtered in fire-clouded corners of the garden while tiny men looked on and laughed.

Leah had waited all day for Mati to ring her back and when he did, he just said he was going home to get some sleep after work and would catch her later. She knew he and Ginny would be in bed for hours after finishing their respective shifts and she sat waiting for them to get up, after the day she'd had she was desperate for someone to talk to. It wouldn't be for long though—they would eat, drink, prepare to go out again, plunging from one hedonistic spree to another. How either of them ever managed to get up for work at all was a miracle. Recently she had felt herself disappointed in Mati. He used to be reliable and house proud like her; he paid rent on time, helped her clean and sometimes even had dinner ready for her when she got in. He left casseroles and dumpling type dishes in the oven, the dishes, he said, his mother taught him to make before he got on that bus and staggered his way through Europe to get here. He'd brought a small bag of herbs with him, picked from his mother's yard; the bag was empty now but it was hanging from the butcher's hook on the kitchen door as though still waiting for his mother to walk in and reclaim it. On cold nights, the fragrance of the herbs still clinging to the fabric of the bag caught Leah's breath as she passed it, bringing her up short to summer. But since he'd met Ginny... since he'd met Ginny everything had stopped. She didn't even live in St Marie; she lived twenty miles away in Liverpool, always missed her train and could never afford a taxi back. Leah, the good landlady, had turned her blind eye, ever patient, ever the diplomat, she had let it all slide. She folded the tea towel, tied the bin bag ready to go out in the morning and made herself a fresh coffee. Mati had been a good friend when she needed him; she wasn't going to forget that.

When she returned to the lounge, the newsreader had moved on to the next news item and the interview with Leah, all forty two seconds of it filmed in front of Pleasure Island, had been left out. Six minutes to fill, a girl missing in Chorley and a major incident on the M6 north of Lancaster, they'd dropped her from the schedules. She'd made an effort to be around when the TV crew turned up, gave them all the background they needed, but yet again, the curse of provincial news had her by the throat. Christ, was she ever going to get out of this bloody place.

'Leah!'

Mati emerged from his room wearing a pink towelling robe and a broad grin, his hairy legs poked out at the bottom like a fairy in drag.

'Where the fuck have you been all day?' she snapped.

She was not going to be derailed by Mati's bonhomie. He always looked like he was in the happy land of the high and sometimes, in fact most times, she now realised, it was just bloody annoying.

'Is cold no?' Mati said, rubbing his arms vigorously.

'Yes it's cold.' Leah replied with a curt glance his way.

'I was tired.' Mati spread his hands wide in apology, head tilted in mock-sorrow.

'I had to clear up again.' She kept her eyes fixed back on the TV.

'I had long shift this morning,' Mati said and laughed. 'And that cycling makes me very tired. Sorry Leah, I'm not call you!'

She glanced over and he was smiling. His teeth were as white as the skin beneath the hairs on his legs; a contrast to the dark that made up the rest of him. She could never stay angry with him for long. Most of the time he was easy enough to live with because he was intelligent, interesting and, most of all, no threat. She preferred his company to that of a woman. He didn't want to be her friend, build confidences and secrets that could be used against her at a later date when they'd fallen out over some tiny misdemeanour that was undetectable to the human brain. And besides, it was Susie who had brought him here one evening, his bag on his shoulder, vouching for him and for that reason alone, she was not going to turn him away. But, all the same, there was only so much she could take of the sight of Mati in a woman's tiny bathrobe and she flicked channels around until she found a documentary on clowns, which didn't seem that funny but was at least better than looking at Mati.

'Go and put something else on though, yeah?' she said.

'One minute.' Mati went into the bathroom. His urination echoed through the half-opened door, then the toilet flushed and he came out tugging a pair of jeans and t-shirt on, grabbed from the drying rail. Neither was ironed —the t-shirt crumpled like a ball of tissue and Leah smelled the mildewed dampness that comes from leaving clothing on a radiator, the hint of leaves under a hedge, the warmth of unwashed skin.

He went into the kitchen and Leah could hear him slamming cupboards, rattling glasses looking for a clean one. He was singing—a good tenor voice, in French, one of his sad songs which, though Leah couldn't understand a word, sounded like those dying breath arias from Puccini. It caught her in the back of the throat, unexpected.

'Vodka! You like?'

Leah looked up. Mati was standing in the doorway with a bottle and two glasses in one hand, a loaf of bread in the other.

'Hey.' He came over, placed them on the table and took her hand. 'What is it my friend?'

'It's just been a long day,' she said, dragging the back of her hand across her eyes, shaking them to dissipate the sorrow that was clinging there waiting, as it always was, to catch her unawares.

'Anyway,' she said nodding at the vodka. 'Yes, thank you, I like.'

The vodka was poured out into her grandmother's tiny glasses, dimpled thimble-sized and coloured in every hue from purple to green to blue. They were cheap and bargain basement, but when she was a kid she would always ask to drink from them even though one gulp and the drink was gone.

'Where did you find these?'

'Back of window cupboard,' he said.

She didn't even know they were there. She tipped her glass to her spectral grandmother, leaned back, let the vodka slip down her throat like syrup.

'Nice huh?' Mati said. 'Is from Daniele, you know, the guy on the building site. For all the help he has me.'

'*From* you,' Leah corrected him.

'From me, da.'

Leah did know. Mati had helped him to dig the foundations for a wall in some footballer's wife's monstrosity of a house at the weekend. They worked solidly through from Friday to Monday *and* he got paid in cash; Mati's kind of work and he never turned down extra

143

work. Mati knew everyone in this town and worked harder than anyone Leah had ever met. He cleaned old farm machinery, dug ditches, picked up building work in the winter and picked tomatoes, beets, leeks in the summer, worked bars in the afternoons. His hands were the colour of magenta ink. He was twenty-four, but looked forty and some days like he'd never make it to thirty. Mati said value in this country was based on how many pieces of paper you owned and he didn't have any. Not in England anyway, in Rumania he had a degree. Here he had his hands and wasn't afraid of hard work. He said English people didn't work hard enough, that's why he was here, doing the work they wouldn't. He was going to save his money, go home and start his own business—a bar maybe, with a dance floor—but the more she got to know him the more she thought he was just a dreamer afraid of returning home, all the time hoping she might be wrong. He had stayed far longer than he intended and now she couldn't see him ever going back.

'Is nice house Daniele builds, no?' he said.

'No,' Leah said, thinking of the black and gold electric gates, the twin Romanesque pillars and the mock Trevi fountain in the front garden.

'Is better than you find in my village,' Mati said.

'If you say so.' Leah wasn't going to argue with that. Mati had shown her a photograph of his home, in a small village somewhere in Rumania where his house, smaller than a penny in the picture, looked like a garden shed. The main road was no more than a rutted cart track and in the distance there they were, the cart and horse, thin and head down-trodden, waiting in a dull light for its orders for the day. No wonder Mati preferred the footballer mansion.

'But in Rumania we have mountains and beautiful hills,' Mati said.

'We do too, just not here.' Leah felt honour bound to defend her country. Mati had no idea what England looked like, he hadn't been out of the town since he arrived.

'Is too flat here, like a pancake.' Mati laughed at his own joke, at his mastery of the English language. Leah laughed too and smiled at him, but his attention was turned towards the television, which was still on. He'd turned it over to the sports channel, some US soccer game; it looked like rugby only flashier and faster. Mati liked football, Leah knew nothing about it, much less did she care.

'These guys.' Mati gesticulated towards the screen, 'They are ballet dancers no?'

'No good?'

'Nah,' he clucked his tongue dismissively, 'Americans can't play football.'

'If you say so.'

Mati smiled, sat back, his wide mouth spread in a surprised grin and his dark hair dried to his face. The biscuity smell of sleep hung around him and every time he moved it made its way over to Leah, which was strangely comforting.

'In Rumania, I was in college team.'

'Yeah?'

'I miss football, I like.'

That's what football was to Mati, home, and Leah envied him sometimes. There was no one left here to root her, no one left to make her feel at home. She had Susie, but she knew that one day Mati would go. They sat for a few more minutes watching the Americans play what to Leah looked like fairly respectable football, while Mati explained what they were doing wrong and what they should do instead. Some of it was in broken English, some in Rumanian, some in French and the more vodka he drank, the worse his English became.

'You working in the club again tomorrow?' Leah asked.

Mati nodded.

'Is it worth it?'

Mati looked at her, like this was too obvious a question to answer, 'Sure is worth it. What you ask?'

'Why,' Leah said.

Mati waved his hand, 'Why, what, is same thing.'

'I mean, you can do better than that dump yeah? They're using you.'

'Is okay, you do your job, is okay, you get pay, you go home. Sorted.'

He laughed, pleased with another word added to his growing slang vocabulary as Leah poured herself more vodka. It was good stuff, obviously the real thing, smuggled not imported. Twelve months of living with Mati and Leah knew the difference.

'My friend Eva, she comes yesterday, she *came*.' Mati corrected himself. He put his finger to his lips, 'But *pssht*, not to tell Ginny, Eva is only friend but Ginny not good on difference, you know?'

Leah tapped an unsteady finger to the side of her nose, secret safe.

'And Eva, she very clever and interesting for you. You must meet her, yes?'

'Maybe,' Leah said. 'She's come here to work too?'

'Sure, I get her job in my bar.' Mati said.

They sat watching the men run around the pitch in silence a bit more. Leah wanted to ask him how this Eva had got here. He never mentioned his mates so she must be someone special, Ginny wouldn't like that. She knew from past attempts not to wheedle information out of Mati; he was as closed as the pine cones he'd collected from the coastal Pinewoods when he first got here. He had bowls of them all over the flat. They were lucky, he said. They would tell them the weather and he was right as it turned out, opening and closing in tandem with the rain and the sun. Tonight they were clamped shut. But still, if she let this moment pass there might not be another. With Frank

146

Molinari's unexpected arrival this could be a coincidence, couldn't it?

'How'd she get here? Same guy sent you from Paris?' she asked as casually as she could. She knew it was one guy who got them the passports, that's how Mati got his.

'Sure.'

'The guy in the café?'

'Sure the guy in the café.'

'Who was that?'

'Dunno, Dan, Tom, Bob—I forget, is contact is all.'

'He was English?'

Mati didn't answer, just started channel hopping with the remote control. This was when he tended to shut down, ask a few questions you got something out of him, push it and he shut down. Like the pinecones on a rainy day.

'Sure is English.' Mati said and found a premier league game on Channel 5, highlights of which seemed to please him so that his concentration switched to watching every inch the ball moved across the pitch while Leah tried to think of another way to ask the questions she had persistently asked him since the day Susie brought him here.

'You didn't tell me he was English,' Leah said.

'You never ask.' Mati shrugged and started shouting at the TV. 'You see these guys, this referee is seeing nothing!'

'How old is he, this guy?' Leah persisted.

'What you wanna know for Mrs Paxman?' Mati laughed, eye still on the game. He knew the extent of Leah's ambitions and *Newsnight* was another passion of Mati's besides football.

'It's something I'm working on, a story,' Leah said.

Mati poured another measure of vodka, almost missing the glass.

'This story is to do with the dead man?'

Leah looked at him. He'd said it so casually it could have been a throwaway comment about the match. She saw his cheek pinch in a twitch, like he'd said the wrong thing. He looked straight at the television screen, unflinching. There was no way he could have known any more than the news flashes had announced.

'How did you know about the dead man?' Leah asked.

Mati threw his hands open. 'News travels fast,' he said.

'This café guy, did he bring Eva over yesterday?' Leah persisted, the door wide open now; she was not going to let this chance slip.

'Dunno.'

'You don't know his name?' Leah tried again.

'Maybe,' Mati said, looking at Leah. 'But maybe I don't know his real name.'

Leah cleared her throat. 'What's he look like?'

'He is lazy man,' this was emphatic, 'and he likes himself very much,' Mati said. 'He knows friend of mine in Paris and says he can get me job in England. What am I gonna say, is hard for Rumanians to come now.'

'You trusted him?'

'No.' Mati laughed, a low forced laugh that made him seem twenty years older, as though there was more to the world than she could understand. The laugh made her feel as small and insignificant as that stupid ball the players were still kicking aimlessly around the screen. He had no right to do this to her, no right at all. He did not have the monopoly on suffering he and his kind, to dismiss her life as though it were a fly between his fingers.

'I need him,' he said, 'and then Eva needs him too.'

'Thought you said you didn't know if he'd brought Eva…'

Mati, coughed, downed another thimble of vodka and shrugged.

'Why did Eva need him?' Leah said.

'She came here to look for her brother, but why you so interest?'

'This man,' Leah said, 'I think this man, your man in Paris,' *should she tell him*, 'might be the dead man.'

He turned back to the screen snorting a laugh again. He drained his glass down in one and pulled a fat grey sweater, draped over the back of the sofa, over his head. She watched him lope into the hall and could hear him dragging his big working boots on to his bare feet, cursing under his breath as he struggled with the combination of laces and drunken fingers.

He came back to the lounge and said, 'I know is dead man.'

And then he was gone, leaving these words hanging.

20

'Sorry, sorry.' Tom rushed into the back room hoping that maybe he'd got the time wrong, that maybe it would have switched back on itself somehow so that he would have been in time to greet his son. That he would have shown himself to be the good father he always hoped he might be. But, Jack was already there. He was watching the new TV with Clemmie and didn't appear to notice that his father had been absent.

'Hey,' Jack said.

The two of them were crammed into the tiny sofa, their combined weight pulling it into a pointed sag in the middle. Clemmie didn't use the front room because when the wind came in off the sea it rattled the tiny leaded panes in the window and blew soot down the chimney. In the back room the fire was lit and Jack and his grandmother shared a bright orange blanket draped across their knees, which used to belong to the cat. The cat that hissed at Tom every time he entered the room but at the moment was nowhere to be seen. They were watching an American crime series where pathologists in shades solved impossible crimes. Detectives swept bright strobes back and forth across patches of invisible blood standing back to watch the patches change colour in front of their eyes like magic.

'You can see everything on this TV,' Clemmie said. 'Doesn't cut the corners off like the last one.'

Tom looked at the huge screen, which filled the wall above the fireplace and the sight of it depressed him more than anything that had happened that day.

'They've dug a body up that was buried twenty years ago. Nothing to go on,' she said. 'Imagine that.'

Was this one of Clemmie's arrows sallied forth to cut through the mess she thought he'd made of his life? Was she highlighting the fact that her beloved granddaughter was reduced to ashes while he stood by and did nothing? Or was it his conscience catching up?

'I can imagine,' Tom replied. 'It happens.' He was not going to have this discussion with her, not tonight, not again.

Clemmie waved a hand towards the kitchen. 'You'll have to make your own omelette,' she said. 'We've had ours.'

He poured himself a glass of cold water and gave in to the nag of the last of the tablets in his pocket, swallowing three of the stronger ones in quick succession. He didn't fancy an omelette so he dug some cheese out, made toast from an old loaf in the cupboard just the white side of blue. He watched the cheese fizz and bubble across its surface under the grill, a dunk of pickle and a mug of tea, which he carried into the room where his son was sitting.

'How did it go?' Clemmie asked not taking her eyes off the TV.

'Oh you know...'

'Gran says you're back at work?' Jack said.

'Yes, well, sort of...'

'That's good.'

'I suppose so.'

He knew he should say something, but couldn't think of anything worthwhile. He ate in silence and the three of them watched the make believe Miami police department solving the perfect crime with nothing but blue fluorescent lights and test tubes; for now, that would have to be enough. He was just happy to be silent.

They had to be up early the next morning so when the programme was over, Clemmie announced she was going up to bed leaving the two of them to flick through channels. At least that meant they didn't have to talk. They watched football, which neither of them liked, then *Newsnight*, which at least gave them something to talk about in a *what's gone wrong with the world* kind of way. When his father was alive, Clemmie took a contrary opinion, always willing to start a fight in an empty room, but after he died the fight left her. It was only after his father's death Tom realised the arguments were her misguided attempt to communicate with a man she had long run out of things to say to.

Tom asked Jack about his mother and was informed she was fine. He wanted to ask more, to know if Louise slept well, ever thought about him, if she had anyone else. But Jack never told him much. The twins stayed with their mother when he and Louise divorced and it was only a year ago, when Susie died, that they had been able to speak to each other again, as they used to. *Why did it take something like that?* But the things Jack told him about Louise's life remained bare bones, which revealed the strength of her, getting on with life instead of dragging it behind her like him.

When they finally went to bed, Tom couldn't sleep. The wind was high again and the big tree in the back garden cast its waving shadow through the curtains of his room, its arms waving in angry motion. He was a child in this room. *Was the bed bigger then or had he outgrown it?* Jack was walking around upstairs. He could hear the low rumble of his voice talking on his mobile to people Tom didn't know, existing in a world he wasn't part of. Too much time had passed between them and if he didn't reach out and pull it back in soon, he would lose the thread of its connection forever.

There was a house before this, a smaller one in a narrow street in a different town when Tom was a boy. He remembered the amber glow from the street lamps outside the window. It would peep in beneath the too-short curtain, the rain at night gathering in the gutters gurgling. He lay awake listening to the swish of car tyres on tarmac, counting them, one-two-three, until he fell asleep. In that house he had a hamster in a cage and built ships out of upturned tables. His father would come in late from work, building his business meant he stayed out all hours, but also that he stayed away from her. But Clemmie would be waiting, always waiting, whisky at her elbow, and then the shouting would begin.

'Jack?' he whispered, tapping on the door.

The boy, who in a heartbeat Tom saw had grown into a young man, came over and opened the door ajar.

'Hey, Dad. Thought it was Gran.'

'Can I come in?'

'Sure.'

He'd brought his school bag, a rucksack in blue and grey, lived in from walking in the rain, from being thrown down on some common room floor. Tom had never seen it before. He thought back to Jack taking off for college the morning of the fire. Louise had to work and rung him to ask if he could drop Jack in Wigan where his college was. He'd taken Jack to the gates and waited no more than a minute at the drop off, watched him saunter away, bag slung across his shoulders, a different bag. The new bag looked like the hours he'd lost in the months between then and now, hours he was never going to get back. The bag was on the table beside the single guest room bed. The room was small and warm, inviting.

'How's it going?' Tom said, for something to say.

'Oh, okay. Just getting my stuff ready for tomorrow you know?'

'You have your ticket?'

Jack shrugged; a lock of brown hair fell over his right eye. 'Yeah.'

'I was just... I know Gran said she'd pick you up from Lime Street later, but I thought I might?'

'Oh?' He didn't look his father in the eye when he spoke. 'Right.'

'It's okay, she was quite relieved when I mentioned it.'

'She gets a bit lost in Liverpool…' Jack laughed with a hitch in his voice.

'So…'

'Yeah, that'd be great Dad, yeah.'

There was little else to say, it was settled. Tom's hand was on the door; *get out now before you snap this moment.* There was so much more he wanted to say.

'Thanks Dad.'

'Night.'

'Night.'

Tom shut the door and went downstairs where he filled another glass from the cold reservoir of the big American fridge Clemmie bought last summer. She had started buying big the year his father died, filling the space he'd left. She bought a king-sized bed, a shed for the garden large enough to fit a car in, the fridge and now the TV. Things he would never have let her buy, things she always wanted. The house was too big for her and Tom wished she would move instead, find her space to fit into, knowing she would never move now that she was free to do so.

He drank the water looking through the notes magnetised to the fridge door—all out of date and useless, some going back three years. One was for a prescription he'd forgotten to pick up. He slugged two more codeine with the cold liquid, a relief to be back on the routine of tablet counting. It was okay to mix that with ibuprofen but no more than eight of each in a day. He'd taken fewer than usual and he hadn't even noticed. He was making up for it now.

He went back upstairs and put the glass of water on the table beside his bed in case he needed anything in the night. He spun the childhood globe, which stood gathering dust, letting his finger fall on the first country it found.

When this was all over, that's where he'd go.

Mexico. What language did they speak? Portuguese, Spanish? He imagined dark skins and dark eyes, black hair. He imagined Dolores. He found her number in his wallet. Like his mother, he never cleared anything out so it bulged with till receipts and car park pay and display tickets. On the back of a dentist's card with a reminder of an appointment he'd also forgotten, he'd written her number and dialled it before he changed his mind.

He imagined her sitting in her red room surrounded by her pictures and her cards which told the future; her window with its view across the seawater marine lake.

The telephone rang out, and out. Nobody answered.

21

Leah lay in the dark and stared at the ceiling. She'd heard Mati come in around 3.34am and stagger around the bathroom. Why did he always have to piss so loudly? She turned over and looked at the red digital numbers on her clock and thought about this Eva. Why was she here and why had Mati mentioned her then looked like he wished he hadn't? He was not a man for loose talk, words thrown out like careless soundbites. When you spoke in a language not your own you had to think about what you said and who you said it to. She remembered her grandmother's faltering English, how she would pause and think about the way she was about to say something so that she wouldn't be misunderstood. Her grandmother was German and had learned to be cautious; she'd seen the same in Mati, the way he raised his head to sniff the air like a cat, searching for the right words. Leah was sure that it was Frank Molinari who had brought Eva. Frank was the man in Paris who had found Mati his job. It was the thing she wasn't able to see before and Susie, she guessed, must have known all along. She was going to tell her that day, that's why they went to the fairground, *but who told Susie?*

She dozed, heard the radio in the kitchen—music, indistinct and distant and then the door slam shut around seven. She heard two sets of footfall, Ginny and Mati leaving for work. The alarm clicked the *Today* programme on, the radio buzzing news around her numb brain. She must have fallen asleep because when she woke it was 10.24 and the flat and the streets around it were silent. She couldn't place where she was or what had happened and for a moment thought everything was all right. She thought she had got Susie out of the burning train and this time the smoke hadn't held her back, she hadn't left her behind, she felt happy.

She put her hand to her throat, as if she could smell the smoke. She could taste it at the back of her mouth. She'd been shouting Susie's name, over and over. Then the crashing pain in her ear came like a white noise and the plateau where the land was flat, no tears, no rage, no grief, only silence.

22

In the night the gales turned into the storm that had been threatening all day. When Tom looked out of his window in the morning, the big tree had split down the centre and lay across the grass now like a great slaughtered beast. The tree had been there as long as he could remember, since before the children were born, before he was born and long, long before that. He should have felt sorrow, the tree forlorn and trashed on the grass, limbs flung asunder and twisted out of kilter. But it had opened the garden which, in the aftermath of the storm, brought the sunlight streaming into it. Now you could see the gardens beyond, fresh lawns and the gentle rising hill that ringed the back of the houses. He opened the window and could catch the iron tang of brine in the air. The glass of the windowpane had a veneer of salt blown there from the sea. He ran a fingertip down its length and put it to his lips, the salt tasted sweet and nutty.

He showered and dressed with an urgency he hadn't felt for a long time then went downstairs. Only Jack was there, the kettle had boiled and he'd laid out two places for breakfast. Tom sat and they began to eat.

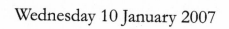
Wednesday 10 January 2007

1

Pleasure Island didn't look so glamorous first thing. It stank of piss and diesel fumes, the storm having blown ever more plastic and debris into its space. Crisp packets and paper cups, plastic drink bottles and cans all piled against the chain link fence. After yesterday's buzz and chaos only a thin police presence remained—a lone officer sat in a yellow mobile surveillance van. Leah could see him scrolling through a mobile phone, one elbow on the closed window. As she came past, he raised his head in a perfunctory *well you don't look like a threat* way, then looked down again. Leah heaved herself against the rusted metal gate hastily erected across the front of the Moroccan archway. It had been tacked up against the walls by a chain, unlocked, and was only there for effect to deter intruders. No one was around. When she crossed the courtyard she hesitated a second, but the door to the office portakabin was ajar. Leah went straight in.

'Good Morning.'

Genaro Molinari was at his desk. He was surrounded by the clutter of two-for-one Chinese State Circus flyers in brown cardboard boxes, piles of folders and files. She knew he rented the car park space to visiting circuses in the spring and summer months, but these flyers looked old and forgotten. An empty bottle of whisky balanced like a high-rope walker on the edge of his desk. It was almost empty.

'Christ you look awful,' Leah said, pushing the door to the office wide open to let some fresher air in.

Genaro Molinari took two tablets from a bottle on the desk and gulped them with something from a polystyrene cup. He didn't seem the least bit surprised to see her.

'What do you want?'

'Can I have a word?'

Leah had to look away from him as she spoke. She was repulsed by the way he had caved in, his height shrunk to the level of his shoulders. Unshaven, his eyes were dragged down by envelopes of skin like a great bloodhound. Too tall for the chair, his shoulders stooped over so that his chin rested on his chest and he kept rubbing a tanned wrist across his forehead, scrubbing an invisible mark. In the growing red winter sunlight, his gold watch with concertina links glittered on his arm. It caught the beams as they filtered in through the murky window. She hadn't expected him to look like this. This was not the way she remembered him. She hadn't expected to feel sorry for him.

The room was stuffy, slept in, the overpowering stench of sweat. She sat in the chair opposite his desk and tried to block the noises from outside—the blue incident tape flapping a low and constant beat, the heavy clang of the fairground machinery creaking in the aftermath of the storm. Genaro Molinari didn't notice. He was already playing the part of a man in mourning, a man who didn't look like he was pretending and that wasn't what she'd come to see. Through the glass, which was so dirty, Leah imagined writing her name on it, she could see the 'Log Flume' and the 'Fire Cat', the blue lights of the 'Hellraiser' rippling along its high curves like the blips on a heart monitor. She looked for a way to begin.

'I'm sorry to hear about Frank,' she said, taking the easiest route.

'Everyone is sorry for me,' Molinari said.

'I know this must be a difficult...' she said but Molinari's laugh interrupted her. It turned into a guttural cough, Leah expected gobs of phlegm to fly out of his mouth and land on her knee, '...time,' she finished her sentence with an emphasis she didn't intend.

'Why are you here?'

Molinari's voice sounded like he was trying it out for the first time. She detected a hint of Italian, la famiglia with an edge of Scouse. As far as Leah knew, the nearest Genaro Molinari had ever been to Italy was Luigi's Ice Cream Parlour on Marine Drive, which he'd owned for years until he sold it to another local ice-cream family. It was still like an out take from a Fellini film, all Italian tricolours and collages of Rimini. Everyone in the town loved it, the new owners had painted and preserved it, as any changes would be made at their peril, but it had pulled in more people than ever, a glimpse of the nostalgic past everyone yearned for. Genaro Molinari spread his hands, palm upwards on the table, a dealer laying out his cards.

'What you want to know?'

But Leah had one thing in her favour and Genaro knew it. She wasn't afraid of him, not the way her father was.

'I'm covering the story,' Leah said. 'I just want to get the facts straight.'

Molinari scowled at her then stood. He stretched and went to the window. He looked out, came back bringing the scent of a heavy aftershave, sprayed liberally to hide the deeper scent of a night spent in this coffin of a room, with him. He studied her for a few moments.

'This a big story for you huh?'

She held his gaze until it slid in an exhausted motion from her face and on to the bottle of whisky at the edge of the desk. She now noticed two cups beside it, polystyrene, one dented and broken. He snatched them and threw them into a black bin bag, hanging on the edge of a makeshift sink at the side of the room. He switched one of those useless electric water heaters on, a splash of washing up liquid and washed his hands. Rinsed them and then washed them again.

'You write only nice things about my brother,' he said. His voice was so quiet Leah had to turn her head round to hear what he said. 'After the last piece you write on the fire you nearly closed me down.'

'You can hardly blame me...'

Genaro turned back to her, drying his hands on a towel that looked as though it had never seen a washing machine. He gave a shrug of the shoulders and that *bpff* sound she'd never heard an English person make—Mati used it sometimes when he didn't want to talk, when he wanted to say *I can't be bothered.*

'No,' he said. 'I suppose I can't.'

Leah had the article she wrote a year ago on her memory stick in her pocket, one of her best, one for the portfolio. She always kept her best work with her, you never knew in this business. The article had suggested that the fire was the result of negligence caused by an exploited workforce. It was nobody's fault, except for Genaro Molinari's, and he'd got away with it. But now, now she wasn't so sure—she hadn't factored the brother, the younger more unpredictable one, into the mix. Nor had she factored in a police force that didn't do its job. At the time she thought she had got her facts straight and she thought losing his brother in the fire was enough punishment. Losing Susie had been enough for her. They had both suffered and lived with the consequences, learning to, or *not* as the case might be. Now he had to go through it all over again.

'But I didn't close you down, did I?' she said.

Genaro took a heavy coat from a hook behind the door, eased himself into its folds and slowly fastened the buttons one by one. He fastened them out of order so that the front of his coat ended lopsided, which he didn't seem to notice. The sight of this rendered his appearance even more pathetic. Leah noticed his hand shaking as he placed it on the door handle, fumbling for keys in his pocket.

'Come,' he said. 'I have something to show you.'

She noticed he locked the door to the portakabin behind him. The police officer was still in his van, still on his phone, and didn't seem to be taking any notice of them; no one else was around.

'I need some fresh air,' he said, but he didn't look any better when he got outside.

Genaro walked towards the far end of the fairground with Leah following a pace or two behind. She was surprised how fast he walked. For someone who looked so tired, someone so exhausted with his life, this was unexpected. They could hear the sea crashing against the new promenade where clouds of sand had gathered in the corners of buildings and rides, covering some and leaving others with bits of metal protruding like the bony fingers of ghosts. This part of the ground was bitter and hard-edged; a place where carousel horses went to die. The wooden rollercoaster tunnelled above them, the carriages sitting up top like disjointed limbs. Nothing moved between the rides. The carriages beneath the tarpaulins, which covered the waltzers and teacups that resembled the spectres of summer punters waiting for the sun to arrive and wake them from their winter slumber.

'Oldest working rollercoaster in Europe,' Genaro said as they passed it.

'When was it built?'

'1913.'

Leah looked up. 'They build them safer then?'

'You think my rides not safe?'

She ignored him; she wouldn't be goaded and besides, there was the twist of a smile at the edge of his lips. They went further back away from the entrance, from the useless policeman in his van, and it struck her that she should have known better. She must have been insane to think she could get the story out of Genaro this way. What was she going to do, just come out with it: 'Genaro, did you kill your brother?' Because that was the only story she had in her head even though, by now, she doubted it. She hadn't really thought this through, just got up, got dressed and made her way. No one else knew she *was* here, she hadn't even told Mike or Arun.

When they reached wherever it was Genaro was taking her, he halted abruptly as a grubby white cat the colour of dirty snow ran out and hissed at them. Others watched boggle-eyed from behind the wooden structure of the rollercoaster. The place was teeming with cats, mainly strays that migrated here for the summer food discarded by the tourists, desperate now in the throes of winter. Molinari dropped down and cooed at the cat in an unexpected and tender gesture.

'You like cats?' he asked. Leah didn't answer. 'I like cats.' Genaro straightened as the cat spun on its heels and ran.

They turned a corner and Genaro stopped beside a piece of flat, scarred ground surrounded by an iron fence that, on closer inspection, was made of razor wire. They were at the back of the ground away from any sign of life; even the sound of the sea had receded like a distant dream. Old rollercoaster trucks lay on their sides across pieces of small gauge railway. The fibreglass head of a red dragon lolled against a fence beside tins of discarded paint. In the distance Leah could just see the tops of the lamps on the new Millennium Bridge. A new bridge in an old style, Edwardian wrought iron with turquoise and white lamps its entire length, solar-powered instead of lamplit—the town trying to reclaim its past. This helped her gain her bearings and she knew then they were at the end of the ground near the ghost train. They had just arrived at it by a different route. She looked up to see the wall of painted skulls with green and black paint chipping off a fibreglass façade, more Scooby Doo than scary. She hadn't seen it since the day Susie died. *Oh Christ* she was stupid to have come here, falling again under the Molinari spell just like her father. He ran around after Genaro, always thinking he had the upper hand, doing what he was told and never, ever, able to say no. But he never had the upper hand, Genaro did.

'The ghost train is closed now, I don't have a key,' Genaro said.

Leah knew he wouldn't open it even if he did. She also knew better than to ask why he'd brought her here as the grey phantom on the front of the ride leered out at them over a train. The sculpture was made from fibreglass and wire, eroded by the acid sea winds its wires like bones eating its flesh away. Leah saw the metal cage that housed the machinery just visible through the steel gate, padlocked for the winter and a door behind, leading to the room where the fire started. She thought of Susie, as no doubt she was meant to. It would take more than Genaro's games to scare her.

'Is where my brother died,' Genaro said. 'The first time.' Leah couldn't read his expression, was it remorse? 'This where your friend died, we both lose someone we love so what story are you gonna tell this time? Huh?'

'This is the story,' he said. 'Frank, my brother, I think he is dead and then puff back he comes like Lazarus. You know Lazarus?'

Leah nodded. But she didn't believe in the dead coming back, even if she believed in their voices, miracles and smokescreens created in the imagination of the living.

'What you gonna say about that? I have him dead to deal with all over again. Frank never does what he supposed to. Now he's really dead. There is no story. Is finished.' He snapped his palms together *slap*.

'But... you have an idea what happened?' Leah said.

Without missing a beat, Molinari turned and studied her. 'I loved my brother.'

It wasn't an answer, but it was all she was going to get. He turned away. A strange walk he'd taken her on, his motive unclear.

They returned in silence, the back way again, this time across a patch of bare land unbuilt on, hemmed by thick wire, fence posts and signs saying guard dogs but none in sight.

'I've heard you've got plans for a casino?' Leah said, looking around her, the ground looked prepared, set aside for something. 'This where it's going?'

'You shouldn't believe everything you hear.'

Leah thought about the glossy brochure and its plans, another set of smokescreens and mirrors, will-o-the-wisp. Was that, she wondered, what Frank had been after? A piece of the action?

'Did Frank know about it?' she asked, feeling braver now that they were back near the Portakabin where they were more visible with the yellow police van within sight. But Genaro turned and offered his hand. The meeting, if that's what it was, was over.

'Don't come back.' Genaro smiled leaving no doubt she wouldn't ever be welcome again. But, there were other ways and she knew how to find them.

'Genaro' she said. 'I...' *what was she going to say?* 'Thank you,' which felt pretty lame. Molinari waved his hand dismissively.

'Is nothing. Your father wasn't a bad man, you are his daughter.'

And he wasn't a good one either, Leah thought, but then Genaro would know all about that. She knew that Genaro would watch her until he was sure she'd left the car park, just as he said, making sure she didn't come back.

As she passed the stationary police van, she noticed a man in a light suit leaning into the window, talking to the officer. A finger from the van pointed to the fairground, to the Portakabin door which Genaro was unlocking. He stopped when he saw the man coming towards him. He waited, then held the door open as the man reached it to let him through and it looked from where Leah stood, as if Genaro had been expecting him.

168

2

'You'll need to sort yourself a car,' Clemmie said.

Tom and Jack were taking the Volvo again. Jack was already in the front, fiddling with the radio.

'Thank you for the loan of the car Mother,' Tom said, his voice on the edge of sarcasm.

'That wasn't what I meant,' she clipped. 'I might need it.'

'*Do* you need it today?'

She went over to Jack and leaned in giving his cheek a kiss.

'Good luck sweetheart,' she said to him. 'You'll be fine.' And to Tom: 'That wasn't my point.'

She stood in the driveway, the housecoat flapping over her nightdress, big walking boots loose-laced on her feet. It was warmer, a better day. When this was over, he'd get himself his own car, somewhere else to live...

'So what time does your train get back tonight?' Tom said, watching her disappear in the mirror behind them.

'Sixish I think...'

'I'll come to Liverpool for you.'

'You don't have to, I can come back here...'

'I do and I will.'

What he should have said, 'I'll come with you, look round the university, I don't need to go back to work today' *Because he didn't*... One of them—him or Louise—should have gone with Jack, but somewhere in the maelstrom of grief and blame and anger, their son had got lost. Jack had reeled his thread behind him, hoping one of them would hang on, but neither had and he could see already how well Jack was managing alone. He didn't need either of them; he'd learned that the hard way. This, driving him to the station today, was a start of sorts, but not enough. No one picked his thread up either when his brother died, not his father, not Clemmie. When his younger brother died he was never discussed again, his room cleared, his name unmentioned. It was so long ago that Tom never thought of him at all, but he was still there, nudging him, and he would do well to remember that.

'Dad?' Jack was watching him. 'You okay?'

'Yes, yes fine,' Tom said. 'So… here we are.' *Why say something useful when you can state the obvious instead.* He pulled up behind the taxi rank in St Marie's station car park, half expecting to see Frank with the blue girl waiting for a taxi.

'Cheers Dad…'

'Text me when the train's at Crewe.' Tom left the engine idling, reached over and gave his son as close to a hug as he could. The boy was startled, but he could feel Jack relax beneath him. 'Good luck son.' The words and the gesture sounded lame, they *were* lame, whoever called their child 'son' anymore? But he couldn't take the words back and he wanted to say so much more. Jack's body stiffened beneath the awkward hug; he pulled himself away and out of the car.

'Don't overdo it today Dad, yeah?' Jack said. His face was pinched with concern. The gesture, which had been intended to reach out, had merely alarmed him.

'I'll try not to.'

Then he was off, iPod in his ears, swaying down the entrance to the station, jeans baggy around his bum, his head already elsewhere. Tom watched until his son was out of sight, aching to call him back.

His phone rang out in his pocket—two missed calls, both from Ruby, no voicemail just a brief text: **where are you?** He looked at his watch—9.32. The hospital was round the corner, a few minutes away. He turned the car round, drove the long way out of the one-way system so that he wouldn't have to go past the station again, so he wouldn't have to see the train leave.

The mortuary was at the side of the hospital, hidden. He had to cross a car park and negotiate a delivery lorry at the back door, which was unloading metal food trays. It occurred that corpses and vacuum packed food would all be delivered through this same entrance like a strange ritual in the loop of life. In the corridor, piles of laundry waited to be collected and the smell of detergent caught in the back of his throat. He realised he hadn't had a cigarette since he left the house that morning. There was no time now. In spite of it being morning, everything had an end of day feel to it. The smell of disinfectant and floor polish was overpowering. The linoleum was shiny and slippery under his feet where the cleaners had come through and washed it, left it to dry. In the mortuary, the slab boys looked done in. They barely lifted their heads as Tom passed their office and he thought he recognised one, a blonde-haired lad with a long fringe that kept catching in his eyes, who couldn't have been much older than Jack. They drank tea out of Bob's on the Job mugs, Health and Safety posters above their heads. A mess of forms and papers were scattered over the desk in front waiting to be filled. They'd probably been here since dawn working on Frank. Tom well remembered Linda's view on commitment to the job—long hours, way over what was required, get the job done. He caught himself—*it took one to know one.*

'Dr Sweeney around?' he said. The blonde lad jerked his thumb to the postmortem room which was just visible through the glass, the slatted blinds half drawn down. Tom could see Linda writing on a clipboard at a desk to the side, concentrating. She had her tongue clamped between her teeth, the tip of it poking out and Ruby Miller was standing to her left, reading a report. Neither was speaking, they had been waiting for him for half an hour.

Tom turned to thank the lad and felt a gear switch in his head—he *had* met him before. The lad didn't recognise him, of course. He was tuned to have all memory erased as he moved on from one set of bereaved parents to the next. It was part of the job description, but Tom remembered him all the same. The mug of tea in the Bob the Builder cup, the kindness, the quiet word, the flick of the hair over the eyes which settled on him that day unafraid to look away. He was much older than Tom had given him credit for now that he saw him again, and it was clear that he didn't remember Tom. Police officers were able to do that too— they couldn't recognise one victim from the next, like they had an on/off button. Tom couldn't imagine what it would be like to be one of them now, even though he knew he had been one of them for so very long. The counsellor they gave him after the accident said that if you lose your compassion, you lose yourself. No, she hadn't exactly said that, it was he who had nudged that one out of himself, but it was true. The counsellor had nodded; surprised, said he'd make a breakthrough. He still wasn't quite sure what she meant. He thought it was what she wanted to hear.

He could see the two women were talking. To their left the bodies—two of them, distinct shapes under sheets. The one on the right, head uncovered, he could see, was Frank Molinari. He'd imagined himself lying there countless times like that and, no doubt, others had too. Louise had wished it, she'd told him: *you should have died instead of Susie*, she'd said, she used those words. She couldn't wish it more than he had.

Neither of the women noticed as he walked into the room. The forgotten sharp smell caught him, made him gag.

'Morning,' he said and they turned and nodded without speaking. *Hello* would have been nice he thought, but Linda was already pulling the sheet right back to expose what was left of the rest of Frank. He didn't look as bad now, apart from the skin greying to a blush of violet before it bloated and mottled black. Blood pooling in corners of the body you would never know existed. Tom thought of a fish rotting in a barrel, of the cockler they'd found a few years back. They'd found him down by the pier in an oil drum, with his fish, lid on, victim of the ongoing dispute over some indistinctive molluscs on a beach and the price you'd get for them. A life reduced to a few empty shells.

Tom looked up to where Linda was pointing, there were pictures on the wall of a brain in thick pale slices, Linda and the boys had been busy parcelling Frank up and sewing him back together again. There was neat stitching around the crown and up his gut in a long neat line, stretched out in a 'Y' at his chest, like Frankenstein and his dead monster. Frank looked different though; his body had reached that state of relaxation in the muscles that sets in after twenty-four hours or so. He looked, as they say (whoever *they* are) at peace. Whatever spirit Tom thought he'd felt yesterday in that fairground, an aura hovering around the dead man's head, was long, long gone. There was a small cavity where the left side of his head should have been but cleaned up he didn't look so bad, he could have been a waxwork. Frank was a tall man—long armed, strong-armed and, if he was honest, not that bad as criminals go. In a different lifetime he might even have liked him, he *had* liked him. It was something else entirely that set them at odds in the weeks before the fire.

'He was killed by a single blow,' Linda said, matter of fact.

'You *are* kidding?'

'Oh you do speak then?' Linda carried on in her stubborn mechanical way. 'Here, side of his head just below the base of the skull.' She moved the head and indicated a small wound like a bruise, which you'd miss if you didn't know where to look. 'There's a vein links to the common carotid artery, which runs up here.' She indicated by running a light finger up and along Frank's skin. 'Any pressure which might be applied to the artery at the sinus, which is just underneath here, can prove fatal even in a healthy person, but in someone with advanced heart disease like our man here it wouldn't take much. There's a mark, look, just here. You could even do it with your hand if you hit the right way.'

'What about the face?' Ruby was reading the notes at the same time as scanning what she saw. She meant the blow to the side of his face, the blow that apparently hadn't killed him.

'Well, none of that's got anything to do with this, that was done later, postmortem, confusing at first I agree. But...' she angled her gloved hand towards Frank's neck, the base of his skull. 'The body bruises or bleeds if it's hit ante-mortem, so this bruise was inflicted earlier. He received this blow after death, I have no idea why but probably to make sure he really was dead. But isn't that supposed to be your bit of the job?'

Ruby said nothing, Tom could see her watching, thinking. Linda's unflinching convictions came back to Tom the more she talked. Working in forensics was like gazing at your own navel. He'd had that conversation with Ruby many times over Linda's predecessor, a taciturn man called Wayne Macdonald who could only hold a conversation when it was about blood and guts. He knew Ruby was thinking the same thing because she was chewing her nails the way she did when she wanted things to happen more quickly than they were. *How did he remember that?* She looked over at him, a quick glance, a smile as she remembered, they were on the same track at last.

He stared at the bruise on the dead man's head, which connected to a long snaking artery, surprisingly prominent on the skin, leading to the brain. It was obvious, even to the uninitiated that Frank had been in bad shape when he died. He'd lost a lot of weight so that the only thing left of him *was* veins, bone and skin. Is that all it would take to kill a man? Tom put his hand up to his own neck; his fingers found the beating pulse, smooth as a train going over a track.

Linda said, 'Traces of cocaine. Wouldn't have helped the heart condition.'

'Recent?' Ruby asked.

'No, but he was a regular heroin user at one time too. See, puncture marks on his arms. No traces now, replacing it with cocaine I would guess. Slipping back into old habits. Might explain the weak heart. Anyway...' Linda rearranged his hands, his arms, to show them. She ran a latex-gloved finger along the purpling flat of Frank's tie-dyed palm. It was impossible to distinguish the lines now and Tom was squinting, searching for Frank's lifeline, which had to be there. Dolores once told him you could cheat death if the lines said so, but that wasn't true. Tom knew that better than anyone.

'All supports what I said, pretty sure he was dead by the first blow, the one to the artery, but then he was finished off just to make sure,' Linda said.

'Same person?'

'Well...' She looked through her sheaf of loose notes on the desk. 'My guess is no. The first blow was at least two hours before the second and could have been accidental. So someone else could have come back to check, or found him and decided...'

'You're sure?' Ruby said.

Linda nodded '...he might have survived the first blow weak heart or no. And...' she continued, '...atrophied muscles, concurrent with someone who used to be very fit, but gone considerably to seed.'

'He used to be a circus strongman,' Tom said.

Linda and Ruby laughed.

'For real?' Ruby said.

He nodded. 'That's how he met Dolores.'

175

There she was, and in the end he was the one who had to say her name. Linda looked at him, eyes thinned wide in blankness.

'Dolores was...' he hesitated, 'she was Frank's lover, partner, I guess you'd say. They weren't married.' *As if that made a difference.*

'Right.' Linda seemed confused, why was he ever mentioning it, and Tom could feel Ruby's eyes on him, waiting for what he was going to say next. He didn't disappoint.

The words trickled from his mouth as though they had been backed up behind his teeth waiting to spill out. 'They met when they travelled round France with the circus, they were just kids. Dolores...' he hesitated. 'Dolores said he ran away from the family, from something...'

'We should speak to Dolores then,' Ruby said quietly. 'She might have seen him before he died.'

'It was a long time ago. And Frank came back.'

The air in the clinical space was spare and cold. Tom imagined he could see his words dancing out there against the white walls, bouncing and spinning. St Marie-by-Sea and its fairground must have been dull after the circus and its delights. The twirl of a Ferris wheel was no match for the excitement of a sawdust ring and the roar of a crowd. He imagined them—Frank and Dolores with her crystal ball and her spells of magic, voices from the past dreaming of a future they were never going to have. But he didn't know what Frank had run from, Dolores had just said 'family' but as far as he knew there was only Genaro. But then running away could mean many things and he thought of Jack on his way to visit a university miles away from home, miles from him.

'Do you know where Dolores is?' Ruby asked him, because she had to.

'No,' he answered. 'No, I don't.'

That much, at least, was true.

176

It was true too about what they said about the dead—they hung around uninvited, long after their time was up. Their silence was everywhere and Tom felt as though he could reach out and touch it, as light as the bounce on a spider's web. He loosened the button on his collar.

'I need a cigarette,' he said and sensed the two behind him exchanging glances of concern, muttering under their breath that he should be at home, that it was too early to come back to work, post traumatic *blah, blah, blah*.

He made his way outside to the car park where the lorry had finished unloading the lunch trays for the wards. A small ambulance marked 'private', the kind that ferried bodies with blacked out windows, was parked to the side and the driver of one of them was leaning against the back wall smoking.

'Alright?' he said.

The community of smokers was shrinking these days; they clung together like survivors on a raft. In a few months they wouldn't be able to smoke anywhere indoors. How much longer before they became outcasts altogether.

'Alright,' Tom replied.

The man offered him a light and he felt energy seep back into his body as nicotine hit his lungs. He thought briefly about the state of his arteries, but then dismissed it. He told himself it was not today's problem. He enjoyed the hit of the cigarette, the pull of the addiction and closed his eyes, leaning against the flimsy shelter of the wall where he was standing. He wondered if Jack had made his train by now, where it was on the long slinking line between here and London.

Two people then—one to knock Frank out, the other to make sure he was dead. Or the same person? Genaro? Dolores? *Always look to the family first* and Dolores was as much family as Genaro, but who was Frank running from those years ago? His mind flicked from one to the other. He couldn't believe either of them would kill Frank. In his career he'd only had to deal with a handful of murders like this, they just didn't happen in this town, or if they did, were more mundane if no less brutal. Domestics or feuds, fits of violence and broken bottles outside a nightclub, hit and runs, all as bad but not as—well, strange. One of the worst disasters had been the fire and now here they were back again. Frank dead once and now dead a second time.

What if it *was* Dolores?

He felt the phone buzz in his pocket and snatched it up but by the time he saw the name it was too late to switch to voicemail.

'Tom.' Louise's voice was small and pale.

Tom swapped the phone to his other ear, tried to lower his voice, moved away from the other smokers.

'He got away okay, train on time, sorry I should have called I...'

'Okay thanks,' she said. He had to strain to hear. 'I just wanted to check.'

He pictured her on the other end of the phone—her silver one with the dent down the side, full of photos of the kids. The image was ten years out of date and she probably had a new one by now that he didn't know anything about.

'Are you back at work?' she said.

'I am.'

'How are you... is that sensible? Tom?'

If this was a trap, he'd fallen into it before, thinking she still cared about him.

'I think so.'

The pain was biting into his head again and he was no longer able to tell if that was a good or bad thing.

'I'm sorry to have bothered you,' she said, 'I'm sorry. I just wanted to check about Jack that was all.'

'I know.'

She sniffed and he heard her light a cigarette, the scrape of match on sand and he saw her hair falling forward against her cheek, she had beautiful skin. She inhaled a long breath of smoke, which he could almost smell through the phone.

'You should give those things up, they'll kill you.'

He knew she smiled but her face was fading. 'Will you be ok?' she asked.

'Yeah.'

'Where are you?'

'At the hospital.'

Anyone else would have asked why he was there but she didn't.

'Okay,' she said. 'Will you get Jack to call me when he gets back, let me know how he gets on?'

'I will.'

She hung up first.

Where he was standing, he was sheltered under a ridged plastic roof, which ran around the edge of the building against the back wall. It was beginning to rain and the roof afforded some small respite from the colder dampness. After the fire they must have brought both of them in this way—him and Susie, through those mortuary side doors on their stretchers, along with the shrink-wrapped food neither aware of the other. Everything the wrong way round. His life, the way things had turned out, things he'd expected to achieved, gone. He was forty-six and in four years they'd try to make him retire so maybe he should quit now and retire on sickness grounds and devote himself to... what? Birdwatching? He'd thought about it, only a few weeks ago because it seemed easier. But then Frank Molinari had to go and die, really die this time. He had to finish this, for Susie, for himself. *Even if it was Dolores.*

The car park was filling with morning visitors. A young lad on crutches with a tattoo down his left arm staggered into A&E, cigarette dangling from his lips. He must have been freezing in a t-shirt, but didn't seem to notice. His phone rang again. He flipped it open without looking at the caller ID thinking it might be Louise again and despite himself hoping it was. It was Ruby.

'Tom?' Ruby said, hesitating, just a small intake like the flit of a bird's wing. 'Dolores has tried to kill herself.'

At first he wasn't sure he'd heard what she said, the sound of the automatic doors to A&E swished to and fro behind him and someone was swearing inside the building, shouting. He thought he heard an owl somewhere in the trees, the movement of traffic on the service road and above all, it was raining again, steady and slow.

'Tom? Are you there?'

'What happened?'

'Coast Guard found her on Formby beach in her car, unconscious.'

In the silence that followed, Tom had an image of them all, years ago—Jack, Susie, Louise and him on the beach at Formby. Susie was five years old, in a blue coat against the bright white sky waving at the birds and Jack was on his shoulders hanging on to the top of his head. Louise had her camera taking the out-of-focus snaps she always made her own.

'Okay,' he said. 'I'll go.'

A bird flew down from the tree above the shelter, long slow swoops and wings the span of a man's two arms stretched wide—an owl, in daylight, hunting for mice.

3

Leah had to be careful not to overdo it. All she needed to do was to give Higson enough to know she had something important. If she played it the wrong way before she'd even said anything, Higson would give the story to someone with what he called 'safer hands.' He would hand it to Mike (who didn't want it anyway) and if he didn't take it there were plenty of other word-heavy idiots who had plodded away here for decades, itching to get a story.

'Frank's lover,' she said, 'has just tried to top herself.'

Bill Higson, his eyelids flickering from lack of sleep, placed his mug of coffee with care on the desk. He placed his fingers together in a steeple, the tips resting against his lips.

'Go on…'

'Dolores Angelhescu was found on the beach by the coastguards a coupla hours ago. She'd taken a whole heap of pills, waiting for the tide to come in. I saw Genaro this morning and was going straight to see her when I heard but…'

'But?'

'Fairfax got there first.'

'Did he?'

'Yeah, and I asked myself, what would he want to see her for, today of all days?'

'How do you know he went to see her?'

'I turned up, he was already there.'

'Did he see you?'

She shook her head. 'He didn't go in though' she said, 'turned round and went right back out again.'

'She might be unconscious?'

'She isn't, I asked.'

Higson thought about this then said, 'You think she killed Frank?'

Leah shrugged. They knew that if it turned out to be Dolores, there were two stories—Frank and his doppelganger, the one who died the first time, and now Dolores Anghelescu. Then there was Dolores's connection with Tom Fairfax, not to mention Genaro. Leah still hadn't decided how he fitted into all this, only that he had to in some way, *didn't he?*

'I need to make connections,' Leah said. 'Dead man not dead, turns out to be long lost brother of Genaro Molinari, and lover of Dolores Anghelescu. Now *he's* been murdered and *she* tries to top herself. I'm thinking she's frightened, why? Could she be guilty, did she try to get him that first time, got it wrong and now...'

Higson indicated with a small movement of his head that it was possible. His fingers were winding themselves in and out of the steeple.

'So we're left with who died in the fire instead of Frank,' Leah said. 'My guess again, it's one of the Rumanian or Bulgarian lads who work for Molinari. As we know they are...' she was careful not to mention Susie's name, 'expendable.'

'Dolores Anghelescu would know,' Higson said.

'That's why I went there, soon's I heard, but they wouldn't let me in. Said I was her niece, said I'd come back later.'

'Which you will?'

'Course.' Leah paused. 'Shall I run with it?'

Leah could see a pile of emails on Higson's desk, to his left receipts in a box and his diary, underlined with meetings that could only be urgent considering the red ink that stood out on the pages.

'I'll get the story for you Bill,' Leah said.

The story was between the spaces, one thing would lead to another and she knew she could find it this time; she had to. She could see Higson hovering, deciding what he thought was the truth. She knew the signs of this, he

182

thought way too long over things, took too much time and then it was too late. She had to make sure he wouldn't do that this time.

'The fortune teller?' Higson said. 'You're sure it wasn't an accident?'

'I went straight to the hospital, asked about a bit. Then I saw Fairfax going in, fag in his hand as usual, he looked like he'd just got up. And then go out again.'

'So she must be a suspect?' Higson said slowly. 'Else why would he go there?'

Leah didn't answer because that's what she'd thought too, at first, but she wasn't sure now. She saw Tom's face when he came out of the hospital and it wasn't the face of a detective investigating a murder, but of a man in pain. She didn't share this with Higson though, nor that she'd seen Dolores the day before in her car by the pier. She didn't tell him that had she gone over to her, she might have been able to stop her. Dolores must have gone straight to the beach from there. Leah never had any real intention of trying to stop Dolores though. If someone is intent on killing themselves, there's no way you can stop them. She couldn't stop her father drinking himself to a slow death and she had wanted to do that, she had tried so many times she lost count. Dolores...well Dolores she cared less about. If it hadn't been for Dolores, Susie might still be alive.

'I'll go back, see what she has to say,' Leah said. 'If Fairfax hasn't seen her yet, I'll still be first in.'

'Arun's working on the casino story.'

Leah leaned forward, 'I know. She's keeping me in the loop. At first I wasn't sure but now, well maybe... there might be a connection. Genaro has some land fenced off at the back of the fairground waiting to be built on. '

And then something else nudged at the fringes of Leah's mind—Eva, Mati's friend. She had yet to be introduced, but she could see how much on edge Mati had been since her arrival. If she had come in on one of those passports that she now knew Frank Molinari had been flogging before he disappeared, *if* Frank had brought Eva here the day before, then she must know something.

'Not that migrant worker thing again,' Higson said. 'Don't go down that route, this'll be something else entirely. Murder is always closer to home,' he said.

Leah just about managed to sit still, bit her lip and waited. She knew from experience that he had to be the one to come up with the way forward.

'Okay,' he said, 'see what you can dig up.' Then he placed his hands in front of him on the table. 'But remember, you're not a copper, right? That's not your job. You have to write the story, *that's* your job. Stick to the facts. Anything else comes out that's a bonus.'

'I know.'

She left the door open as she went out, she could feel Higson hadn't moved behind her and the energy draining out of him, leaking out through the door. Even a story like this might not be enough to keep the paper going, but what else was there to do, for any of them? She had to keep ahead of the nationals; they were going to get this story anyway. It was barely forty-eight hours old and hardly any details had got out. She still had time to hang on to it.

Arun was waiting for her at her desk.

'You got a minute?' she said.

'Sure.'

'Listen.' Arun looked around, checking for other ears listening in. 'There's a copper involved in all this and I don't know who it is.'

Leah remembered who she'd just seen in the hospital, his face, his fear.

'Fairfax?'

Arun shrugged.

'I have no idea, all I know is Genaro is pally with someone in the force, quite high up and they hang out sometimes, no one can be specific enough that's the problem, trying to blend in is the word, hide. How many high up coppers you know in this town?' she asked.

'But Fairfax's been a vegetable for months, no one's seen anything of him.'

'Says who?'

Well, Leah didn't know to be honest. She cast about thinking of who else it could be and came up with no one. There was literally no one else it could be but then Fairfax wasn't that high up so...

'How do you think Molinari gets his licences, huh? Not through planning applications is my guess. And now if he's planning a casino he'll need a special licence.'

'But Fairfax doesn't deal with all that stuff and anyway, he *has* been out of stuff for a year, we all know that.'

'So, maybe it's not him then...' Arun said, 'even if you want it to be.'

'I don't.'

'Whatever you say.' Arun was already walking away. 'Anyway, it's yours now, do what you want with it.'

Something else, something in the past knocked at Leah's head, told her to watch what she was doing. She sat and stared at her blank computer, switched it on and waited for it to load up. When it did, the image of a falcon, small and weightless like a flake of snow drifted across the screen.

4

Twice he'd got as far as the door to the ward, twice he'd turned away.

'Can I help you?'

'Senior Nurse Emily Roberts,' Tom read on her badge.

'I'm looking for Dolores Anghelescu.'

'And you are?'

He pulled his warrant card from his jacket pocket and handed it to her. She peered at it.

'I was younger then,' he said, indicating the photograph.

She smiled. Senior Nurse Roberts was young and pretty, neat as a new-done sum, but weariness had changed the angle of her smile. Today she looked like she just needed a good night's sleep. She pointed him towards a curtain.

'Don't be long, she's very tired,' she said, as if speaking for herself.

Maybe she won't be there; maybe it isn't her. He moved forward, raised his hand and opened the curtain.

'Have you brought me some grapes?' a voice said. He knew then that Dolores had been expecting him.

'They only had green.'

Tom placed the brown paper bag on the bed. She looked up at him, her eyes light as clear water. He found himself knotting his fingers inside each other to stop them reaching out for her. The scar etched into the side of her face was clearly visible, staring at him in defiance. A sour tang of vomit clung to the air.

'If you came with pity,' she said, 'I don't need it.'

'I haven't come with pity.'

'Then what did you come with? Besides grapes?'

Her mouth moved, lopsided—was it a smile? The edge of a tooth snagged her lips and he was caught off guard with an image in his head. His thumb hooked in the corner of that mouth, her teeth biting into his skin. He remembered the way he carried the smell of her on his fingers all day.

'I have to talk to you Dolores...'

She looked away towards a window opposite her bed. The window lead to the red wall of a distant ward, to another window, the rail of a curtain around another bed.

'I have to talk to you about Frank,' he said.

Her hands moved, smoothing the bedclothes, counting the stitches, 1-2-3, moving her fingers along them, picking, 4-5-6. He watched her nails—red, slashed across the centre with a line of white, the way punters used to cross her palm with silver.

'You knew he was alive,' he said.

She seemed to be gathering her thoughts, looking across to a place where the past might be. It was a past that, simply by crossing the threshold of her hospital ward, Tom had opened up for both of them. She turned her head back towards him and returned to the room. The small light at the side of the bed illuminated her face so that half was in shadow and half in relief. She looked like alabaster, her skin pale with a sheen like snow, the thread of veins barely visible at the base of her neck.

'Frank,' she said, looking at him for the first time. 'He came back, yes he did, and he called me.'

'When?'

'Two days ago.'

'And you saw him?'

She nodded.

'Did Genaro know?'

She shook her head, thin skeins of sweat lingered in the creases of her forehead where her long auburn hair had been wound in a messy pile on her head. Fringes of silvered grey nudged at the edges, silver that was not there before. Tom's fingers moved as he remembered the weight of her hair in his hands, tangled in his fingers. Sometimes he would find a long hair on his clothes or in his car. Their secret was something he carried like a dead weight in his soul.

'He thought his brother was dead,' she whispered.

'Like we all did,' he said.

'Frank owed money to some people who want to kill him. What else could he do? What could I do? He has to hide.' Her reply was swift, angry.

'How much money?'

Her fingers went on counting, 7-8-9...

'Who'd he owe the money to, Dolores?'

She shrugged.

'People—gambling debts. Horses. You know Frank,' she said.

He did.

'So why did he come back now?'

'Maybe he missed his brother?' She laughed.

'Did he miss you?' he asked, but he already knew the answer to that. For a moment neither of them spoke.

'Where was Frank all this time?' he said.

'Paris.'

'Paris?'

She looked at him and that's when he realised. She knew, all this time she knew.

'I sent him there. It is our city.'

He dragged back the story she'd told him one night about growing up in Paris as a child of the greatest circus family in Europe, a trap she always wanted to run from. The city where she'd met Frank, the story he'd started to tell Ruby and Linda in the hospital only a few hours ago. He felt bile rise in his throat, the bitter taste of it. Frank saved her back then, she'd told him that but he'd only half listened. She owed Frank. She was never going to leave Frank for him. There'd been women before, others, but he'd never cared that much about them and Louise, if she

188

did know about them, never said anything. Dolores changed all that, probably because he couldn't keep her.

'You had a lucky escape yesterday,' he said.

'It wasn't luck.'

Her voice was like rainfall, slipping away from him.

'Then what was it?'

'I had a lot to drink,' she said.

'I can smell it.'

'They pumped my stomach.'

'What did you have?'

'Vodka.'

'And?'

'Pills, lots of them. There were boys skateboarding, and then I start driving, I keep going. And then I don't remember...'

She looked straight at him then, the uplift of a heavy eyebrow. Her eyes were like small dots in the shadows of the ward, all brightness gone. Her fingers kept on counting, counting, tapping the rhythm of lost time into the stitches of her sheet.

'I'm frightened, Thomas,' she said, saying his name in her own singsong way: *Tomass*.

He put his fingers on the edge of the bed then and this time she found them. 'Did you kill Frank?'

Did she? She dropped her eyes, twisted her head, dragged the fingers back away from him. *No.* 'But now they will be coming for me.'

'Who?'

His eyelids pulsed with pain, the lashes twitching, scratching. It was not going to happen a second time. All he wanted to do was to lie on the bed with her and sleep. But he didn't move.

'No,' he told her. 'No they won't.' *I won't let them.*

He reached up, put his finger along the scar. The edge of it felt hard, a ridge under her skin, which ran from the top of her cheek to the edge of her nose. It was deep and long and violent and angry. She recoiled, a misjudged gesture he wished he hadn't made and couldn't take back.

'I didn't know you were hurt,' he said. 'When they found me you were gone.'

'Your daughter...'

'She died, but you know that.'

'I am sorry Thomas.'

'In the fire.'

'I'm sorry.' She was crying, saying 'I'm sorry' over and over.

Why was she crying? He watched her face change, the tears. What was it?

'Why are you sorry?'

'We didn't know she would be there.' She said simply.

He wanted to say something, but no sound came out, nothing. *The fire*, she knew about the fire before it happened.

'Why?' he asked. 'Why would you...'

'We were afraid, Frank was afraid. It seemed...' she looked straight at him, clear-eyed in sorrow, '...the only thing we could do.'

'But Susie?' he couldn't speak.

'I'm sorry,' she said again as if it would be enough. It would never be enough, nothing would ever be enough now.

'Who died instead of Frank?' He heard his hard cold voice and recognised it as his own.

'I don't know,' she said. This time he didn't believe her.

5

The bird was being flown when Leah arrived—from one barn roof across to the other. The barns were on the outskirts of St Marie; they had always been there, perched on a low-lying stretch before the marshlands of the bird sanctuary. Far enough not to threaten the wild birds, but close enough for temptation. She was learning to know what to look for; Susie had taught her well. The falcon coasted the curving roofs in a dance through the sky as, on the ground, Rich whistled, his gloved arm outstretched, waiting for her. She alighted on the leather gauntlet with a bounce. Each was aware of the other's presence as surely as a spider knows a fly is on its web.

'You try,' Rich said.

Leah waited because she knew Sky had clocked her too, was uneasy about her. She stood as still as she could, arms loose and fingers tensed for when the bird would swoop down. The first few times the bird ignored her, whirling down before rising again to the safety of the barn roofs.

'Hold your ground.' Rich handed her a larger piece of meat, a claw hanging yellowed and scrappy.

The falcon saw the meat, hesitated then in a dive came down, took the claw then returned to the barn before Leah had a chance to react. It sat on the eaves with nonchalance assessing its next move. A minute, maybe two passed until down she came again, carving a slice of morning from the air. This time she landed feet-first, easy as a dandelion clock on Leah's glove where another claw waited. She raised her head while she ate, her black bead of an eye catching Leah, keeping her fixed tightly within her gaze.

The spell had been broken.

Tom drove. No plan on where he was going, heading west out of town on the Blackpool road. The radio was on loud, a discussion about the Iraq War with words not details. 'Next of kin have been informed,' said a newsreader's voice and he whispered at the radio it was a lie. It didn't get any easier. They always told you it would, but it didn't. *I should know.* The anger pulled his grief taut like the skin on a drum.

He turned off on to the coastal road. The flat landscape was bleak, relentless with the sea staying just out of sight. It hovered on his left, across the marshlands and pools of stagnant water, always on the edge of his vision. The catch of salt air hit his face through the open window. He threw a dead cigarette butt out of the window, lit another and felt the pain in his shoulder searing through his bones.

He drove with one hand on the wheel trying to light the cigarette from the car's ancient cigarette lighter with the other. On the sands, waders pecked around the rising current and starlings caught the lilt of the wind. They threw themselves high in wild formation before dropping back to earth like a bag of pebbles. This was the point where he could go home, to his pills and bed and nightmares, give it all up. He did not have to do this. It was not his case anymore. He stopped at a petrol station at the start of St Marie's one dual carriageway, the one that would take him from the town, and pulled up in front of the kiosk. He searched through the glove compartment for painkillers, throwing debris to the floor, the overflow of Clemmie's life tipping its contents into the passenger well of the car. As he reached across, his right shoulder was wrenched blood from bone from socket as if a knife was hacking at the nerves in his neck. There was nothing there, nothing to take the edge off the pain. *Damn...*

He pulled himself upright, cramming everything back into the glove compartment and fished a cigarette from his packet, the only sedative he had. He closed his eyes, pulled the smoke in, let it out in a stream then lit another. The smoke shifted into his lungs like quicksilver as he looked around. There was a man in the kiosk watching, waiting to see what he would do. The man looked almost as old as Clemmie. He tried to smile but had the feeling it didn't come out right because the man turned away. Serving a customer, glancing back to see if Tom was going to come in or not. *Time to go.* He turned the car around, moved back into the road towards the roundabout, swung in the opposite direction and headed back towards town. He took his time, deep breaths, one after the other, moving his shoulder and neck as little as he could to hold the pain in. When he hit the crescent of shops at the Royal Botanic Gardens, he threw the car into a space and got out, *taking it easy.* Behind the pharmacy counter there was a young woman, a teenager, no older than Jack. She wasn't going to ask questions so he reeled off his list: codeine, ibuprofen, aspirin and a bottle of water from the fridge. She didn't say a word even though he danced on the spot while he waited, like a boxer, fidgeting to keep the pain at bay. He took the water and pills and drove to the seafront, swallowed six tablets and waited ten minutes to buy himself time. The medley of tablets did their work. He needed to remember, to think...

Dolores was lying—she knew who died in that fire but... she didn't know Susie was there, she couldn't know, she wouldn't... *she just wouldn't.* The question repeated: *how well did you really know her?* A row of black-headed sharp-eyed gulls sat huggermugger on the sea wall watching him, like pegs on a line. The beach huts were closed, locked up with padlocks and long bolts. In summer you could hire them for fifteen quid a day. They booked up first thing, filled with families with spades and windbreaks and picnics spilling out onto the coastal path, blocking the way. Sometimes one came up for sale and its owner tried to make it into a bijou hideaway with curtains and plants. Never lasted, there was no place for nostalgia. In the bleak winter light, he could imagine the owner locked up inside, hibernating, waiting for Spring to show its face. Hiding. *You only saw what you wanted to see, what she wanted you to see...* He needed to get someone to talk to Dolores who didn't know her. He opened his mobile, dialled a number he hadn't called in a long time.

When the phone was picked up he could hear the song of a bird, an imperceptible cry of joy borne on the echo of a breeze. He heard Leah Barnes hesitate. She said something to someone next to her, a shuffling with the phone and her voice came on louder, clearer.

'What do you want?'

He could hear the wind in the earpiece of the phone as clearly as a sigh.

'Are you with the bird?' he said. 'Please...' he jumped in quickly because he could hear her hesitation, '...don't hang up.'

A beat and then, 'What do you want?'

'I need your help.'

Leah had spent hours the night before hunting for information about Genaro again—for anything that would link him with a bent policeman. That policeman could have been the man who was on the end of a phone asking for her help. How strange then that he should read her mind when she had shut it against him. She would let him speak. She would see what he had to say.

She made him wait then said, 'What kind of help?'

'The other body we found—in the fire that day when...' Leah knew he didn't mean Susie, but she would not make this easy for him. '...I need to know who it was. Frank started the fire. Whoever died in there, I think Frank killed him,' Tom said.

'What do you want from me?'

'Dolores Anghelescu knows who it was but she won't tell me.'

194

'...and you think she'll tell me?' She'd laughed at that bit, why would someone she'd never met tell her something she didn't want anyone to know?

'Yes.'

But then, where else was she going to go? What other leads did she have? She had never met the famous fortune-teller, not properly. More than anything she wanted to see what everyone else seemed to see in her. Then there was the famous scar, the one that marked her to Tom forever. That marked both of them irrevocably to Susie's death. No matter what they thought they could do to change it.

'Where is she?' she'd asked even though she already knew.

'Still in the hospital, but don't say...' he paused. 'I'd rather you didn't say you were doing it for me.'

'I'm not doing it for you,' Leah said.

'Right.'

'It's a story,' she said. 'And it's Susie's story, I'm doing it for her.'

She heard him swallow. 'Of course. You have my number so when you speak to her, if...' he hesitated, '... you will let me know what she said?'

Leah scuffed the ground with the toe of her shoe. 'Sure.' But she wasn't sure, and they both knew it.

'I'm doing it for Susie too, Leah,' he said and she didn't answer.

Then he was gone, the air was still and the bird was back in the tree waiting for its orders.

Leah bent to pick a thread of chicken from the pail at her feet and placed it between her thumb and forefinger so that Sky could just see it. The bird narrowed her eyes, fixed on the food. In Egyptian mythology, the falcon was the bird that represented the soul of the departed. It was the spirit of the dead vanished into the ether represented on earth by this thin, picky little bird. The falcon's head was strong and muscled despite its fragile bones and Leah looked up, shielding her eyes from the bright morning to watch the bird descend towards her. She felt herself move towards it as though she was skating to her through the air.

6

It was the same guy she'd seen at the fairground, the guy in the light suit who'd gone to see Genaro. He arrived just before her and as she fastened her bike to the railings at the side of the main entrance to the hospital, she clocked him striding in looking like he owned the place. He expanded into the pavement he walked on, his back straight and shoulders easy. She waited until he was out of sight then made her way over. Not that the guy would have seen her earlier that day, but you could never be too sure and she had a strong feeling he was going to visit Dolores.

She found the hospital florist and went in to buy a small bunch of flowers, choosing freesias that smelled like springtime. She carried them close to her nose bringing the freshness of a field into the noise and hammer of a hospital in full flow. Reception told her that Dolores was in Hesketh Ward, but when she got there she was told visiting hours were between three and five and it was only 1.30. Leah smiled her best smile. She'd replaced her cycling jacket with a smart silky sort of t-shirt, which smelled, only just slightly, and paired it with a black suit jacket. Her navy trousers made her presentable, so she knew she looked at least ten years younger than she was, which was sometimes a bonus and sometimes a drawback. Today it was a bonus.

'I've just cycled here from Southport; I came earlier. It's my aunt...'

It was a different nurse at the ward station from the morning so she didn't know any different. '*Senior Nurse Emily Roberts*' her name badge said, and Leah thought she looked kind with her blonde hair curled beneath her cap and so decided to let her in. Closer inspection showed that her hands were red with angry patches of eczema forming on the skin's surface and eyes were heavy with worry and sleep. She smiled at Leah and waved her hand. *Oh okay you can go in* the smile said. She had so much to do, too much to worry about to question whether Leah was who she claimed. Leah had long learned that the nicer you were to people you wanted something from the likelier you were to get it.

'Don't stay long though, will you? She needs rest. That's why we've moved her to a private room.'

'Oh!' she shouted after her. 'I forgot… she already has a visitor,' which Leah had already guessed.

She sat on a chair close to the room where Dolores was, and waited.

A patient was wheeled by on a trolley, feet first flat, covered in a blue blanket staring at the ceiling. Leah watched it go past like a sailing ship, smooth movement, rubber wheels going thunk-thunk on the shiny floor. The last time she was in this hospital, three years ago give or take, was the night her father died. Her mother called her in the middle of the night at her college rooms in university. She'd only been there seven weeks; she had a window overlooking the quadrant from where she could see a fresh green patch and a large gate, the buzz of a magical city just visible in footsteps beyond. She had been looking forward to sitting on the grass in the summer with a novel, a bottle of water. In her mind's eye she had seen herself with someone's head in her lap, dreaming. She'd only met one candidate so far, a German student from somewhere in the mountains of Bavaria, which had fairy tale houses of Grimm Gothic chic and canals that wound like mazes through rickety streets. Gilda had painted a picture of a beauty she must have guessed that Leah would like and so far it had worked. The previous night they'd walked home along the river, held hands all the time knowing they were going to end up in bed together, longing for it. Leah lied to Gilda that she was estranged from her family, a lie decided on the day she arrived there. It was a lie that felt more like the truth the

198

more she said it. She was good at lying then, before she met Susie. She never lied to Susie.

Gilda was asleep when her mobile rang in the early hours of that morning and the small bed was even smaller, the room airless. Leah forgot where she was, staggered into the sitting part of her college rooms and fumbled for the phone. She heard her mother's calm, slow voice.

'It's your Dad,' she said, which was all she needed to say.

When Leah left, the quad was silent. Gilda had never even woken, in spite of the noise she made making tea, shuffling clothes into a rucksack. In the early morning light the grass seemed greener than she'd seen it, even on that first open day she came to look around. Her watch said it was just past five in the morning. Oxford was a pale watery blue when she left it behind, the first time it had ever looked as beautiful as she'd always imagined it could be. She knew she would never see it again.

She caught the first train from Oxford, changing at Wolverhampton, the train gathering the damp dawn on its windows the further north she went. Her mother met her at the door and Leah went to kiss her, but she moved away. They should have found comfort in each other, wasn't that how it went? She never tried to hold her mother again, not even on the day of the funeral. So they were on their own, just the two of them, and it went back to the way it was when she was a kid and her father left them then came back and nothing was said—about where he'd been or why he changed his mind. When they got to the hospital her father was lying on a trolley in a side room, waiting. He didn't look like her father and Leah wanted to ask somebody—are you sure? She put her hand out to touch his face, but there was nothing there, nothing at all, his face impassive. The wheelings and dealings that had made up so much of his life had passed away with him. She thought about what a waste his life had been and most of all about how Genaro

Molinari had played him like bloody fool. She looked at him, she thought all this and then she walked away. She was not going to end up like that.

A few weeks later, after the funeral, she saw the reporter's job in the newspaper and that was that. Well they had to give her the job didn't they, ex-editor's daughter, sympathy vote and all that, and then there was Oxford, even one term was enough to impress them. For a while she had intended to go back even though she didn't tell them that, but in the weeks following her father's death, St Johns felt a long way behind her. She didn't want to stay with her mother, but she knew she couldn't leave her even if she wanted to. Her mother who sat in a chair all day, starting her journey on giving up on life until eventually, a few years later, she did. Sitting on her chair outside Dolores room Leah told herself, when this was all over, she would go back, finish her degree, it was never too late. That's what Susie always said she should do. Maybe this time she would.

She looked at her phone—13.42—then wandered back to the nurse's station, where the same frazzled girl was fielding phone calls with a cold mug of tea at her elbow, the film of tannin settling like an oil slick on its surface.

'This visitor, with my aunt...' Leah said. 'He say who he was?'

'Police I think...'

'Oh.'

'He say his name?'

'I didn't catch it, sorry.'

A cleaner was working his way towards them, brushing the floor with an electric polisher, side to side. It made a low hum, sweeping a swathe of shine down the low-lit corridor. The door to Dolores's room opened and the 'policeman' stepped out.

'Oh, here he is now, I'll just...' but Emily had already forgotten her, head down on spreadsheets and a buzzer going while somewhere down the corridor a medley of room bells demanded her attention. Leah left her to it.

The man was tall, black hair cropped quite close to his head and a snatch of grey near the base of his skull which leant him an air of glamour enhanced by his solid physique, broad shoulders and long confident legs. He didn't look like a policeman and he didn't so much as glance at her when he came out of Dolores's room, but Leah knew him; he was the man she'd seen at the fairground. He shut the door and walked with big strides up the corridor and away, stopping some way down where the long windows in the middle looked out on to a courtyard. He looked out of the window, but he was also looking behind him, to where Leah was still sitting trying not to watch him. *Was he trying to work out where he had seen her before?* She kept her head down willing his memory to fail him. The floor polisher stopped and sat on the windowsill a few inches from where the man stood, catching his breath and it was only this that interrupted him, made him move. He turned and his footsteps in his suede brogues tapped heavy rhythms on the linoleum as he walked out of sight. Leah waited until he had gone then put the flowers in a firm hand and opened the door to Dolores's room.

7

Tom followed the labyrinth of thin-walled corridors until he came to the boardroom where the team were talking. He could hear the rumbling murmur as they waited for the meeting. He had a moment of panic almost turning back, before he took a deep breath, put his palm to the door and pushed it open. The room opened and time slid away. He was back where he was, one year ago in the place his days always began and ended with the briefing in the morning, the quieter conclusion of the afternoons. He felt, with relief, that it might be easier than he anticipated it was going to be. *It felt like coming home.*

To call it a boardroom was being kind. It was a badly-lit cubbyhole at the rear of the building, which looked out on to the back wall of the Magistrate Courts and the Multi-storey NCP. There was barely enough space for everyone to squeeze round the higgledy row of tables. Boxes of leaflets and paper were stacked against the wall along with teetering piles of vending cups and an overflowing bin of dreggy coffee with the only light coming from a small window, blocked by a police surveillance van parked in front. The window was jammed shut and the door was a fire door on a spring hinge, which wouldn't stay open. The room smelled of unwashed skin, which nobody else seemed to notice. His nose was too sensitive. He'd been away too long.

He went to the only table and sat, everyone else was huddled, perched on chairs or standing, there were five officers but he knew only two—Ruby Miller and Doug Hughes. The other two constables—young and fresh-faced, a woman and a man—were new, drafted in, he didn't know where from. He nodded to them. Hughes ignored him, which didn't bother him much. It wasn't true, he reflected, about absence making the heart grow fonder.

Everyone was watching him; he could feel it, wondering what he was going to do next. He stayed silent, sipping the water, waiting for someone else to begin. *Don't show your hand too soon.* Ruby moved to the head of the table and sat, riffling papers in front of her.

'So,' she said. 'Our dead man is Frank Molinari killed Monday night, as you know, by a blow to the head; initial PM report suggests the first blow might have been an accident, the second series of blows weren't. He had advanced heart disease, which probably caused a heart attack within seconds.'

'Probably?' Hughes said.

'Bradycardia,' Ruby's voice gathered a hard edge of confidence that Tom was witnessing for the first time. 'His carotid artery, which runs up the side of the neck here...' She moved to the whiteboard, which she'd set up behind the desk, and drew a quick sketch of the head. *Was there nothing this woman couldn't do?* '...takes blood to the brain, but right here at the base of the neck near your ear it splits like this.' She drew a fork. 'The external carotid remains near the surface, the internal goes under the skull. If pressure of some kind is applied or a person is hit, even slightly, caught by say a ring or something—wouldn't take much, on the carotid near the sinus, just here—like Frank was, it can cause bradycardia, which basically means a slowing of the heartbeat bringing on a heart attack in people with underlying heart problems which Frank also had. In spades.'

There was silence. Ruby moved back from the board suddenly self-conscious and someone sniggered; Tom glanced across at the sound as Hughes folded his arms and stretched his legs out in front of him, crossing them at the ankles. The young woman constable was scribbling in a red spiral bound notebook and her male colleague seemed to lighten up as Ruby's calm delivery shifted the atmosphere in the room. Tom relaxed, glad for once that he wasn't where

Ruby was. It was good being back here, with the others, where he could hide. He could get used to this, even with Hughes. There was a quiet movement behind him, the shift of the door, a click and from a hush in the room, he knew, without turning round, that someone senior had entered. Robert Nardone sat away from the others to emphasise how important he was and mouthed 'sorry,' indicating through saying nothing that they should go on. Tom realised that everyone was trying hard not to look at him too.

'So,' Ruby acknowledged Nardone's presence with a glance, 'we need to know the last person who saw Frank alive. His brother has an alibi, I've spoken with him, DI Fairfax accompanied me, but we need to speak to him again, in more detail.'

Nardone turned his head slowly towards Tom, raised an eyebrow with a silent question: *so you're well enough now are you?* then turned back to Ruby. 'I was the leading officer on the fire when DI Fairfax was…' he hesitated, 'So, I'll go, it's the least I can do.' He smiled.

Smug fucking bastard. Without missing a beat Tom blurted, 'What about Dolores Anghelescu, his girlfriend, she's in hospital having her stomach pumped. I saw her earlier.' His words came out in one long stream, without breathing, he had no way of stopping them, even if he wanted.

'Did you?' Nardone said nodding his head to the slow rhythm of the outburst. It wasn't a question, but it was out there and everyone knew what it meant.

Tom met his eyes and clenched his fingers into a fist beneath the table. Nardone's jaw would fit into the knuckles of his hand like a glove. Ruby was watching them, brushing a strand of hair from her eyes and Tom wanted to reach out and tuck it behind her ear. If he could do this for Ruby now, he thought, somehow it would make everything all right.

'But the other body, from the fire, if it wasn't Frank back then, who was it?' Ruby said.

'First body has to be a Rumanian or a Serbian, obvious,' Hughes said. 'Molinari has loads of them, how he runs his business, sneaking them in, those countries aren't legit. Cheaper.'

'Right then,' she said, winding the discussion up. 'As it's your call Doug you check on all workers at the fair, *legit* or otherwise.' She emphasised this last bit then continued, 'Constable Rimmer will go with you. Anyone still missing, any contacts who've disappeared, you know the drill. Anyone who knew Frank—or Genaro.'

Ruby sat on the edge of the table. Rimmer was the young woman PC. Her face couldn't hide her disappointment at being sent out with Hughes and Tom noticed the exchange of glance with Ruby. Hughes made his presence felt on everyone, never in a good way.

'Any questions?'

'Excuse me Sir.' Hughes turned to Nardone. 'I'm just wondering, dental records... why weren't they checked? How did the original investigation miss it wasn't Frank?'

Nardone coughed, leaned forward clasping his fingers. Everyone's eyes were on him, waiting for his excuse. He was wearing another of his natty light woven suits, the glint of a ring on his left hand catching the one shaft of light trying to struggle through the dusty window. *The same ring he was wearing yesterday, but now it looked familiar. Why?*

'The body was too badly burned to be identified,' he said. 'In circumstances like this, dental records are hard to get, sometimes impossible. You know that... and resources were limited and we had evidence that it *was* Frank don't forget...'

'So who did identify him?' Ruby said. 'I can't remember who did...'

'Genaro Molinari. From a ring that survived the fire... gold will survive you see. And there was one gold tooth, you'll remember that?' Nardone said.

'Vaguely...' but it looked like she remembered very well.

'Then of course...' he looked at Tom, '...there was Dolores Anghelescu. She ID'd him too, confirmed he was there.'

'That's it?'

He coughed again and Ruby's mouth pursed, maybe to stop herself asking any more questions. She shouldn't question a superior officer in an open situation like this, undermining his authority.

Tom could see the protocol whirring around her head, but then Nardone said, 'It's no good going over what did and didn't happen. This is a live situation. If we don't come up with something concrete in the next twenty-four hours, everything will go cold. We need to know who Frank was running from. Find out everyone he knew, who he owed money to and how much. Someone must have seen something.'

Just like that Nardone had taken charge, taken the words out of Ruby's mouth and set himself up as the expert. A phone rang, intrusive in the small room—Nardone's, he dragged it out of his pocket and looked at the number on the screen.

'Sorry, I'll have to take this...' he said.

He stood and raised a hand to push the door open and as he did, the silver band glittered once again on his finger. Tom watched the door after he'd gone, *something wasn't right*.

'Sir?' Ruby said.

'Nothing,' Tom said, but he'd marked that she called him Sir. Acknowledging him and dismissing Nardone in one swoop.

As everyone shuffled out, the spring-bound door whipped back on itself each time someone left the room. Each bang left a bigger dent in Tom's headache. Eventually only he and Ruby were left. He was twirling a polystyrene cup someone had left on the table in front of him, twisting and poking it, liking the feel of his nails digging into the surface.

'Sir?' Ruby said, watching him.

He was thinking of Pleasure Island and what this had to do with it all. He wasn't at all sure it had anything to do with it other than being a convenient smokescreen.

'I don't know,' he said. 'Something... just something Nardone said or did, I don't know...'

The cup was disintegrating in his hands now, collapsing into fragments.

'You want me to have a word with him?'

'God no! But if you... could you just keep an eye on him that's all? I need to talk to Genaro again, at the fairground...' he said. 'I think that's where I have to go.'

Back to the place the whole damned thing started.

8

Something gnawed at Tom all the way there, a persistent voice that wouldn't let up. By the time he reached Pleasure Island's front gate it was so loud it blocked anything else in his head.

In the event of an emergency—scream!

The sign was spattered across the front of the Hellraiser ride where everyone could read it, in day-glo letters three foot high. It was supposed to be a joke, but it read like a warning—the kind you could do nothing about. The ride was off, the neon amber lights sparking up and down the side, the red on the top brighter to signal its height.

He parked the car in the ride's shadow and walked to the side entrance where he knew no one would see him approach. There was less police presence now, just one squad car, quiet and hidden. He nudged the door to the Funhouse and was surprised to find it open. Within seconds he was standing in front of the carousel, the echo of his breathing quick and sharp in the closed space, which he knew was closed despite the ease of his entry. Yesterday Genaro had given the impression of normality; today he'd known better, he was nowhere to be seen. The coffee urn was switched off, the shelves stacked with food, still waiting. No one would be coming.

He had to work fast. Across the far wall behind the food shelves he found what he was looking for—the photographs he'd noticed the day before. He went straight to the one of Mama Molinari. Mama's face looked out at him from the glare of the Italian sun—Salerno, Genaro had said it was taken. *That was in Italy, wasn't it?* Tom turned it over, on the back he read—Sylvia, Orkney, 1952. *Not Italy then.*

She was seated on a wall and behind the sitter, there was a flat calm sea and sunlight. She held her arm up to shield herself from the sun where the silver ring on her finger caught the light—*Nardone's ring* and Genaro's lie. The photograph was no bigger than a postcard. He put it in his pocket and then he got out of there as quickly as he could before anyone had noticed he'd been in there. In the car, his phone rang almost as soon as he started the engine.

'It's me,' Ruby said.

He swapped the phone to his other ear where the tone of her voice was quiet, with something low and urgent about it.

'I just took a call from CID in Blackpool.'

'Yes?'

'And they wanted to know if we'd heard from Superintendent Nardone.'

Tom felt the air thin in his lungs, the breath sucked out of him.

'Why?'

'He's gone AWOL, they didn't know he was here.'

'Where is he now?'

'I don't know. Haven't seen him since the meeting, not answering his phone.'

Tom looked around, he saw only the slow heavy jitterbug of the lights around the edge of the ride and the black evening coming in across the bay.

'Didn't he say he was going to speak to Molinari again?' she said.

'He did.' But there was no sign of him, no sign of anyone around the bleak concrete site. Tom took the photograph from his pocket and turned it over—Sylvia, Orkney, 1952. It was him; Nardone. He looked just like her even down to the fingers on her left hand against the sun, a silver ring, glinting around the black and white edges of the fading print.

'We have to find him,' Tom said, 'fast.'

'I know…'

He looked at his watch—he'd forgotten about Jack.

'Shit! I have to go, pick Jack up from Lime Street. Find him, Ruby. I'll be back as soon as I can'

But Tom already knew what Nardone wanted and that the chase had begun.

9

It was as if Dolores had been waiting for someone to ask her what had happened.

'Eva is one of my girls,' she said.

One of her girls... Leah watched Dolores picking at the bedclothes; her fingers twitched along the seam and Leah thought of the girls in the flat on Hamilton Street above the chemists raided a few months before the fire. No one was any the wiser, no one saw what was obvious. Except Susie who had watched and waited. Then she told, not her father, but someone else, someone higher. Susie had told Leah her father hadn't been happy about that, but she said she couldn't trust him. 'Why?' one answer: 'Dolores.' Susie found her crusade and Leah had... well, Leah had the start of her story and now here she was, sitting in front of Dolores trying to find an end for it.

'It's not like that...' Dolores read what Leah was thinking. 'They clean and cook and waitressing,' she said.

'For Genaro?'

'Not for Genaro, this was Franco's work,' she said. 'Frank just does passports, I do rest of organising.'

'Why?' Leah looked at Dolores and didn't see a wealthy woman. She looked tired and drawn, her skin in patches flaring with dried red skin. She looked like a woman who had worked hard all her life.

'Someone helped me once,' she said. 'I help them. But...'

She hesitated. She looked straight at Leah, her gaze steady.

'...but Frank has other ideas. Frank needs money.'

'Did Frank bring Eva yesterday?'

'How you know Eva?' Dolores's voice was sharp, on her guard.

Leah shrugged, 'I have my sources.'

Dolores didn't answer, but her silence confirmed the truth.

'Why would he risk that?' Leah persisted.

'Because I ask him, this time, to come…'

Something she wasn't saying, something Leah had to read between the lines. 'Why?' Leah couldn't work it out. 'I still don't see…'

'Because,' Dolores said, 'someone has to pay… how do you say… the ferryman.'

'I…'

'If he is not paid then the soul has no home, it will wander like ghost.'

'Frank's soul?'

'Not Frank's no…'

'Then whose?'

Outside the ward, Leah could hear the evening meal trolleys arriving—the clang of metal lids over warm food, a drawer being shut and voices calling out options. Lights up to bright, then down again as doors in the corridor opened and closed. Dolores was lying back on her pillows. Her dark hair bundled on her head, had fallen away from its pins and spread waywardly about her.

'My soul,' she said. It was a whisper, nothing more.

'What have you done?'

'It's what I didn't do,' Dolores replied. 'Eva will need to know. Tell her I sent you. Tell her I am sorry.'

She wouldn't say any more. Leah left her, her fingers still moving, feeling the edges of the hospital sheet as though she were nipping stitches into the fabric of time.

10

When questioned later, Senior Nurse Emily Roberts would say Dolores Anghelescu had seemed unhappy when she left but because she was calm they let her go. As a rule, they wouldn't have discharged her so soon, but she wanted to go home and, besides, they needed the bed.

Emily had been on her feet nearly eighteen hours when Dolores was brought in. She was working an extra shift because two others called in sick, but as soon as she could, she moved Dolores to a side room because she liked her. It was usually reserved for private patients, but the ward was slow. She told all this to Ruby Miller in her statement. Dolores was nice, she told her, didn't give you any bother, you don't get many like that.

Before she left, Dolores read Emily's palm. Emily didn't believe in horoscopes or fortune telling, but all right she said, it couldn't do any harm, could it? She knew what she wanted out of life, but it would be nice to know if she had any chance of getting it.

'This is your lifeline, here,' Dolores told her, 'you see like a moon shape? This tells how long you live. Long means a good and healthy life, broken or stopping halfway then, well, not so good. Yours is strong—see at the top here is youth, the middle adult and the bottom old age.'

Dolores moved her finger across the line, the edge of a red nail tracing the curve on Emily's palm.

'This is the one we need to know about—how old are you?' she said.

'Twenty five.'

'And you're healthy, see a strong line tells you.'

'I don't feel it!'

Emily laughed, her hand felt weightless in Dolores's palm. 'What else does it say?'

'Well, these small lines here tell me you're easily controlled by others. Do you think that's true?'

Emily thought of her boyfriend Zack who was trying to persuade her to emigrate to Australia because he didn't have enough points to be allowed in whereas she, as a nurse, had plenty. They could start a new life, get married he said, then he'd be allowed in too. She didn't want a new life; she wasn't even sure she wanted him.

'No,' she told Dolores, 'I don't let anyone tell me what to do.'

Dolores let go of her hand. Emily looked at it. The lines seemed to crisscross in a way she had never noticed making her, for some reason, seem older than she was.

'Would you tell me if like I was going to be really sick or die or something?'

'The lines never lie.'

'That's not an answer!' Emily said. Then, 'Do you ever read your own?'

Dolores turned her palm over and showed Emily the lifeline, which was strong for the first few centimetres and then stopped, halfway up to her thumb where the rest was a lurid pink scar of new skin. There were no other lines at all.

'How did that happen?'

'I was in a car accident.' Dolores said. 'Time is running out for me.'

'You can't just give up because of a line on your hand!' Emily said.

What else could she say? Dolores had a thin scar all the way down the side of her face too; from the same accident she'd like to bet, what could anyone say? She was still beautiful though; anyone could see that. Emily could see that even if Dolores couldn't. Emily knew she should call someone in psychiatry or social services, but she didn't want to because she knew that would only cause more problems for Dolores. She'd end up on some ward miles away, next to people who screamed and rocked themselves all day, and Emily didn't like to think of her there. Best let her take her own chances, with her own life, whatever she wanted to do with it, so she called Dr Amin who discharged her. Two hours later a surgical patient with a ruptured hernia occupied the bed. Emily's shift ended and Emily went home where she told Zack that she wouldn't be going to Australia with him after all.

Emily told Ruby Miller that Dolores had two visitors before she left. One said he was a policeman. He was rude she said, didn't even ask to go in just marched straight into the room and shut the door, snapped the shutter down on the little window. She walked up to the door several times just to check everything was all right, but all she could hear was the vibration of the policeman's voice low and Scottish, or Irish, it was always so hard to tell wasn't it? The second visitor was a young woman in a smart jacket; she brought flowers. She seemed nice and Dolores seemed to be calmer after she'd been. It was after the girl left Dolores said she wanted to go home, that she had things to see to, that the girl was going on ahead to prepare them for her.

'Don't know what she meant by that,' Emily said. 'But you know, we can't keep them. If they want to go we have to let them.'

And by the next morning, Dolores was dead.

11

Leah didn't know where Eva lived, but she knew who to ask.

Mati was reluctant, but she spun him some story about having information from Dolores Eva needed to know. Like any man, she thought, he didn't ask enough questions so it was easy to get it out of him. He could only give her a vague address though, just a road.

A flat at the end of Moorland Avenue, he said. Next to the posh ones. Leah narrowed it to the luxury flats in the converted warehouse, the ones that only footballers and solicitors could afford, which left them vacant and lifeless for the majority of the year. Just like every other new build in the town. She chained the bike to some cycle stands in front of the warehouse flats and made her way along the street, knowing she was going to have knock on several doors before she found the right one. The new flats were smart and clashed with the old buildings nestled so close beside them. The town didn't need them, no one would live in them. All the local papers were full of happy councillors shaking hands with some 'property developer' or other, which seemed a bit of a grand title for someone trying to hide money where it couldn't be found. All you had to do was provide a hefty backhander and the rest was profit. Was this the kind of thing Molinari was desperate to get in on, surface legit and a route to acceptance? But Leah had to catch herself, she knew that in spite of this it didn't make him a bad man. It just made him a man who wanted to fit in, like everyone; who wouldn't want that?

She had to be careful. She did not, on balance, tend to change her mind about things, but she *had* changed her mind about Dolores. The woman was not what she expected. It was her sadness, her resignation. Something she had done—something that might be to do with Frank

Molinari's death. She had written 'the ferryman' in her notebook. She knew who the ferryman was—the payment of a penny or something to go across a river, the Styx was it? Death, that's what Dolores meant. Pennies on the eyes of the dead, a weight to keep them closed. *Who else was going to die?*

She settled on a large Edwardian house, split into flats on the corner of two dividing roads—on one side the newbuild, on the other, the house. Back to back, a down at heel reminder of the Victorian redbrick grandeur the town once possessed. Once, one family owned these houses with servants with a row of bells in the corridor ringing in distant cellars. The Victorians would promenade along the seafront sashaying in and out of its grand ironwork canopies like peacocks, taking the waters and seeing the sights. The house was just shy of the promenade, but even so its stained glass had been left to the mercy of the sharp sea wind. The glass was cracked green squares and what used to be the front garden was paved over for cars. A big red wheelie bin lurked in the corner beside a Fiat Uno with foreign number plates and 'SRB' on a bumper sticker—where was that... SRB? Serbia? It was as good a place as any to start.

The woman who came to the door was tall and skinny and nothing like Mati had described. That was the first thing Leah noticed. The second thing was her smile, or lack of it. The woman's face looked like good news was a long time coming.

'Can I help you?'

The accent was thick; it sounded East European.

'I'm looking for Eva,' Leah said.

The woman looked her up and down, beginning to close the door, ready to bolt if she so much as shoved a foot in it. That's how she knew she had the right place.

'Who wants her?'

So that she wouldn't slam it shut, Leah thrust her press ID through the crack in the door.

'Leah Barnes. From the local paper. Dolores sent me.'

The woman took the card and studied it, but it was only for show. Leah could tell she knew exactly who she was talking about and not only because the door was still open.

'Where is she?' the woman asked.

'She's in hospital, she's ill.'

The woman didn't show any emotion.

'She hurt?'

'No, no,' Leah said. 'She's going to be okay.'

The woman opened the door wider, gestured for Leah to go in.

The house stretched back to occupy the triangular area of land it was squeezed into. As she entered the hall, Leah could hear traffic coming down the roads on either side, creating a rumbling like bowling balls down the corridor. It was claustrophobic, lined with a pile of rucksacks, coats and boots. Many people lived here and it looked like the worst kind of student digs. In the atmosphere Leah could smell the damp that came of inadequate heating. A radiator lined the length of the hall, hung with wet clothes, nothing quite drying, the smell filling the height of the gloomy corridor. Sour condensation dripped on the window ledges down the dank walls and pooled in grey puddles on the old white paint.

The passageway seemed endless. Leah felt it had to be brighter when they reached the end of it. She half expected to come out somewhere in Eastern Europe—a Berlin Speakeasy with red Tiffany lamps and a Maître D, a jazz band breaking into music. The woman, just ahead, opened a door at the end of the corridor into a brighter room where a gas fire belted out a dry artificial heat. The contrast between the damp and the heat made Leah feel tired on impact. There was a smell of cooking, garlic and some kind of herb. The smells reminded her she hadn't eaten anything since breakfast. She swallowed hard, tasting the food at the back of her throat, feeling the cramp in her gut.

'This is Leah,' the woman said to someone she hadn't seen when she walked into the room. 'Says Dolores sent her.'

In the corner away from the door, a dressing table had been set up on what was the dining table. Mirrors and pots of makeup and cream, a bottle of Evian, hair curlers covered its surface and there was an old-fashioned hairdryer beneath which another woman sat swaying her head, drying her hair. She wore a thin yellow dressing gown, and her black hair, spiked with orange at the tips, flew about her head like a Medusa. Her eyes were closed, but Leah knew she'd seen them come in. The two women were wary of her, challenging her, and she glanced back at the corridor wondering if she should quit while she was ahead. It was a hell of a long way to retreat without losing face, without at least explaining herself. What story would she have then? The woman stopped drying her hair, reached up with one hand to switch a dial to 'off' and opened her eyes.

'Who are you?' she said.

'Eva?'

Eva came out from under the dryer and pulled the robe round her.

'My name is Leah Barnes.' Leah put her hand out, but Eva ignored it. 'I'm from the local paper here, *The Courier.*'

'Well,' Eva said. 'I don't know what you want with me but sit down Leah.' She pronounced her name the way Susie did, like the princess in the space film, Princess Leia, *Lay-a,* but there was no smile. She looked bored, interrupted. Leah found herself sitting on a small velvet vanity stool with thin gold legs. She didn't feel she had a choice.

The two women faced her on hard, upright chairs, arms folded.

'Dolores said that I should see you, but you know my fr... my flatmate, Mati...' Leah said, deciding to start on safer ground.

'Mati?'

Eva was the younger of the two. She was smaller; her neat bones blended into her chair, metal-legged with a velveteen seat more suited to a conference suite. One chair leg was unbalanced and would have tipped anyone but this slight, tough little girl on to the floor. She didn't answer at once, narrowed her eyes.

'He's a Rumanian guy, lives in my flat, he's...' Leah stopped. *What was he?*

Eva shrugged.

'Sure, maybe. If you like.'

Eva laughed, looked at the other woman and they laughed, *why were they laughing*. Leah shifted. The stool was too small even for her and she felt the bones of her backside catch the edges of the dainty frame beneath the cushion, terrified it would give way and make her look a fool, which she was certain was their intention.

'You want a chair?' the other woman asked. Leah didn't answer. She took a deep breath, looked down at her notes, catching her professionalism by its tail and told them both what had happened to Dolores. Dolores hadn't told her what she should tell Eva so it seemed the best place to begin.

'Go on...' Eva said.

She closed the notebook, looked Eva in the eye. She told her first about Frank, and then she told her that Frank was dead. She'd seen *The Courier* on the table when she came in, so she knew that they might have already guessed this, but what the hell. There was a ripple across Eva's face all the same, a pucker of the lips at the corner of her mouth. She told her that Dolores had tried to take her own life, she wasn't sure why and this made Eva look at the other woman before turning back to Leah.

'She's going to be all right,' Leah said. 'You don't need to worry.' She couldn't imagine either of these two being worried about anything, but said it anyway, still unsure how all this fitted together.

'That why you come?' the first woman said. She hadn't given her name and Leah felt it was too late now to ask.

'Yes.' This hovered somewhere around the truth.

'To tell us this. No more?'

'Yes.'

But neither of them moved. They seemed to be waiting for more.

What more did she have? Suspicion hung in the air like the powder on the makeshift dresser in the corner of the room. She knew she only had a few more minutes until the shutters came down. She took a chance, pulled a photograph from her pocket. 'This is the man who died,' she said.

It was a picture of Frank Molinari, a few years old, the one they'd used in the paper the day after he 'died' in the fire over a year ago. There had been no picture in the paper this time; he still hadn't been named. Eva's eyes flickered again, just slightly, but enough to betray that she did.

'What has this man to with us?' the other woman asked, too quickly.

'He's the man killed in the fairground yesterday. Frank Molinari. Dolores said you knew him.'

Eva looked at her friend then back at the photograph and then at Leah.

'It's not in the paper,' she said. 'Why would she say that?'

'She said he was the man who got you passports to come here,' Leah said.

Eva's eyes were steady.

'Did she?' she said. She looked at her friend again, who nodded encouragement.

'Okay, so maybe he is man who brings me here from Paris,' she conceded. 'But this all I know.'

'Why did he bring you here?'

'Dolores help many people for job,' she said.

'You have a job then?'

Eva dismissed this with a wave of her hand. 'There is time; I am clever. I will find a job.'

'Mati told me,' Leah said, '...that your brother used to live here too?'

Eva's gaze never wavered. 'Is this your business?'

The silence was heavy between them now. Leah could see Eva weighing her options, deciding what to say. *Deciding what not to say*. 'I come here to find my brother,' she said. 'My brother Stefan gives me Dolores number, is long time ago. I hear nothing from Stefan, I try to call him but nothing and then I think there is this man Frank. I remember Dolores is knowing Frank and he is in Paris and he brings me, but when I get here, Frank says my brother is gone.'

'Now she must work to earn enough to go home,' her friend said.

'Without Stefan...' Eva's voice was quiet.

'Did your brother work for Frank?' Leah asked.

Eva laughed, spitting the words out, 'Frank works for *my* brother; my brother is powerful man. Now my brother is gone. Now Frank is gone.'

Leah didn't ask what Eva's brother did; she didn't have to. She could take a guess. Frank worked for Eva's brother; Frank probably owed him money. Now Frank was dead. She thought about the body in the fire with Susie, the one that was not Frank. She shouldn't have come here, and worse, she now doubted that Genaro had anything to do with this. She was beginning to see that he was, in all probability, an innocent man. And she didn't want that. Above all, she didn't want that.

'Did Mati know your brother?' Leah asked.

Eva hesitated then stood. 'Mati is my brother's friend,' she said.

Leah knew her visit was over. Eva's eyes were brittle, torn of sentiment. Leah had a fleeting image of the eyes she'd seen on news images only a few years before during the Balkan War. The faces of people trekking over mountains in the snow and rain, people hardened by and focused on survival of the kind she couldn't imagine. Here she was stuck in a safe urban backwater desperate to quit. Leah realised that was all she knew of these people—of Eva, of Mati, even of Dolores who had come long before them. She had built a picture based on images in a television newscast. She knew nothing about them at all.

Eva didn't need Leah to tell her that her brother was dead. Just by coming here, by telling her that Dolores had sent her, she had exposed the truth. And just like yesterday, when she saw Dolores sitting in her car on the sea front, it was too late to go back. It was too late to do anything about it.

12

Tom pulled in to the packed station forecourt at Lime Street Station in Liverpool and threw the door open,

'Get in.'

'Nice to see you too Dad!' Jack said. It was 5.21pm, which meant Tom was twenty minutes late after taking a meandering back road that should have been the faster route. Forty minutes round the back winding lanes through Netherton and then down and along the dock road in heavy traffic, crawling, had left him in a stinking mood. He wasn't where he wanted to be and he had to get back as fast as he could because all he wanted to do was find Nardone and find out what the hell he was up to because since that meeting and his 'phone call' he had vanished off the planet.

'Sorry, sorry...' Tom said 'Bad traffic...'

'I did say I'd get the train...'

'I'm here now, aren't I?' Tom snapped.

'Okay, okay, calm down. Fucking hell. It *was* your idea!'

'Don't swear, you sound like your sister.'

Wrong thing to say, but it was out there and, in rage at himself, Tom reversed the car round the swollen taxi rank just missing the bumper of a black cab. It resulted in a stream of abuse from the driver. Tom pulled over into the side. He breathed in and out. The great arches of Lime Street station glowered over him, a cathedral of steel and glass. When he was a kid, getting the train to London, it was the most exciting thing to come here—see it above his head stretching, the start of something exciting. That's what it had been for Jack today and he had to go and spoil it.

'She did swear a lot though, I'll give you that,' Jack said, saving him.

He nodded a smile of assent then moved from the kerb and back out into the city.

He found himself in the new one-way system taking a wrong turn near Moorfields Station, heading back down towards the docks again. Jack fiddled with the radio, flicking backwards and forwards searching for a sound he liked.

'Can we leave that off?' Tom said, then remembered to add, 'Please...'

He tried to find his way down through the twisting roads, passing the law courts on their left where Louise might be working even now. Maybe he should have let her pick Jack up today but... *no this was up to him now...*

'Whatever,' Jack said and swept his hair out of his eyes. He leaned back in a sulk.

This was a bad idea. *Was Jack thinking the same thing?* He should just have told Louise he couldn't come. Found an excuse like he used to do. He always got lost in Liverpool and it annoyed the hell out of him even though after all these years he really should know where he was going.

'Mum always goes left here,' Jack said, reading his mind.

So he turned down a road he wasn't supposed to take and suddenly they were heading the right way.

'Thanks,' Tom said.

'No worries.' Jack settled back into his seat. 'So I need two As and a B to get on to the course,' he said, monotone.

Tom whistled and Jack laughed. 'I know, mental...' he said.

The traffic was backing up again and even though Tom tried to stay calm, he wasn't concentrating. He tried to be interested in Jack, but he had one steady eye on the clock. He should be somewhere else, his default setting for so long was being in one place while being pulled towards another. He was so close to getting sucked back into work, work that would chew him up and spit him out again. *How did that happen?* This was not what he wanted. But then this wasn't really about work, was it? This was about Susie. He looked round for a free lane, an exit where he could double back. *It was always about Susie.*

'Susie would be happy if I get into UCL anyway, she liked London,' Jack said, reading his mind.

'What?'

'Susie,' Jack repeated. 'She liked London.'

'Yes she did.' Tom said and he saw her in a London she would never see. He saw her young and free and alive and had to squeeze his eyes, to trap the sorrow there. When he opened them again, on the dashboard he could see his phone flashing.

'Can you answer that?'

Jack reached forward and scrolled through the menu before pressing a key and sticking the phone to his ear. Tom resisted the urge to tell him to hurry. He had forgotten how much Jack lived his life in slow motion. Two speeds—dead slow and stop, Clemmie called it.

'It's that girl, Susie's mate. Leah Barnes,' he said. 'Wants you to call her back, says it's urgent.'

She must have found something

'Blimey,' Jack said staring at the phone. 'Haven't heard from her in a while.'

The traffic crawled. Liverpool was choked with road works blocking up all the arteries in the city. Cranes the size of skyscrapers grew above the skyline from ground level, towering even above the cathedrals high on their plateaued hill. To Tom's left, a row of black warehouses converted into upmarket apartments stood empty. The old 1980's Garden Festival site was reduced to rubble with a brand new casino where there should have been sustainable parkland for the city. That was the promise. The reality was different—the casino was swanky and neon lit, surrounded by high end cars, the sign of new money in a city that was never short of symbols. It was always a city reinventing itself, against the odds. In spite of everything, he had to admit, it did look impressive and it never failed to lift his

226

spirits. They passed the Liver Building, still standing proud beside the ersatz glitz of the new hotels springing up around it. St Nicholas's church jostled for space in the middle, holding its own with ancient dignity. Tom took the fork down to the dock road, choosing a different way rather than taking the top road back again. It was his father's route, 'just me and the taxis,' he would say. He prayed that the traffic would be better here. He hadn't gone more than a few hundred yards before he was stuck once more in a line of spewing exhausts. That was when he gave up, wound the window down, lit a cigarette. Jack's eyes were drooping.

'What about your carbon footprint Dad,' he muttered.

'What about it?'

'You should quit that.'

'I know.'

Jack's face in profile was so like his sister's. When Susie was alive, Tom got on better with her than he did with Jack, but Louise was always telling him he didn't get along with anyone, *hadn't done for years*. That made him sound like a tosser, which, come to think of it, he probably was. Just like Nardone. That must have been what Louise saw in them both once. *Nardone*. He tried Leah Barnes's phone. It switched to voicemail so he left a message, tapping his fingers on the open window frame.

'Shouldn't use a mobile while you're driving,' Jack mumbled.

'I'm not driving.' Tom waved a sarcastic hand at the traffic.

'Still shouldn't.'

'Shut up and go to sleep.'

Jack smiled openly for the first time since he'd got in the car.

Tom tried Ruby who told him Dolores Anghelescu had been discharged. Where'd she gone? Home, Ruby thought. Did Nardone know where she lived, would he go there?

Ruby couldn't say, she still hadn't managed to track him down and anyway, she said, what's that got to do with Nardone?

'Keep trying,' he told her. 'Just trust me on this.'

He clicked the phone off as the traffic inched along, doing his best to keep calm. With every tyre roll forward, this was getting harder. By the time they got moving again, Jack had already fallen asleep.

13

'You finished early today or what?' Ginny said.

Leah hadn't expected anyone to be in. Her head was full of everything that had just happened and she didn't like what she'd come up with. Ginny was still in her dressing gown, without makeup, watching reality shows on the TV in the front room, *Leah's* front room. Mati was nowhere in sight. Without her slap Ginny looked much younger and more vulnerable than she was.

'You done anything today,' Leah said, 'at all?'

'Nah, I'm out later, thought I'd chill for a bit.'

She flicked around the channels, not taking notice of anything she found. A pot of green nail varnish balanced on the edge of the sofa and a pile of cotton buds was scattered on the table in front of her. She had her hair in a turban, looking like a before and after model on daytime TV, the before bit. Leah snatched the pot of varnish and screwed the lid back on slamming it down on the table.

'You wanna come?' Ginny said ignoring her irritation.

'No thanks.'

'Whatever.'

Leah went into the kitchen and loaded what she could see into the dishwasher. She made herself a ham sandwich from some curly bread left on the side all day, shoving it into the toaster to make it more palatable.

'You going to clear that mess?' she asked Ginny coming back into the room.

'Later.' Ginny was still watching the TV.

'Everything is later with you.'

'Oh chill out will ya,' she said. 'Who knocked your donkey over?'

'It's my flat Ginny, my home. You don't even live here…'

Ginny turned back to the TV, unscrewed the lid on the polish and painted her toes. They sat in silence, the TV muttering inanely in the background. Leah was too tired to argue.

'You ever come across Rumanian girls in the clubs?' she said eventually. She'd been forming and reforming the question before it fell off the end of her tongue and into the open.

'How do you mean?

'Working and stuff?'

'What do you mean "stuff?" Like Mati?'

Leah shook her head, 'I went to this flat today and there were these two girls living there.' Leah hesitated, she didn't know how much Ginny knew about Eva. 'Rumanian I think,' she said, 'or Serbian.'

'Oh you have to watch the Serbians,' Ginny said. 'They're up to friggin' all sorts, drugs and shit. Rumanians are cool though, they're okay.'

'Yeah?'

'Yeah.'

'Anyway,' Leah went on, 'the Rumanian one, she was wearing like a leotard or something, like in the middle of the day.'

'She fit?'

Ginny turned, pushed her feet under her bathrobe and seized the opportunity to quiz Leah about her sex life or, as she saw it, the lack of it. Leah felt herself redden, she knew what Ginny was up to. Ginny didn't understand her but Ginny didn't judge her and, she supposed, this was the one thing she did genuinely like about Ginny. She treated Leah just as she treated everyone else, food for gossip, food for fun and right at this moment it was just what she needed. She felt her irritation slip, coming out of herself back to someone she used to be.

'She was nice,' Leah said. 'Pretty.'

She was. Leah thought of Eva under the dryer, her hair flying around her head, the sharp-boned cheeks and blazing eyes. She had the look of someone outside on the edge of looking in, just like Susie. Ginny was watching her.

'What?' Leah said, caught out.

'So, are you going back there?' Ginny asked.

'Gin' it's not…' Leah knew what Ginny was hinting, a raw nerve in her emotions twitched. She switched tack. 'The leotard, what do you reckon that's about?'

Ginny turned back to the TV and yawned. She'd lost interest.

'Maybe she's a lapdancer, plenty of 'em about. And none of 'em speak English.'

'Have you seen a lapdancer?' Leah said.

Ginny drew a low rolling laugh from the depths of her young belly.

'Christ you're so straight Leah!'

'And…'

'Fucking boring if you ask me, and now there's that limo thing goes round the town full of boozed up staggers, with the pole in the middle or something.'

'A what?'

'Limo, it's a lap dancing limo. Christ knows what they'll think of next. Wouldn't even be enough room to have a wank in there shouldn't wonder.'

'Ginny!'

She still had her eyes on the TV. She laughed again. 'You are so easy to wind up dude,' she said. 'Got any more beer?'

Leah went into the kitchen, pulled two beers from the fridge—Becks, her favourite, Susie's favourite, and put one back. She took a San Miguel for Ginny instead; she wouldn't know the difference. Ginny took it without a word.

'I don't think this woman is a lap dancer,' Leah said.

'Ask Mati.' Ginny swigged from the bottle. The bottle popped as she pulled it from her lips and she smacked them *aagh* as she swallowed the cold beer. 'Good beer mate,' she said. 'If she's Rumanian, chances are he'll know her. They tend to stick together.'

Mati.

'Where is he?'

'No idea,' Ginny said. 'Said he was meeting a mate, won't be long.'

It was Eva's brother, had to be. It was Eva's brother Stefan who died in the ghost train instead of Frank. Leah went through it, step by step. *And Frank?* She went back over what she could remember about Frank Molinari, but all she could come up with was what he looked like and even then his face was vague. Just his sharp suits, his swagger. That was all she remembered. He didn't seem like the type would plan a murder. Rewind—*anyone is capable of murder.*

Tom told her the fire was deliberate—he said Dolores told *him* that. That she was sorry and she told Leah to tell Eva she was sorry. *About what exactly?* Sorry didn't come close. So, what? Did Frank kill this Stefan or put him in there before the fire started or… or what? And—if Dolores knew then did Genaro? She left Ginny painting another coat of green across the top of her nails and went into the kitchen. She dialled Tom's mobile. It was already dark outside. She pulled the cord on the blind and eased it down shutting the darkness out as she listened to the voicemail recording. She left a message: 'It's me, we need to speak yeah? Soon as…' Then she dialled her editor. Higson picked up on the first ring.

There was a pause on the other end, which told her that Higson wasn't alone. She heard a shuffle and then a door closing. Her one good ear was getting better at compensating for the bad one. She missed nothing.

'Everything okay?' Leah said.

'You better have something good,' Higson said. His voice sounded like it was coming from a long way off; weary, lost in a tunnel somewhere.

'I have,' she said, coming to a decision. 'The fairground fire...'

'What did I...'

'Hear me out,' Leah cut across him. She heard him sigh.

'Remember the dead guy who was supposed to be Frank?' Leah said, 'Well I think I know who it was.'

She could hear his breathing slow. 'Go on.'

'Some guy called Stefan. A Rumanian, connected with Frank Molinari, not sure exactly how but through the girlfriend, Dolores.' She still couldn't connect Genaro so she didn't mention him. '*He* died in the fire,' she said. 'I think that's why Frank was murdered. Someone getting revenge, payback, something like that...'

She didn't mention that Frank and Dolores had started the fire. She would hold that one back.

'So Dolores you think?'

'Possibly, although...' it could have been Dolores she was the obvious suspect. But she seemed to want Leah to tell Eva, why did she want that?

Eva... She was starting to have a bad feeling about this, all of it.

'You have proof?' Higson said.

'Not yet, but I have a source.'

There was another pause. 'You can't run with it you know, not 'til you're sure,' Higson said.

Sure on all counts, including who started the fire and killed Frank. She had to get hold of Tom, now.

'Don't worry,' she said, 'I'll be sure. It's just that it's... well, it's messy at the moment. Just wanted to know that as soon as I have it all, we can run it?'

She pictured Higson alone in the dark office. She could imagine everyone else had gone home. Mike was leaving in a week or two, he'd be cruising his hours at work until he

233

was gone. Arun was away somewhere, on a story. She was always away somewhere and the temps would work to rule. Leah felt she could almost reach out and touch the silence behind him.

'Oh we'll run it.' Higson said. 'You bring it in, we'll run it.'

'Thanks Bill.'

Neither of them said goodbye.

Leah tried Tom again but there was still no answer. She hadn't switched the kitchen light on. The blue light from the television in the other room flickered in shadows across the kitchen, catching chrome and paintwork. Disembodied laughter filtered through the door, Ginny humming, the sounds echoed in the hum of the fridge and the flash of the rain on the windowpanes. She needed to speak to Dolores again. She would have to go back to the hospital and deal with this without Tom's help.

14

Only when Tom hit the bypass did any kind of free road open. He put his foot down, making up time between the roundabouts then losing it again when a red Mercedes pulled out in front of him straight into the inside lane. Tom swerved, missing the wheels of an articulated truck by inches. The ruck's horn bellowed like a bull across the carriageway, waking Jack.

'Whoa, what the f...'

But Tom took no notice; he was watching the Mercedes. It was the same colour, the same model as the one he'd lost. The one that nearly killed him. A classic Mercedes 190 with red paint faded to pink in patches from age and weather, chrome-nickelled with scabs of rust. The car slowed and Tom overtook it. A man was driving and as they cruised past, Tom felt he was looking at himself in another lifetime, in a parallel universe where nothing had happened, where everything was still as it was. The man was a similar age to him, similar build, fair reddish hair and a beard, but Tom didn't have a beard, he looked nothing like him at all. A coincidence that's all. Tom tucked in between the Mercedes and the truck, which was ahead now, where he preferred it. He kept his alternative self in sight in his rear view mirror. Their speeds matched, the distance between them equal until they reached the edge of town and the Mercedes accelerated, overtook them, then disappeared.

Had it even been there at all?

He glanced at Jack to see if he'd registered anything, but he was still staring out of the window, barely awake. On the road ahead the sign for tourist attractions lit up in his headlights. The billboard of the famous Winter Gardens, a watercolour of its heyday, Victorian ladies sashaying along the promenade with frilled parasols held to the ground just so. Wind and rain-battered, the sign had been there for decades and signalled the boundary of St Marie-by-Sea before you reached the old town gates. The name of the town was worked around the gates in wrought iron—gilt and black-filigreed letters welcoming visitors.

The lights changed and in the distance he thought he could see the taillights of the Mercedes, nothing more than an illusion to pull him home. He should have been relieved, but for some reason—maybe the Mercedes, maybe the growing cold and rain of the night—there was no relief. When the phone rang Jack answered it.

'Yeah, I'll tell him,' Jack said.

'That Leah again,' he told his father. 'Wants you to call her soon as...'

Tom accelerated the car again; it couldn't be soon enough.

15

The front door slammed in the hall and Ginny squealed. Mati was home. Within five minutes she was curled against him on the sofa, his muddy boots still on his feet. He usually took the boots off as soon as he got in, but tonight they stayed welded to his feet, mud and all. He flicked the television over to the news while Ginny, having finished with her toenails, started on her fingers.

'Alright?' Leah said.

Mati was preoccupied, frowning. His hair flopped over his forehead was soft with rain and when he reached up to push it from his eyes, she could see the dirt ingrained in his fingernails. His fingers, calloused and cracked with soil.

'You want a beer?' Leah asked him.

'Sure.'

Mati took the beer and glared at the news on the TV. He ignored everything Ginny said until the report was over, seeming to be waiting for something. She was wittering on about who was going to the Limelight tonight and what time they should go, but Mati wasn't listening to a word. *What on earth did he see in her?* Her words floated into the shadows above them with the flickering TV screen giving out the only light.

'You got a minute?' Leah said, gesturing her head towards the kitchen.

Mati got up and followed her, like he'd been expecting it. Ginny didn't even notice. When they were alone in the kitchen, Leah pushed the door gently to. She faced him. 'I saw Eva today.'

Mati's silence told him that he already knew.

'I was given some information,' she continued.

'What information?' Mati went to the sink and washed his hands. He poured a glob of washing up liquid from a great height and started scrubbing his fingers together. 'Eva is a tourist, what can tourists know?' The black soap suds flew about the sink like gnats. He picked and peeled at his nails, prising the dirt from beneath them.

'Come on, Mat, tell me...' she said.

Mati didn't flinch. 'I know her brother, Stefan. I meet him in Paris and I come here with him but he gets into bad things and now he's gone. I look everywhere, maybe he is gone to London is what I think. So I tell Eva and of course, she comes to find him.'

He rinsed his hands under the tap, the water washing the black foam away. His back was still turned. He looked for the tea towel. Leah handed him kitchen paper.

'Why didn't you tell me before?' she said. 'I thought we were friends?'

Mati chucked Leah on the shoulder. Mati was strong and it hurt. 'What should I tell you?'

'It might have something to do with the story I'm working on.'

'How?'

'I think Stefan is dead,' Leah said.

Mati glowered from under his dark eyebrows, eyes like Eva's, freezing her out.

'Of course he is dead,' Mati said. His voice in a whisper filled the tiny kitchen. Mati didn't move. Their faces were so close now that Leah could feel the sour warmth from his breath. This man had lived here in her flat for all this time, but now looked like a total stranger.

'You know who killed him?'

'Do you?' Mati replied.

'What are you two doing in here?'

Ginny stood in the doorway, blowing on her wet nail varnish.

'Just talking,' Leah said without taking her eyes off Mati. 'Work.'

'Hey,' Ginny said, 'Leah met a tasty girl! Rumanian, she might need a translator!'

238

Mati turned to Leah as though this information was new.

'Yeah? What's her name, this Rumanian girl?'

'Eva,' Ginny said.

'A good name.'

Leah went to the fridge and took out another beer. She didn't want it but she needed to buy some time. She passed one to both of them. Mati's fingers brushed hers as the bottles were exchanged.

'Cheers,' Mati said, emphasising the word, the English language tripping off his tongue as if he was showing off. Then he followed Ginny out of the kitchen and went back to the sofa.

The front door was thirty feet away, through the hallway. Leah did not have to pass through the lounge to reach it. She put the unopened beer back on the side and waited two, three minutes. When she heard them talking quietly, settled, she made her way out, closing the door by squeezing the latch behind her. It was pitch dark outside and she had to scrabble around at the back of the building to find her bike. She unlocked it, glad that she was still wearing her jacket, feeling the bite and the blur of the beer sloshing around her head. She hadn't eaten that bread she'd toasted, she'd forgotten. How had she forgotten to eat? She felt nauseous, the beer bitter between her teeth, no longer riding on the confidence of alcohol. She had to lean against the wall of the building to catch her breath.

Mati knew Stefan was dead. *How did Mati know?* Thanks to Leah, Eva had a good idea that Dolores was mixed up in all of this, but then maybe she'd known all along? It was Frank who brought her here in the first place so maybe Mati had told her and that's why she was here? But could Eva kill Frank? Didn't seem possible, a small bony girl like that.

Eva knew about Frank and Dolores, she knew about that. *Dolores.* In all this she'd forgotten about Dolores, again. She called the hospital where they said she'd been discharged; she was at home. *Damn, damn, damn.*

She headed for the seafront where a damp drizzle drenched the night air. Her phone was in her hand, jammed against the handlebar, ready to ring. She took off. Her tyres flew over the rain on the tarmac with the low steady rhythm of wet wings.

Tom picked up Leah's messages as soon as he reached Clemmie's house. Her voice was urgent and scared. She said Dolores discharged herself from the hospital hours ago and they had to get to her. She knew where she lived and would meet him there. She didn't need to tell him, he knew where it was and he didn't want to go back there. *Anywhere but there.* But he knew from Leah's voice that he had no choice.

Clemmie had the TV on as usual, volume turned up loud. Tom thought that the screen seemed bigger each time he looked at it and each time he thought this, it depressed him more.

'How'd it go son?' she asked Jack as he plonked down on the sofa next to her.

'Corrie on yet Nan?'

'Soon.'

Tom stood behind them, the images moving with lazy ease across the screen. His feet itched to get away. Clemmie asked Jack about his day, asked all the right questions he'd not thought to ask in the car. *He'd got it wrong again.* He smelled food in the kitchen, lasagne or something. He was starving, torn between staying, pretending he'd never got Leah's message and knowing he had to go.

'Look, I need to be somewhere,' he said. 'I'm sorry.'

Clemmie nodded.

'Off you go then,' she said and Jack just raised a hand.

He grabbed a brown banana from the fruit bowl in the kitchen, crammed two paracetamol in his mouth and swallowed them with tepid tap water noticing as he did that his head had stopped hurting hours ago. *How come he hadn't noticed?* It was well past seven when he got into the car and drove towards Dolores's flat, almost two hours since Leah Barnes had first called him.

In less than a mile it went from darkness to pitch black. Tom pulled into the small curve of the Royal Crescent, but could see no more than a few feet in front of him. The red of the grand Edwardian buildings had faded to dirty grey, barely visible. He turned the corner and slammed straight into what, at first, looked like fog. As he edged closer it engulfed the air until he couldn't see anything. He had to leave the car at the opening to the Crescent because two squad cars and a line of incident tape formed a barrier across the end of the road. Clumps of people were scattered at the barrier, in pyjamas and overcoats, a dog here and there, a cat in a carrier. His dry eyes watered as smoke poured from the windows of the building ahead. Dolores's building, the top floor. The acrid stench of burning furniture, melting plastic foam, clothes, bricks, lives, stuck in his throat choking his breath. Fire crews were snaking hoses to the upper floors blasting water at the highest windows, but there was a lack of urgency about it, as if they had already done what they could and now they were just trying to put the fire out so that they could go in and bring out whoever was still in there. He could see it on their faces because he'd seen it before, too many times. The resignation and the wait as all hope drained away. He saw Leah Barnes, outside the cordon of people, leaning on her bicycle watching and went over. Leah turned round and smiled joylessly.

'Too late.'

'I was in Liverpool picking my lad up.'

'Both of us. We were too late.'

She didn't say, although Tom could have finished it for her—*again*.

A fire officer came over, a dark stocky man with heightened colour from the fire. Len Roberts, Tom knew him because he was on duty the day Susie died and came to see him later to offer his condolences. Louise told him that Len brought Susie out, in a body bag, shrunk to almost half her size, her bones like a small sack of sticks that sagged in the middle. No weight. Tom didn't have to be there that day to imagine what that was like and he didn't have to imagine that it was going to happen all over again.

'Someone still in there?' he asked.

Len nodded,

'Couldn't get to her,' he said. 'Saw her, shouted, but she seemed to be asleep. Flames were too bad, couldn't reach her. Maybe she was unconscious from the smoke, hope so.'

Len coughed, hacking the smoke up like a sloop of tar. The heat was overwhelming all of them. Shards of ash flew into their faces, melted on their skin and burrowed its blackness into their pores. Tom didn't need to ask who. He looked up and saw the window jagged and white from the heat, the frame and paint melted. He imagined her, eyes closed, his fingers brushing the edges of her eyelashes in sleep. *Dolores.* He stood and watched as the fire, like the edge of his reason, raged on.

Thursday 11 January 2007

1

Genaro Molinari stared straight ahead. He wouldn't drink, wouldn't move. He wouldn't speak.

They brought him in for questioning as soon as they could find him, but so far he'd given them nothing. He asked for his lawyer and the guy who came in looked just as crooked. Tom knew him from an earlier case, a local solicitor who reeked of expensive aftershave and smiled and simpered his way through the interview. Each thick finger sweated as he turned the pages in his bulging file. He had the soft skin of a man who didn't know a hard day's work from a bung off a client. Tom wanted to wrap his stupid striped tie round his neck and hang him from the iron ceiling girders. Ruby Miller was asking the questions, but he'd sat in with her, wanting to jump in, wanting to scream at them. The pair made him sick.

The lawyer spoke for Molinari. He was nowhere near Royal Crescent last night, he was at the fairground then he went on to the new club he was hoping to buy near Church Lane. Genaro had not seen Dolores Anghelescu to talk to for at least a year, but it had come to his attention in the past few hours that she had been in touch with his brother Frank. Who, the lawyer said in a slow and measured way, it appeared had not died after all in *that* fire. They had nothing to hold Genaro on, the club had been packed last night and plenty of people had seen him. Tom leaned forward, deciding to take a punt on an idea that had been swilling round his head.

'Can I ask you something,' he said. Genaro turned towards him. 'Do you remember a Superintendent Robert Nardone? You would have met him at the time of the fire?'

Ruby Miller was frowning at him, but he ploughed on even though Molinari was staying silent. He thought, though, he really thought, that he saw a tightening in Genaro's jaw and a definite shift in his seat.

'No comment,' Genaro said and they had to let him go. *What else could they do?*

'What on earth were you playing at back there?' Ruby Miller hissed when they got outside the interview suite.

'I think he knows Nardone,' Tom said. 'Better than he's letting on.'

'Well that's not exactly a leap,' Ruby said. 'He *was* the investigating officer on the fairground fire!'

'But it would mean that maybe, just maybe, Nardone...'

'He's not involved in all this, surely you don't think? Come on...'

'I'm not saying he *is*, but...' Tom was thinking about how you would hide something you didn't want in the open. Maybe that was what Nardone was doing, covering up something, for someone else. 'I think this goes back to the day of the fire.'

'Well I know Nardone screwed up spectacularly but even so...'

'Where is he now then?'

'That,' Ruby conceded, 'I don't know.'

Molinari followed them out of the interview suite with his lawyer. They shook hands, the thick fingers on the lawyer's free hand gripping Molinari's shoulder in reassurance. No charge. *For now.* The lawyer left and Genaro turned to Tom and Ruby, he would like to see his brother's body if they would be so kind. They exchanged glances—it couldn't do any harm. *Could it?* Frank was still with Linda at the hospital, so they took a patrol car, Ruby driving, Tom riding shotgun in the back with Genaro. The whole way, apart from a crackle on the radio, not a word was said.

Tom hadn't mentioned the state Frank was in because he figured Genaro already knew. Genaro had found the body so he must have seen. As soon as the metal drawer slid out of its socket in the wall, however, Tom realised he'd badly misjudged him. The big man seemed to diminish as he stared down at his brother's destroyed face.

'How did this happen?' he said quietly.

Tom looked at Ruby, she back at him. A shrug, *I've as much an idea as you*... then: 'It was you called the police yes?' Ruby said, suddenly, as though something had just occurred to her. She glanced at Tom, who was already following her line of thought.

'I called...' his hesitation answered her question.

'You called Nardone,' Tom finished for him.

He didn't deny it.

'I suppose you are now going to tell me you already had his number from Frank's *first* death?' Tom said.

Tom was aware of Ruby behind him, leaving the room. He knew where she was going. Her phone was already at her ear.

'You think I could do this to my brother?' Genaro said so softly Tom had to lean forward to hear him.

The faux Scouse accent had gone. In its place was a trace of the roots he'd lost long ago. He reached out and touched Frank's face, laid the back of his palm against his forehead then turned and walked away. Tom nodded to the mortuary assistant to replace the drawer. It was the same blonde lad from the day before. Linda Sweeney was nowhere to be seen.

'What's your name?' Tom asked.

The lad sniffed, gave him a crooked smile.

'You're Fairfax aren't you?'

Tom nodded.

'I remember your girl. I'm sorry.' He slid the metal box into its socket, it sounded long and thin and hollow. It

249

sounded like it would keep on going and never reach the back. 'I'm Mitch,' he said.

'You think that man could have killed his brother Mitch?' Tom asked.

The boy shook his head. 'You wouldn't think it,' he said. 'Some people come in here and they just don't care, you know? He weren't one of those.'

'Thanks.'

'No worries.'

In the lobby, Genaro Molinari sat on a hard plastic chair against the wall. There was a 'No Smoking' sign over his head.

'Thing is, Genaro,' Tom sat next to him, offered him a cigarette, 'Thing is, we have two people dead now. Two people who were connected with you.'

'I did not kill my brother.'

'I'm not saying you did.'

'Then what are you saying?'

'Who did Frank owe money to?'

Genaro looked at his cigarette. He filled the chair and most of his bulk spilled out on to Tom, almost touching him. In the distance between the station and here, something had changed in both of them. Genaro looked like someone whose sorrow was kept deep in his pocket. *It took one to know one.* Tom knew how that felt.

'My little brother was not...' Genaro smiled, '...how do you say... the brightest yes?'

'You could say that again,' Tom said.

'But it was not to me he owed any money,' Genaro said. 'He wanted me to help him. He was dealing in passports, nothing more. I didn't know for certain, but when I hear that Dolores...'

'Who you hadn't seen for a year...' Tom cut in.

'When I hear that these Rumanian girls are suddenly here in St Marie,' Genaro continued smoothly. 'I'm thinking, this is Dolores. And if it is Dolores, then who is helping her?' Genaro sighed, leaned back on the chair. The plastic ached and creaked beneath him. 'You are remembering my waitress at the Fun House?'

'Suki?'

Genaro nodded. 'One of Dolores's girls, she tells me and I put two and two together to make Frank.'

'It wasn't a shock to see him then?'

Genaro smiled. 'You didn't know my brother. This time, I'm thinking he went too far. In France, he is doing something else, I'm not sure what.'

'Enough to get him killed?'

Genaro tut tutted, *no*. 'Whatever he was running from, he ran into much worse here...' He stopped for a moment, then said, 'You know her name, Dolores, "Anghelescu" it means "angel"?'

Tom didn't know that.

'Her family died in Auschwitz, they were Roma. Her mother escaped, they hid in Paris until after the war.'

'But,' Tom said, 'she told me that she met Frank in a circus in Paris. She told me that he ran away and found her...'

Genaro tipped his head back and let out a deep chuckle. 'Who told you that?'

'Dolores, I...'

'Frank was never in no circus.' Genaro was still laughing quietly; he seemed to enjoy this image of his brother.

'He wasn't a circus strong man...' Tom felt stupid even as he was speaking. The laugh rolled from Genaro even more. 'So how... how did he meet her?'

Genaro placed his hands on his knees as he turned to Tom. 'She read my fortune, many years ago—is why I come here, buy this place. She read Frank's too, and you know the rest. My brother, he loved Dolores.' Then he added, 'You loved her too.'

Tom didn't need to answer that. He saw her going to sleep in that bed in the alcove in her flat surrounded by drapes and her Indian summer bells and knew that once the fire started she wouldn't have stood a chance.

'There was a man,' Genaro said. 'A Rumanian. He worked for Frank. Maybe Frank didn't pay him?' His shoulders drooped and he seemed to be sinking into the chair. 'Frank never liked paying. He liked money but he didn't like paying. I told him—you don't trust drug dealers. This man...' he paused. 'I have heard that he was drug dealer.'

'Frank was dealing drugs?'

Tom remembered the track lines on Frank's arm in the postmortem.

'No,' Genaro said. 'This Rumanian, he helped with the passports. The drugs were a sideline, but it seems neither of them were very good at it.'

'So maybe Frank owed him, for the passports?'

'Maybe.'

'Or for drugs?'

'Perhaps,' Genaro said sadly.

The smoke from Tom's cigarette drifted above their heads. 'When Frank came back from the dead,' Tom asked, 'did he come back for the money?'

'Sure he came back for the money.'

'And you didn't want to give him any.'

'Not me. Frank is my brother.' Genaro was adamant. 'Besides, I don't have that kind of money.'

Tom raised an eyebrow.

'I don't care whether you believe me or not.'

'Someone else, then? You were going to ask someone else for the money, weren't you?'

The way Genaro looked at Tom then, was it pity or something else? When Tom thought about it later, he didn't know how he hadn't known it all along. He didn't know how he hadn't seen the truth way back when he first met

Frank with Dolores all those years ago, questioning him for something else he hadn't been able to pin on him. Too many years to count had passed between now and then, gone in a second. The number of years didn't seem to matter any more.

'Come on Inspector, I don't need to spell it out.' Genaro said. 'There are three brothers, and Roberto won't miss Frank as I do.'

And suddenly there it was—the likeness in Genaro's face, the sallow skin that seemed out of place in the gloom of an English winter, the droop of a lazy eye. The man he should be looking for wasn't sitting beside him in the mortuary lobby. Wherever Robert Nardone was, though, Tom knew he had to find him before he found Genaro.

'Do you know where he is?' Tom asked.

Genaro turned to him. 'No. But I hope I don't find him before you do.' Molinari stood, handed his unlit cigarette back 'I don't smoke.'

Tom replaced it in the box, still warm from Molinari's fingers.

'You'll have to make a statement,' he said.

'I know.'

'And you know that Robert will be looking for you now?'

Genaro nodded 'I am not afraid of him' he said. 'Frank was, but not me, not any more.' He turned to go, put his hand out.

'I am sorry for your daughter, I know you won't believe me, but is true.'

Tom's hand was engulfed by Genaro's firm grip. He *did* believe him. Something had passed between them that neither of them had expected.

'Be careful,' Tom said.

Molinari smiled. 'I always am.'

Tom held the door open for him, followed him out. 'And Genaro,' he said to the man's retreating back. Genaro turned, his eyes red, 'I'm sorry about your brother too.'

Genaro raised a hand behind him and walked away. He reached the taxi rank, no longer looking like a man who was going places. He didn't kill Frank and Tom was sure now he hadn't killed Dolores. Maybe he had been exploiting a desperate workforce, they hadn't even mentioned that, but in Tom's book—and he knew he shouldn't think like that—there were worse things you could do.

In the office outside the mortuary, it was still quiet. Linda was still there, as she always was, filling forms, ticking boxes. She waved him over.

'Are you okay?' she said.

She stood at the doorway and this time did look tired. Tom shook his head, pushed his thumb and forefinger into his eyes and pressed hard until he hit the pain spot behind his eyelids. 'I'll be better when this is all over.'

'Well, I hate to tell you this, even though it was probably a good thing in the circumstances. Dolores Anghelescu was already dead before the fire started.'

Tom looked up, 'She was?'

'Well, fire report is still to be filed and that will be conclusive, but they can't even say conclusively that the fire was deliberate. Probably a cigarette.'

'Len Roberts says if you want to hide a deliberate fire you start it in a chip pan, or drop a cigarette. No chip pan but they've evidence it could be the latter.'

'And she had either been drugged or drugged herself. The latter is my guess. Traces of dihydrocodeine in her bloodstream—co-dydramol to you. A painkiller she'd been prescribed at the hospital along with several dozen paracetamol.'

'They sent a suicidal woman home with a bunch of lethal painkillers?' He thought of his own stockpile at home. *What was the difference?*

'They wanted to get her home, I guess,' Linda said.

'I bet they bloody did.'

Linda was watching him. He hated the way she did that, like she was trying to find a connection between them that wasn't there. It was hard for him to tell if it was concern. *Maybe he was imagining it.* He was thinking of something else, something Linda just said. In the morning with Dolores, he'd light up, first thing. He'd sit in bed, smoking and she'd open the window, watching him. Linda said it was probably started with a cigarette, but Dolores didn't smoke.

Mitch appeared with a mug of coffee for each of them. 'Thought you two could do with this,' he said.

The lad's arms were freckled where his sleeves were rolled up, which made him look even younger. Tom took the mug of tea from him, but in his head he was going over it—why didn't Dolores have the window open, she always slept with the window open. If she had then she'd have heard them coming, she could have been rescued. *But she was already dead and she did that, no one else.*

'You look shattered,' Linda said.

'I am.' He closed his eyes, hoped that when he opened them again there would be no one there but him.

2

Tom went back to the station. The young woman PC, whose first name Tom had learned was Cheri, was talking on the phone writing stuff on a pad in front of her. Ruby was in her office, the door was open and she was typing into her computer, tap-tap-tap. Hughes sat to one side chewing a pencil watching her. Sheaves of papers and empty sweet wrappers covered his desk, a can of Coke balanced on the perimeter like a cliff jumper and he had his feet propped on an open drawer. Just the sight of him set Tom on edge.

Tom took a deep breath. 'Any news?'

Hughes didn't move at first, then he turned. He wound his head in a slow rotation towards the sound of his old boss's voice with no urgency at all. 'No.'

'Sir... you got a minute?' Ruby was standing in his doorway, a scrap of paper in her hand. 'We had a lead, on a woman seen with Frank yesterday. CCTV picked them up in the station, traced them back to John Lennon airport. She came with him from Paris.' She did not mention that Tom had seen Frank and the girl in the station, that in fact this was *his* lead. Hughes was still listening in.

'Anyway,' she said. 'Tracked her down and it seems she's disappeared.'

'Anyone looking for them?'

'What's the point?' as he spoke, Hughes pulled a grey rag of a handkerchief from his pocket and wiped the back of his mouth with it. 'Long gone,' he said.

'Did even you try to find them?'

'Of course,' Hughes said. He folded his arms with defiance.

'And?'

'Vanished into thin air.'

In his head, Tom counted to ten.

'Keep looking,' he said, 'Try your bouncers—your pals on Mount Street, since they always seem to know so much.' The latter delivered with sarcasm, anything more challenging in terms of leads was beyond Hughes and his detecting skills.

Tom felt the walls moving in, closer. He pushed past Hughes in the doorway... breathing slowly—out, in, out, in. He stumbled his way to the locker room where he found a packet of dihydrocodeine in his kitbag. He remembered the printed list of drugs on Linda's report sheet. It was the same drug Dolores had used to kill herself. He washed two down with water from the tap before looking at himself in the mirror. *He was not ready to be here.* He should have gone away, far from here. He'd talked about leaving with Dolores all the time, starting again somewhere Frank couldn't find her. He believed her when she'd said she had to get away from him. *Why didn't she leave the window open, why did she fall asleep?*

He went into the canteen and bought a coffee and a meat pie. The place was almost deserted and the food was old and stale, but he was ravenous with hunger. He had forgotten everything he felt, everything he thought. It was as though there were holes in his hands through which the pinpricks of his conscience had leaked out facts and memories like water through a sieve. He paid for his food, heard his footsteps hollow as he walked out. In the background he could hear someone buying cigarettes from the machine, the clunk of the packet landing in the tray. He was desperate for a smoke and retraced his steps back to the office to get his cigarettes from his coat not expecting what he found when he pushed open the door.

Only two people now remained—Hughes on one side, sitting at his desk and Ruby Miller standing over him, her arms stiff by her side. She was holding them for the moment in check. Her fists opening and closing in her palms.

'What's going on?' Tom said.

'Ask him,' Ruby said without taking her eyes off Hughes.

'Well?' Tom looked at Hughes.

'You want to tell him or shall I?' Ruby said.

Hughes cocked his head, like he could care less.

'It was a joke,' he whined. 'Just a joke…'

'He said you were fucking me,' she said, then added, 'Sir.'

Hughes was smirking, his chair tilted back like a kid on the back row of a classroom, waiting for chalk to fly. Tom looked at Ruby's pale face red with anger and, for a moment and knowing it was the wrong way to feel, didn't know whether to be flattered or insulted. Ruby was clearly the latter and he pulled himself up. Hughes hadn't finished.

'With your track record is all I meant,' he said then went back to shuffling paper on the desk. Shoving them in a drawer, already on the back foot. 'Fuck's sake,' he muttered. 'Where's your sense of humour?'

Tom moved from the doorway in the time it took for Hughes to finish his sentence. The coffee went one direction, the meat pie the other as Tom kicked the chair from under him and he went down. The tilt of his spine hitting the floor sounded with a dull cracked snap. Hughes staggered up, his face white, his mouth open in a jagged split. Blood poured from his front teeth.

'Apologise,' Tom spat.

Hughes raised his fist and Tom caught it mid-air, their faces inches apart, close enough for Tom to smell the whisky he knew Hughes kept in a hip flask in his pocket. He should have seen this coming. Ruby had taken her eye off the ball, trusted her team too much and Tom should have been here to help her. Hughes and his hatred lashed out at anything and everything, it was what he did. Ruby Miller was just in the way and they had both underestimated him.

'Tom, please…' Ruby said.

Hughes's arm loosened then dropped. He gave in.

'She provoked me,' he sneered.

'Apologise,' Tom said.

Hughes righted the chair and took his coat from the back jamming it hard under the desk and without looking up, headed for the door.

'Fuck you,' he said. 'You haven't heard the last of this!'

Tom looked from Ruby to Hughes—there were only three of them in the room, no witnesses. No CCTV.

'Nothing happened here did it?' he said. 'You see anything DI Miller?'

Ruby shook her head. 'I didn't see anything.'

Closing ranks, he wouldn't stand a chance if he took this higher. Hughes let the door go as he left the room and it banged hard enough to make the thin walls of the office shake. Neither Tom nor Ruby spoke for a few moments.

'I'm sorry,' he said. 'About him.'

She shook her head, *it doesn't matter, let it go.*

'There was another phone call…' she said. 'I didn't want him to know.'

'Genaro?' He'd half expected it and she nodded.

'He said you'd understand what he had to do.'

Ruby was watching him.

'The fairground!' he said, answering the question she hadn't asked.

Then he was grabbing his jacket, his keys and was already at the door.

'Get back up and call Leah Barnes,' he shouted back over his shoulder. 'Tell her to meet me there.'

3

Leah checked the time on her phone. That Miller woman had told her to wait for Fairfax by the gate. She'd sounded frantic, said she was on her way there too but that was ten minutes ago and there was still no sign of anyone. She was about to go in when she caught sight of Tom Fairfax's long thin frame coming across the car park towards her. His legs hit their stride on the tarmac, his coat flapped around him as though he was being carried towards her on the wind. He had something on his head. As he drew closer, she could see it was a hat with fur flaps pulled firmly around his ears. They drew level and the hat made her smile, soften. Fairfax still looked unshaven and pale skinned as though he spent too long in the darkness without light, but the hat… the hat made him seem almost human.

'You okay?' Tom said

Leah nodded, grinning at the hat, the incongruity of the situation not lost on either of them.

'Very fetching,' she said and he managed a smile back.

'Genaro around?'

Leah shook her head. 'There's no one here. What's going on?'

'Come on.'

Tom led her across the tarmac towards Genaro Molinari's office where they found the door unlocked. They went straight in.

'You think it's Genaro?' Leah said. 'You think he killed Dolores?' They were in the office now and she was talking, hardly drawing breath, thinking as fast as the words came out. 'I came to see him,' she said, 'after the murder and there was a bloke in here watching us. Like waiting for me to go, and it's been bugging me because I've seen him again.'

Tom stopped.

'Where?'

'In the hospital visiting Dolores. Nurse said he was a copper.'

Under his breath Tom said,

'He is.'

'Who is he?'

'Superintendent Robert Nardone. I think he killed Frank, maybe Dolores... if we don't find him, Genaro will be next...'

Leah heard Dolores's voice in the hospital in her head. She remembered Eva and her friend sitting like two monkeys on a bench: see no evil, hear no evil. *Speak evil* that's what Leah had done. *She had told them.*

'He didn't kill Dolores,' she said.

'How do you...' Tom started to say.

'Eva's brother Stefan,' she said. 'He was the one died in the fire... Dolores told me. I told Eva.' She felt the weight of the knowledge, her words, falling from her. 'I told her.'

He hadn't known. She could see it in his eyes, reassessing her.

'You asked me to speak to her. That's what she told me,' she said.

'You believed her?'

'I met Eva,' she said. 'Yes I believed her.' She thought, for a moment, that whatever he had come here to do, he had changed his mind about it. He stood, dithering. This wasn't what he'd wanted to hear, that much was obvious.

'Eva?' he said. Then he remembered the girl in blue with Frank at the station.

'So if Eva killed Dolores, maybe even Frank...' Leah said, 'what does this other guy...'

'Nardone...'

'Not the guy who was on the case when Susie...' she said then stopped, changed her tack. 'What does he want with Genaro?'

'He's his brother,' Tom said.

'You're fucking kidding me!' What had Arun said about some high up cop knowing what was going on, signing off papers and stuff? Not Tom Fairfax but this man. 'Why though,' because it didn't make sense, 'why would he want to kill his brother?'

'Oh you'd be surprised,' Tom said. He was always surprised, at what people would do to one another, for money, for love. For the lack of both. He could imagine Nardone following Frank and Genaro here, finding them, pressing his nose to the glass of their lives begging to be let in. He could imagine them keeping him out, his refusal to be sent away.

The back door of the office banged in the wind. Someone had left it open. The winter light seeped in through cracks in the gloom. A coffee mug on the desk was half filled with coffee. Tom picked it up—still warm, and Leah followed Tom's eyes to the door then moved back to him both, in the same instant, sharing the same thought.

'The ghost train!' Leah said, out before Tom could stop her.

Tom stabbed the keypad on his mobile and Ruby picked up. He gave her his location, told her to get there as fast as she could. What was less obvious the day before now seemed stark and dangerous in the failing light. High metal barbed fences menaced them as they ran. Faces leered out at them—clowned faces with split red grins and wide mouths, hanging down from the fascias of rides long out of step with their time. Police would soon flank the front of the fairground. In the distance, like a building swarm of bees, they heard the sirens making their way in easy stages towards them. No one was getting out easily but if they did, Tom would see them first. He didn't think Nardone would be expecting any of them.

He ran out, the way Leah Barnes had gone, into the fairground, but she had vanished. There were noises everywhere. Everything louder than it should have been, like that day, in the car, when he was trapped and his legs wouldn't move. He could hear voices, as he did then, somewhere not far away, getting louder, more insistent. He heard feet running, which turned into something else in his head—the burning ghost train, the stench of smoke, a car out of control, sand and wet earth, silence.

He would not let this happen again.

He was running. Someone was running with him and turning he saw Ruby Miller beside him. He brushed her hand, her fingers folding tight.

'You take that way, I'll head down the back,' she shouted and he did as he was told, ending up where he should have been in the first place. Leah was crouched on the ground, running her hand along a bleeding jaw. The ghost train loomed in front of her.

'He's in there,' Leah said.

Tom looked at the entrance, the mouth of the ride waiting for him. *Where else would Nardone go?*

'I'm going in!' He shouted and as soon as it was out of his mouth, it sounded ridiculous. He knew that instead of a gung-ho hero, his voice sounded like a flat line of pain. Everyone looked at him, but no one tried to stop him. Not even Ruby.

'Find Genaro,' he shouted at her. 'He's here somewhere.'

Then he walked forward, swallowed by the darkness.

He could hear his blood, rapping its rhythm against the walls of his heart. He inched forward, the walls of the ghost train throwing dust and cobwebs into his face as he groped forward. He reached into his pocket, drew out his Zippo lighter and flicked it. The walls flared up. Skeletons grinned over the rusting rails like animals in a grotesque zoo, leaning down as if they would fall and crush him. In the pitch darkness he felt the souls of the dead rushing through the tunnel, sucking the life from him. He lurched and stumbled as the low walls pressed on him. The ceiling was less than six inches above his head. He could feel drops of moisture, cold, down the back of his neck. He slapped his face, hard, and went on, listening.

The train rails ran out. He'd gone some distance, felt himself somewhere in the centre because the sounds from outside were more muted now, the air colder. He felt along the wall, easing along. He turned and came out into a wider space, a cavernous space that must be the ride's epicentre. The air gathered height above him here and up somewhere at the top, light filtered in. As his eyes adjusted, he saw he was in some sort of siding. Carriages were discarded on their backs, rails twisted and upended, broken in half and rusting. Something brushed past, an invisible hand. He found himself thinking of that game he played as a kid: guess the ghoul in the box. He'd been blind then too, blindfolded, fingering things in a half-light in hidden boxes, no idea what they were. *He had no idea where he was now.* Something touched his arm in the blackness and he saw her there, beside him, it couldn't be, it was...

'Susie?'

'If only...' a voice said.

In the shadows, Tom made out Robert Nardone's heavy frame. He could smell him only inches away.

'Go away Tom,' Nardone said. 'This is not your fight...'

'You killed your brother.' Tom found his voice calmer than he felt.

Nardone drew a patient breath in.

'No,' Nardone said. 'He was already dead but...' and he laughed the laugh of someone who didn't see the joke, '...I did make sure, even so.'

Tom didn't think Nardone knew where he was, that he could see him. He listened, was anyone else behind him? Where was Genaro? Where was anyone, the darkness was buying him a little time. He inched forwards and then he saw, a few feet away as his eyes adjusted, Nardone's shape become more defined, sharper. He couldn't tell whether he had a gun, a knife, but he wasn't going to take any chances. Nardone moved, towards him or further away, the perspective changing all the time. All Tom was aware of was the sound of someone moving. He knew Nardone wasn't looking for *him* but even so, he knew now that he was collateral in whatever battle Nardone thought he was fighting. Nardone flicked his lighter and for a second his features flared in the darkness. The red flame around his face made his flesh translucent, highlighted the creases in his cheeks, the hollows of his eyes. And then he was gone again. When he next spoke his voice was muffled, further away.

'Genaro couldn't deal with Frank,' he said. 'It was always up to me. But I didn't kill him.'

He believed it, Tom could hear it in his voice that unshakeable faith he always had in himself. *Where the hell was he?* This was turning into some mad game of cat and mouse and Tom knew he was fast becoming the mouse. Two mice—Genaro was looking for Nardone too. Jesus he'd forgotten about him. *Where was he?*

'You can't change the past, Robert,' Tom said into the darkness, buying time.

But nobody answered; Nardone wasn't there.

'Robert!'

And then, a few feet away, he saw the silver flash of the end of a gun, pointed at him. Later he would remember a draft of air as he threw himself into the depths of the pit of shadow in which he was hiding. Nardone must have mistaken him for Genaro, *or maybe not.* He was alive. He had to keep him talking.

'Why was Frank hard to deal with?' Tom said, keeping his voice steady.

'Frank was greedy,' Nardone said.

He knew it was him then, he was going to take out both of them. A neat synchronicity, Tom thought, to die where Susie had died. Only, he didn't want to die.

'About what?'

'You think you'll get me that easy?' Nardone whispered. His voice skimmed the surface of the shadows.

'What happened to you,' Tom tried again. 'You had everything.'

Nardone laughed hollow and dry. 'I had nothing. They had it all, Genaro and Frank.'

The gun was lowered a fraction and Tom took his chance. He threw himself back behind the carriages, into the wall, crouched into the hidden shadows. He heard Nardone, angry now, throwing things in his path aside. But Tom had the advantage; Nardone couldn't see him. He flattened himself against the wall, deeper into the murk. He thought he'd got away with it and then the hammer of the gun clicked, close. Too close. There was nowhere else to go, the cold fibreglass wall at his back blocked him. He looked up to the crack of light above, the distant echo from the entrance to the tunnel as he heard voices. It was too far to run now, even if he'd wanted to. They would not get there in time.

'Everyone will think *you* killed Frank.' Nardone's voice came at him through the darkness. 'You had the motive. You're so out of your fucking head with those pills you don't know what you're doing.' The voice continuing, steady, calm. 'A crime of passion. When you heard Frank was back you had to get rid of him. You had to have your gypsy girl!'

And then a movement, through the tunnel behind Nardone. Imperceptible between the light and shadow. *Ruby*, it must be Ruby, he had to let her know where he was.

'Why would you do that to your brother Robert?' he said, loud enough for her to find him.

'You wouldn't understand,' Nardone said. 'You never had a brother. You never had to share anything in your life.'

Oh but I wish I had he thought and almost gave in then. He felt Susie's hand beckoning, pulling him towards her, *you'll be okay, Dad* she was saying. He could feel a pain, a heavy pressure on his leg. When he'd thrown himself down, he'd knocked a girder, or something from the tracks. He was trapped and as he tried to free himself, reach with his hand, he sprawled too close to Nardone.

'Dolores…' Tom managed to get out in a whisper, in pain.

'Oh that wasn't me,' Nardone said. 'You should listen to the reporter girl, she knows far more than you…'

The words in the cold air of the tunnel stayed where they were. Tom was defeated. He could hear nothing. The shadow in the dark had stopped; no voices came now from the entrance to the tunnel. No one was coming to help him. Like his daughter before him, his time had run out. The gun was close enough to smell the wet metal, feel the rush of air as Nardone's finger squeezed the trigger. The last thing Tom saw was his face, the hatred, raw, before he lifted it and fired.

4

Leah rubbed her chin; her hand came away wet. Blood was on her fingers and a tooth clinked to the floor.

'Where's Fairfax gone?'

That copper Miller was there talking to her, staring into the ghost train. She followed her eyes and they all watched the mouth of the tunnel expecting Tom Fairfax to come back the way he'd gone in.

'What do we do now ma'am?' someone asked.

Miller looked scared. Her face was whiter than ever against her red hair and then someone else spoke, a man— a tall, dark-haired man, tanned. Leah didn't register until she heard him speak that it was Mati.

'There is two exits,' he said. 'This one door and another round the back.'

Miller looked at him, like she was thinking—*how do you know that*, which was also what Leah was thinking. But instead she signalled without speaking that Hughes and some young woman constable should go round the back while she and the two male officers with her would go in the front way.

'He has a gun,' Mati said.

Again she looked at him, but this time she didn't need to ask the question.

'I saw him,' Mati said. 'I come to find Leah.' He nodded towards Leah. 'And I see him, the man, running in. Before the other man.'

Miller accepted what he said; she had no choice. Mati went to Leah, pulled her up by her hand from the ground and held her. 'You look like crap.'

Leah let herself be lifted, was too stunned to answer. She didn't know what Mati was doing there. She did know she didn't want him to be, but when she turned to look for Miller, for anyone, she realised they were alone. Miller had disappeared into the tunnel and the others had gone round the back. Nothing moved, not a sound broke the cold snapped air. Leah felt that if either of them breathed or spoke then something might happen to break the spell so they didn't breathe, they just stood and waited. Two, three minutes passed, maybe more.

'Eva told me after you visit her, she knew what is happened to Stefan,' Mati said into the silence.

Leah stretched her jawbone, checking nothing was broken. 'Where is Eva?'

Mati tilted his shoulders. 'I don't know.'

Leah looked hard at him. 'What the hell are you doing here Mati?'

'Eva is gone. I don't wanna lie to you man. She's gone. The fire, she...' but his voice trailed off.

'What about the fire?'

Mati didn't answer, he didn't have to; Leah just had to look at his face.

'She started the fire? Last night?'

Mati looked at her, his eyes impassive.

'She knew about what happened to Stefan? The fire—Dolores and Frank?'

'Yeah man, you told her.'

Leah fell back onto the ground. But she already knew that right? *Fuck*. Later, when she would learn that Dolores was already dead when the fire started, she thought it might make her feel less guilty and for a moment, it did. But then it came back, that creeping, aching guilt that would never let her go entirely even if it *was* what Dolores wanted. Dolores must have been desperate and with Frank dead, what did she have to live for? And Leah could have stopped her, twice. Atonement? Was that was Dolores was after? She'd got what she wanted. She sure as hell was dead now.

'What about you?' Leah asked and Mati smiled, like he didn't understand. 'Why didn't you tell me?'

'I tell you now.'

'Not the same though is it?'

'No,' Mati agreed. 'Is not the same.'

'How did you find me?'

'I figure it out for myself. Doesn't take rocket science,' Mati said, sitting on the ground next to her. 'Is okay though?'

'No it's not okay Mati,' she said. 'It will never be okay.'

They waited. It was like a film running with the action set to pause. They heard noises, voices raised, shouting and one voice louder. Should they run, or stay here? What if the man with the gun... what if Nardone came out this way and here they were? Waiting. What then?

'Stefan died in there?' Mati said.

Leah nodded.

'So no one is looking for Stefan now Eva is gone.' Mati said simply.

'Was he a drug dealer?' Leah asked.

Mati shrugged.

'Maybe. Sometimes. But he is not a bad guy.'

'They never are,' Leah said.

'Should we help?' Mati said but she didn't catch his reply.

She heard the gunshot—muffled, dampened by the narrow walls of the tunnel. The noise ping ponged from one side to the other, echoing. Its final cry as clear as anything she'd ever heard. So was the silence after. Into her ear, the one that had been closed for so long, came waves, fresh seawater, sound. She turned to watch the entrance of the ghost train. Ten minutes later, they carried the body out.

5

He was still alive, but Nardone was dead.

Tom flipped the Zippo open following the sound he'd heard seconds before, the sound that had told him that someone else was in there with him. Someone else had fired the shot. Nardone's gun lay uncharged beside him, the tang of iron and gunpowder clinging to the air. In the thick blood next to the dead man, Genaro Molinari stood in the gloom of the tunnel shrunk to half his size.

Ruby Miller's face peeled away the ink-black darkness.

'Are you alright?' she said.

Tom moved his head and she bent to him, put her hand on his shoulder. Genaro stayed with his brother. Stefan, Frank, Dolores, Nardone. *Dominoes*. Tom looked across at Genaro then leaned his head to Ruby's hand on his shoulder, closed his eyes.

It was over.

Summer 2007

When he emerged from the ghost train with Molinari, Tom saw a row of faces. So many faces—people he hadn't expected, people he didn't know. It was Hughes stepped forward, took Molinari from him, lead him away. As he watched him go, Tom felt part of himself leave too. He wanted to call him back, tell him something he'd forgotten. Only, there was nothing left to say.

Closure. Tom had told Robert Nardone there was no such thing, that day in the pub, with the shrimp, a lifetime ago. He would never know what exactly happened, but he was certain somehow Dolores had killed Frank without meaning to and then Nardone... well, he had done the rest. Frank was always in the way, the opportunity was there and Nardone took it, he was just making sure Frank was never coming back.

Some days Tom saw himself stopping Frank at the station, talking to him, turning the clock back. Those were the best days when things took a different turn and Dolores was still alive. Other days, his hands shook, his eyelids flickered in a tired rap and he relived all the things he couldn't change. *Hadn't changed*. On those days he didn't have answers, he didn't know what had happened to Susie, everything remained unknown. They were the worst days.

Today though... today was a good day.

The falcon had reached the outer edges of the field where the lane divided into two forks, lined by ditches on one side and low white thatched almshouses on the other. It was a quiet out of the way place where they wouldn't be pestered with questions and wide-eyed alarm. It was the right place and the right day. The bird sat impassive on a fence post, her pale colour blending into the withered line of hedges and the stone of the wall beneath it. Her perch made her invisible and strange, her feathers the colour of pale yellow Cotswold stone. Leah had her arm held out, a torn piece of rabbit sinew sticking out between finger and thumb. Her hand was steady, her fist in the glove secure.

'Come Sky,' she whispered.

Jack and Rich stood aside. The bird was watching Leah, aware of them all watching her. She weighed her options, to stay or go. Behind her the blue sky stretched into a summer morning as bright and endless as the day was long. She dipped her head, launched herself skywards, came swooping low and slow over the grass, stealthy as silence and easy as light. She jump-landed on the glove with barely a bounce as her talons found the rabbit, the leather of the glove and Leah's fingers beneath.

'Thing is,' Rich said. 'You see her as a romantic thing when she's a hunter. You got to see her as she is.'

'Beautiful,' Jack said.

'Aye she is that too.' Rich laughed.

Sky rotated her head slowly as though she had all the time in the world, watching, always watching. A figure was coming towards them, which unfolded into two figures as Tom and Ruby came into view. They were talking in a way that made them look as though they had things to say to each other. They were gesturing, laughing and touching each other as they walked, feeling themselves still too far away to be observed. Leah tracked them coming closer, one eye on her bird, one on Jack who caught her look, a smile, who'd have thought it? Stranger things had happened that year.

'You going to show us what she can do then?' Tom said and Leah threw him a smile as she balanced her weight evenly between her tiptoes. She felt the contact her bare feet made with the ground. She could feel the warmth of the June sun on her neck, hair and face and she could see the expanse of sky above her stretching on and on, free. Jack, Ruby, Tom, Rich, their faces were turned to her, their shadows falling across the grass like the arm of a sun dial carving a slice through time.

She leaned forward, stretched her arm wide and with her wrist threw a flick-switch and Sky leapt up and up, following the currents of air far and away until she was no more than a dot against the clouds.

LEAF BY LEAF